He stole her

They called him The Priest. Maybe because of his billowing black robes and the steel crucifix that hung around his neck. Or perhaps it was because those who met him were compelled to pray. But Duncan Mackay was anything but a saint. He was a sinner—a paid mercenary. Until he met her, and she made him want to change his ways.

Lady Heather Sutherland, has never been compelled to follow rules. And this time, she's gone too far. Following in the footsteps of her brothers and cousins, she chooses to join the fight for Scottish freedom—and gets herself abducted by a handsome, rogue warrior, whose touch is sweet sin.

Duncan's duty was clear—steal Heather away from Dunrobin Castle. What he didn't expect, was to be charmed by her spirit and rocked by her fiery kiss. Now, he doesn't want deliver her to those who hired him, instead he wants to keep her all to himself.

Praise for **The Stolen Bride Series**...

"For fans of Highlander romance, this series is a must read!" ~Night Owl Romance

The Highlander's Reward – winner of InD'Tale Magazine's Best Historical Novel 2012

The Highlander's Reward – *"The powerful yet sensitive Magnus and the saucy and beautiful Arbella are a winning pair in this Scottish themed romance that even boasts cameos from William Wallace himself."* ~Publisher's Weekly Reviewer for the Amazon Breakthrough Novel Contest

The Highlander's Sin

Eliza Knight

The Highlander's Sin

Book Six: The Stolen Bride Series

By
Eliza Knight

The Highlander's Sin

****

FIRST EDITION
October 2013

Copyright 2013 © Eliza Knight

THE HIGHLANDER'S SIN © 2013 Eliza Knight. ALL RIGHTS RESERVED. No part or the whole of this book may be reproduced, distributed, transmitted or utilized (other than for reading by the intended reader) in ANY form (now known or hereafter invented) without prior written permission by the author. The unauthorized reproduction or distribution of this copyrighted work is illegal, and punishable by law. The characters and events portrayed in this book are fictional and or are used fictitiously and solely the product of the author's imagination. Any similarity to real persons, living or dead, places, businesses, events or locales is purely coincidental.

Cover Design: Kimberly Killion @ The Killion Group, Inc.

Copy Editor: Joyce Lamb

****

Also Available by Eliza Knight

The Highlander's Reward – Book One, The Stolen Bride Series
The Highlander's Conquest – Book Two, The Stolen Bride Series
The Highlander's Lady – Book Three, The Stolen Bride Series
The Highlander's Warrior Bride – Book Four, The Stolen Bride Series
The Highlander's Triumph – Book Five, The Stolen Bride Series
Behind the Plaid (Highland Bound Trilogy, Book One)
Bared to the Laird (Highland Bound Trilogy, Book Two)
A Lady's Charade (Book 1: The Rules of Chivalry)
A Knight's Victory (Book 2: The Rules of Chivalry)
A Gentleman's Kiss
<u>Men of the Sea Series:</u> *Her Captain Returns, Her Captain Surrenders, Her Captain Dares All*
<u>The Highland Jewel Series:</u> *Warrior in a Box, Lady in a Box, Love in a Box*
Lady Seductress's Ball
Take it Off, Warrior
Highland Steam
A Pirate's Bounty
Highland Tryst (Something Wicked This Way Comes Volume 1)
Highlander Brawn (Sequel to *Highland Steam*)
The Rebound Pact – A Sexy Contemporary Novel

Coming soon…
The Highlander's Temptation – Prequel, The Stolen Bride Series
The Dark Side of the Laird (Highland Bound Trilogy, Book Three)
My Lady Viper – Tales from the Tudor Court
Prisoner of the Queen – Tales from the Tudor Court

<u>Writing under the name Annabelle Weston</u>

Wicked Woman (Desert Heat)
Scandalous Woman (Desert Heat)

Notorious Woman (Desert Heat)
Mr. Temptation
Hunting Tucker

****

Visit Eliza Knight at www.elizaknight.com or www.historyundressed.com

Eliza Knight

Dedication

To my sister, Katie,
who proves that a sassy woman can indeed find true love.

Acknowledgements

Special thanks go out to Lizzie, Andrea, Vonda and Merry! Thanks so much for your willingness to read!

Eliza Knight

Prologue

Dingwall Castle, 1277
Highlands, Scotland

Screams echoed off the walls, bouncing from one end of the castle to the other like banshees in the throes of a haunt. Young Duncan MacKay huddled beneath the altar in the family chapel tucked behind the great hall, frightened beyond measure.

Today he was his day of birth. Seven years. But from the sound of it, there would be not celebration this evening.

Nightmares were supposed to happen only at night, awakening one in a cold sweat with tears streaming on heated cheeks. Duncan was not asleep. Nay, he was very much awake. And 'twas not entirely dark. A few candles were lit, causing shadows to bump in and out of their glowing light.

'Twas about an hour after dawn, and he'd come down as he was supposed to for morning Mass before his family would break their fast. The only thing was, he was the only one who'd arrived. None of his sisters, brothers, parents, nor his aunt and uncle who'd been visiting with their four children. He had none of them to comfort him in this terror that did not disappear no matter how many times he squeezed his eyes shut or blocked out the noise with his hands. The only one present was their family priest, his tutor, Father Bernard.

A loud crash from somewhere in the castle made him jump, and he bumped his head on the wooden crossbeams of the altar. But he didn't whimper. Warriors never cried. He would prove to them all that he was worthy of such a title.

"Dinna move," Father Bernard whispered, pressing a small but thick silver crucifix into Duncan's hand. "I'll be back before ye can recite Ezekiel 33."

Duncan wanted to grab onto Father Bernard's hand, tell him not to leave, that he didn't want to be alone. But that would have been cowardly, and he'd already caused enough of a stir today.

The screams of pain were his fault.

"*Son of man, speak to the children of thy people, and say unto them, When I bring the sword upon a land, if the people of the land take a man of their coasts, and set him for their watchman: If when he seeth the sword come upon the land, he blow the trumpet, and warn the people…*" Duncan frantically repeated the verses from the Bible, praying all the while that Father Bernard would be back before he finished.

He'd only wanted to pick the most beautiful gillyflowers for Mother. Today was her birthday, too. A crown of gillyflowers would have looked so beautiful on his mother's soft, golden hair, for the evening celebration Da had planned. Now that he was seven, he would be fostered out next year, and he had to make sure his mother's celebration was extra special. He'd woken early, before the whole of the house, to go and find them.

But now it was ruined.

A bloodcurdling scream made Duncan squeeze his eyes shut so tight that pain seared down the middle of his forehead.

He clutched the cross, pressed it to his lips as he continued to recite, *"Then whosoever heareth the sound of the trumpet, and taketh not warning; if the sword come, and take him away, his blood shall be upon his own head. He heard the sound of the trumpet, and took not warning; his blood shall be upon him. But he that taketh warning shall deliver his soul."*

If only Duncan hadn't sneaked out the side gate, leaving it propped open with a rock so he could slip back in unseen. At dawn, the men changed shifts, and Duncan had noticed the guards who stood by the side gate would disappear for a quarter hour. Just enough time to gather the flowers.

And apparently enough time for a stealthy enemy to lay siege. The sound of Da bellowing from the great hall made Duncan tremble. Da would fix this, and then tan his hide, but Duncan would gladly take a beating.

Beyond the chapel door, Da shouted something about bastards stabbing him in the back.

Duncan wasn't sure what a bastard was, but it sounded awful coming from his da's lips, and if the noise coming from all around was any indication, they really were horrible monsters. If only they'd stayed home at Castle Varrich like Mother had wanted. But Da had said this meeting with the Sutherland clan was important, could strengthen their own clan. They'd met here with a brother of the Sutherland laird.

"But if the watchman see the sword come, and blow not the trumpet, and the people be not warned; if the sword come, and take any person from among them, he is taken away in his iniquity; but his blood will I require at the watchman's hand. So thou, O son of man, I have set thee a watchman unto the house of Israel; therefore thou shalt hear the word at my mouth, and warn them from me."

The battle sounds raged closer. Duncan tucked his knees up toward his chin, his face buried. He tried to slow his breathing, to calm himself with the reassuring thought that Da would make everything better. That his mother wasn't screaming. That he wasn't all alone. Oh, what a coward he was, hiding when people were dying all around him. Dying! He may have been young, but he wasn't stupid, and the sounds he heard were of people in agony, people vanishing from this life into the next.

"*When I say unto the wicked, O wicked man, thou shalt surely die; if thou dost not speak to warn the wicked from his way, that wicked man shall die in his iniquity; but his blood —*"

The door to the chapel creaked slowly open, and with each screech of the iron hinges' protest, gooseflesh rippled from his ankles to the top of his head. Boot heels clicked ominously on the stone cobbles, echoing inside Duncan's head. Not the shuffling steps of Father Bernard. Not his mother's reassuring movements, nor the steady, measured footfalls of his father. These were the footsteps of an enemy. If they'd come inside the chapel, then they must have finished with everyone in Dingwall.

Da hadn't won.

Da was— Nay. He couldn't even think it.

Duncan slipped the crucifix into his left boot and reached for the handle of the *sgian dubh* his father had given him, stashed in his right boot. He gripped it tight, the hilt digging into his palm, a palm his father had promised would grow as big as his. Duncan held his breath, praying whoever walked toward him couldn't hear the sound of his heartbeat, for it boomed loud in his own ears.

A screeching sound pierced the air, like a sword being scraped deliberately across the stones, making Duncan's teeth chatter. He clenched his jaw tight, refusing to let this nightmare rule him. The screeching lasted for several seconds, drowning out the sounds of footsteps, and stopped just before the altar.

Definitely not a friend. Did he know Duncan hid in here, hoping for sanctuary? He gripped the little knife harder, swearing that he'd use it if the enemy discovered him. Only seven summers, he was still a warrior, a true warrior, and he'd protect his family's honor, even if he was the only one left.

Duncan's lungs felt on fire from holding his breath. He wouldn't be able to hold it much longer.

The door to the chapel burst open, crashing against the wall, just as his breath rushed out, and he gulped in another.

"Ye dinna belong in here." Father Bernard's voice was calm but loud as he spoke.

"Get out of here, Priest. Dinna make me murder a man of the cloth." A man. Sounded much like the Sutherland contact his parents had supped with the night before.

"Ye wouldn't do that. Such an act would only damn ye forever," Father Bernard protested, his voice still tranquil.

A chilling laugh came from the warrior who stood only a foot or so away. "Och, Priest, my own chaplain forgave me for all sins committed today."

"I sincerely doubt he meant for ye to commit such a sin today." Father Bernard's tone took on an edge Duncan had never heard before.

"Doesna matter what he meant. Ye're a part of Clan MacKay. All MacKays die today."

"Was this your chief's plan all along?"

The warrior laughed cruelly. The Sutherlands had betrayed them. Duncan pressed his lips together to keep from making any sound. If he made it out alive today, he would not rest until he'd sought revenge on them.

"There was never going to be an alliance." Father Bernard sounded dejected.

Moments later, the whistling sound of a sword slicing through the air was followed by a guttural, choking grunt and the thud of a body hitting the ground. Without looking, Duncan knew exactly what had happened. The warrior had felled his tutor. Father Bernard was dead.

Gripping the *sgian dubh* so tight his knuckles whitened, Duncan jumped from behind the altar, letting out a battle cry he copied from his father.

The warrior whirled, his sword still dripping from the blood of the priest. Crumpled on the floor behind the warrior was Father Bernard. Tears stung Duncan's eyes; he blinked them away and forced himself to stare at the warrior who smiled cruelly down at him. He seemed tall as a mountain and cruel as the devil.

"Why did ye kill him?" Duncan asked.

The man didn't answer. He was indeed the Sutherland relation. Hair dark and cut short, with a long beard sprinkled with gray. His eyes were dark as a nightmare, shirt and plaid covered in blood.

"Did ye kill...?" But he couldn't finish his question, didn't want to know for certain if Ma and Da were lying dead on the floor of the great hall.

"Are ye MacKay's son?" the warrior asked, flipping his sword around in one hand, making a wide circle. Droplets of blood splattered Duncan's cheek.

A chill skated over Duncan's skin. He knew that if he told this man he was the son of Chief MacKay, he would die, and yet, he wanted the chance to look this man in the eye and say who he was before he stabbed his thick neck with the *sgian dubh*.

"I'll take your silence as an aye." The warrior drew out the *y* in *aye*, his fingers flexing on the hilt.

Duncan mirrored his movements, clenching the *sgian dubh*.

"Will ye fight me, wee lad?"

Duncan bared his teeth, but was still unable to find his voice.

The warrior tossed his sword from hand to hand, taunting Duncan. "Come on, laddie, try to jab me with that wee blade."

Anger speared through Duncan, but the man in front of him was easily five times his size. How could he win against such a giant?

"Look, here," the warrior said with a laugh. "I'll even set down my sword and let ye have a go while I'm unarmed." He tossed his sword to the ground behind him, the metal clattering as it skidded away.

Duncan's chances were slightly higher. And yet, still slim.

"Come on now. Ye're the last of your line. Dinna ye want to at least go down fighting as your ma and da did?"

That was the last straw, confirmation that his parents were indeed gone, his entire family annihilated. He couldn't let this *bastard* get away with it.

Duncan lunged at the large warrior, jerking his arm forward. The warrior grabbed him around the middle and knocked the *sgian dubh* from his hand.

"A good effort," the man said with a cruel laugh.

"Ye're evil," Duncan said.

"Nay, just loyal, and now—" But his sentence was finished with a grunt as he doubled forward and dropped Duncan to the ground.

Behind the warrior, Father Bernard had managed to stand. Blood soaked the front of his lustrous gray robes and his hands. He held the sword hilt, its tip buried in the warrior's back.

Father Bernard nodded to Duncan, sadness surrounding his eyes.

"Go," he urged Duncan in raspy tones. "Go to Pluscarden Abbey, lad. Seek sanctuary with my brothers."

Duncan nodded, his throat tight and eyes stinging from unshed tears. He ran toward the door to the great hall, but the last words of Father Bernard, spoken to the dying warrior, burned into his ears.

"And I will execute great vengeance upon them with furious rebukes; and they shall know that I am the Lord, when I shall lay my vengeance upon them."

Eliza Knight

Chapter One

Dunrobin Castle, Scottish Highlands
Summer, 1300

Stone cobbles were certainly the most uncomfortable place for knees to rest. Lady Heather, youngest sister to the powerful Earl of Sutherland, knelt before the altar in the family's chapel. Even with the protection of layers of fabric between her bones and the flooring, she could feel bruises forming beneath the calluses on her knees.

The castle's drafts had yet to reach this corner of space within the towers, and as a result, sweat dripped in unladylike fashion down her temples and spine. What she wouldn't give to at least be able to fan herself, but she dared not move her hands from their place firmly pressed together in prayer.

Today would prove to be sweltering if the heat before dawn was any indication. And since Heather had an aversion to heat, she was more than likely going to be in a sour mood. The heaviness of the many layers she wore didn't help the situation. Nor what she was about to do.

The chapel was dark, save the four candles she'd lit. The sun had yet to rise, and the three narrow windows, newly fixed with stained glass, let in none of the moon's silver light.

Heather came to pray each morning, every morning, before the family rose. Typically because she had a lot more to confess than most. She was the first to admit she was not easy on her older brother, Magnus. Nor her aunts, any of her siblings, cousins and the staff in general. She might even be willing to admit that she single-handedly provided for their chaplain's wealth, given that she was constantly slipping coins into his purse as penance or to buy an extra blessing.

But today was different.

On this day, she was going to change her future, forever.

The Scottish rebellion still raged on, despite the horrendous loss at the Battle of Falkirk. Heather wanted to be a part of it. Why should her brothers and cousins have all the fun? Before the rest of the household woke to say prayers, Heather planned to be well on her way to finding William Wallace. The man had taken a step back in the war for freedom. After their great loss, the warrior must have felt downtrodden, for he simply handed the reins of battle over to another. She was going to persuade him to rise up once more, to fight for what he thought was right, what she knew was right.

Robert the Bruce was not yet king—and though he was rumored to have sided with the English, Heather just couldn't believe it. After all, Bruce and Red Comyn were now overseeing the resistance, but they lacked the heart of Wallace. The way Heather saw it, Wallace could turn a sheepherder into a seasoned warrior, and might even have the power to turn Englishmen into Scots—the latter was a bit of a reach, but just went to prove how much she believed in him.

A scraping to her left jolted Heather from her prayer. She sat back on her heels, hand falling to her hip where a twelve-inch dagger was slipped into its sheath.

"Who's there?" Her voice echoed through the chapel.

A shadowy figure lurked just beyond the benches in the corner where their chaplain's chamber was. Looked like a hulk of black. If she'd been more superstitious, she might have thought the devil was coming to pay her a visit like Aunt Fiona always threatened.

"Father Hurley?" She swiped a drip of sweat from her eyes. "Is that ye? Come away from the shadows."

A shiver of fear skittered over her spine, settling like a solid stone in her belly.

The figure didn't move.

Heather swallowed her fear and stood up, straightening her shoulders as much as she could, squaring her jaw. "Come into the light at once," she ordered.

The shadow moved along the wall toward the front of the chapel. Heather followed him with her eyes. 'Twas not the devil but a man. Most definitely not Father Hurley. He was taller by at least a foot—and wide by about the same. His black robes billowed around his form, swishing around his ankles with each step, and sending whispers of fear with every move. The silver chain around his neck swung the large crucifix it held like a pendulum. Back and forth.

A man of the cloth? Her hair prickled. He looked like death come to take her.

Heather stared at the cross, at the man in robes, hypnotized by his stealthy, calculated movements, her eyes wide and immobilized. She finally blinked when they stung with dryness.

"Are ye new to Dunrobin?" she asked, refusing to believe he might be the reaper and wondering why no one had told her there was a new priest.

He stopped a few feet away, just outside the line of light from the candles.

"Nay." His voice was deep, dark, and slid over her body shamefully, in a way that made her want to hear him speak again.

Lord, help her impetuous nature.

Heather made a sign of the cross. "I've not seen ye before now." The slight quiver in her tone made her angry.

He didn't answer. A long pause of silence ensued, making her uncomfortable. Her skin prickled.

"Where is Father Hurley? What are ye doing in here?" The questions tumbled from her tongue.

The man pointed toward the chaplain's chamber. "He is there. Sleeping."

Again that voice. Why did she like it so much? "And ye? What are ye doing out here? I'm…I'm praying. I want privacy." She lifted her chin another notch, hoping the odd priest would leave her be, that he hadn't noticed the slight stutter of her words. When she saw her brother Magnus, she was going to tell him about this odd priest and how uncomfortable he made her. *Zounds!* She wouldn't get the chance before she left… The dawn of her new life would begin today. A note then. She would tell Magnus in a note.

"I'm afraid ye won't be getting any privacy, my lady." Confidence dripped from his words and slid over her skin in a way that felt wicked.

"Ye are not to talk to me in such a manner." No matter how hard she tried, she sounded petulant rather than in control.

"And ye need to hold your tongue, ye saucy wench."

Heather gasped, blanched. Pressed a hand to her chest and took a step back in shock. "What?"

"Ye heard me." An underlying tone of amusement captured his voice.

Indeed she had, but no one had ever, *ever*, talked to her like that before.

"How dare ye?" She seethed, gripped her fingers around her dagger, though what she'd do with it, she had no clue. Killing a man of the cloth was a sin she'd never be able to pay her way out of.

"Enough bluster, my lady. I need ye to come with me."

"Come with ye? I'll be doing no such thing." She shook her head vehemently and took another step back. Only about a dozen more, and she could bolt for the door.

Perhaps today was not a day to run away. Outside dangers had never been a consideration before now. She'd just assumed she'd be able to reach Wallace's camp unharmed. With her dagger, a bow and arrows, she could protect herself. Keep hidden in the bushes and not get caught.

But that was before being confronted by this man who made her feel…scared and hot all over. Now she just wanted the safety and tranquility of her bedchamber. How naïve she'd been to think her plan was solid.

"My lady," he said in his calm, smooth voice. "Ye must. There is no choice in this matter."

"Or what?"

Slowly, he opened one side of his robe, and she squeezed her eyes shut, not wanting to see what he revealed.

"Open your eyes," he demanded.

She shook her head, bit her lip. But when she heard the click of his boot heels on the floor, her eyes flew open. He stopped moving, maybe a dozen paces away and removed the hood from his head. Beneath his robe, he was cloaked in a white leine, leather jerkin and tightly pleated plaid of dark colors. But what she couldn't take her gaze off of, was the cruel-looking battle ax strapped to his chest with a leather belt of sorts. The ax glittered where it caught the light. Silver carved on its handle. It wasn't a regular ax blade either, but elongated, curved and hooked where it should have been flat and triangular.

Heather raised her eyes to his. He'd stepped far enough forward that the candles lit what parts of his face weren't hidden by the hood of his cloak. Strong chin and nose. And his eyes, they flashed out at her like blue lightning, ready to snuff out her life with one blink. His hair was pulled back in a queue, but shaved along the sides, making him resemble a savage.

Her hand involuntary rose to her chest as she pressed against her quickly beating heart. Realizing what she'd done, Heather forced her hand back to her side, not wanting the stranger to know how much he was affecting her.

He touched a strong-looking hand to the handle of the ax. "Dinna make me use it, lass. I'd hate to mar your pretty face."

He thought her pretty? She almost cocked her head and gave him a coy smile, until reality struck and she again realized who he was. A stranger who was attempting to abduct her. A savage-looking warrior priest who threatened to cut her with that horrid-looking blade.

"My family will be here any moment. My brother Magnus, the *earl*, will not be pleased with what you're attempting to do. I suggest ye leave now, and I'll not scream. Ye can get away, and this will all be a figment of both of our imaginations." Heather thought her terms quite reasonable and was more than shocked when the strange man shook his head *nay*.

A cruel smile edged up his lips, his eyes brightening. "Och, your brother." He tugged on the ax. "I hope he comes. I hope he comes right now. Will ye scream for me? Hurry him along?"

The chill of fear that made her tremble turned to an icy knot of terror. This man wanted to kill her brother. Hoped that she'd alert the household and send Magnus rushing in here so he could plant his disgusting ax in her brother's chest.

"What do ye want?" she asked, no longer caring about the tremble in her voice. She just wanted him to go away.

Magnus had taken care of her for as long as she could remember. She'd only been a few summers when their parents had been murdered. Now at nineteen, she still looked up to him, even if she was planning to disobey him once more by joining the rebellion. Heather would not be the cause of her brother's death.

"'Tis as I've said. I want *ye*. I need ye to come with me."

Heather shook her head in confusion. "But why me?"

"Dinna ask questions ye dinna want the answers to."

Words that chilled her. "But I do want the answer."

The man took a few steps closer. He was easily a foot taller than she, and Heather found herself tilting her head back to stare up into his face. If he hadn't been so wicked, she would have thought him to be incredibly handsome in a rugged, dangerous sort of way. Heart-throbbing, finger-tingling, handsome.

She sucked in a breath as he moved forward another step, until his feet were within inches of hers. His size was overwhelming. Never one to faint, Heather was actually feeling on the verge of doing so.

The man closed his priest's robes, covering the frightening ax. He took hold of her upper arms and probed, looking at her oddly. No doubt he could feel how many layers she was wearing. Heather squared her shoulders more and looked him in the eye.

"Get your hands off me," she said through gritted teeth.

That only made the man's grin widen. "Ye're a feisty one, I see." He tugged her closer, her breasts bumping into his chest.

She gasped and wriggled, but he had an iron grip on her arms and hauled her flush against him. Alarmingly, warm sensation spread into her belly from where her breasts were crushed to his chest.

"I did not give ye permission to touch me." Her struggles seemed futile to this hulk of muscle.

"I dinna need permission. I'm taking ye away from here, and I'll do whatever I like to ye. I just need to make sure I deliver ye alive."

"Deliver me?" Where and to whom was he to deliver her? Dear God… "Ye're a—"

"Never mind what I am. All ye need know is, if ye do what I tell ye, then ye'll arrive unscathed."

Heather bit her lip. "And…with my honor intact?"

The man chuckled. "That I canna promise."

Dread, cold and heavy, sank into her belly. Why did the thought of this wicked man taking her innocence send a thrill of excitement thrumming through her veins? "My brother will pay ye double whatever ye've been paid."

"No doubt he would."

"Aye!" She nodded empathically. "He will. I promise."

"'Tis not just about the money, lass." He pressed his nose to the hair above her temple and breathed in deeply.

Heather held her breath. She'd never been embraced like this by a man before. Never had one breathe in the scent of her hair. There'd been men to dance with at feasts, even a couple who had stolen quick kisses, but never crushed her to them.

This man was her captor. She should have wanted to vomit in his tight hold, but instead, her body betrayed that notion, warming and tingling. This would simply not do. She couldn't allow him to treat her this way, and she couldn't allow herself to like it. 'Twas absurd. She shoved against him, her moves futile against his hold.

"What *is* it about?" she asked, instead of demanding he unhand her. The man struck her as someone who didn't do so well when being issued orders.

"Nothing to get your pretty little head wrapped up in."

Heather chose to ignore his condescending answer. Being called pretty at the same time as describing her head as little— in essence, calling her stupid—didn't go over well with her.

"I assure ye, my pretty little head *is* truly concerned."

Whatever his answer was, she had no choice in going with him. If she refused, he'd slice her up with that gruesome battle ax. At least alive she had a chance to escape. Besides, she'd planned to leave today anyway. At least leaving with him, she'd have protection against the would-be outside threats.

"Och, lass, we'll discuss it on the way. We'd best be leaving. As ye said, your family will be here any moment—and your chaplain is bound to wake."

"How did ye sneak in here?" she asked, glancing around.

"The same way we'll be leaving." He tugged at her to follow him, but Heather rooted her feet to the ground, refusing to leave. 'Twas taking a chance, aye, but she had a feeling he wouldn't slice her up just yet.

The man turned on his heel and gave her a warning glance—one that said if she didn't move her arse, he'd sever it from her body.

Hmm. Maybe he wouldn't have any qualms about it. Still she forged on.

"I will not leave until ye tell me your name." She was stalling, and he probably knew it, but she couldn't just run off with him without having a chance to leave her family a note or know where she was headed so she could somehow figure out a way to leave a clue.

"Priest."

"Priest?"

He nodded, his mouth in a long, grim line. "Dinna ye see the robes?"

"Men of God dinna take ladies as their hostages."

"'Haps I'm not a man of God." His expression was unreadable.

Heather's brows wrinkled with bewilderment. "But ye are a priest."

"Aye," he drawled out.

"I dinna understand."

"Good thing for ye, understanding was not part of the plan. Let's go." He tugged on her hand, his overlarge palm engulfing hers, but Heather yanked back.

"Where are ye taking me?" she demanded.

"South."

"*Where* south?" Lord, he was infuriating.

Instead of trying to keep tugging on her, the man swiveled, his face an inch from hers and his warm breath washing over her skin. He smelled of mint and the earth.

"If ye dinna move your feet and shut your mouth, I will tie ye up and gag ye."

He did not sound as though he were bluffing. Heather nodded in answer.

"Let's go," he said.

She inched forward, finding it hard to walk in all the layers of clothes.

"Wait," she said, stopping.

Priest turned, growling under his breath. "I warned ye." He pulled rope from somewhere beneath his cloak.

"Nay!" She held out her hands in a motion for him to stop. "There is no need, I'm not trying to stop ye, I will go with ye. 'Tis simply that I've forgotten my bag."

Priest laughed as though she'd just told some genius joke. "How stupid do ye think I am, lass? I'll not allow ye time to go and pack for our journey. Do ye nay understand? I am *abducting* ye."

Heather shook her head and pressed a hand to his arm, feeling flashes of interest fly over her fingertips. His muscles were bunched beneath his shirt and cloak, and she had the insane urge to pull back his layers and lay her palm flat on his muscled flesh. "I've already packed. My bag is just there."

Heather pointed toward a bench beside the altar where her leather satchel sat, filled with a pouch of coins and a few provisions.

"Nay," he said, studying the satchel like she'd asked to take a week's worth of manure with them.

"Please, I need it."

He shook his head. "Nay. And I'll not hear another word on it."

Heather chewed the inside of her cheek. The priest settled his expression grimly. "Time to go."

"If my family sees my satchel filled, they'll know I planned to run away but was not able to do it on my own. They will know as soon as they arrive here for morning Mass that I've been taken. We'll barely make it a mile before they're on our tail."

The priest growled again, and beneath her fingertips, Heather felt the frustration ripple through his muscles.

"All right. But I'll be holding onto it. No need for ye to try and stab me in the back." As he said the words, he dragged her to the bench, took the satchel, and then whipped the dagger from her hip and shoved it into the bag. "Let us be on our way. One more word out of ye, and ye'll be tied and gagged."

Heather nodded, not wanting to answer him and test his resolve. Truly, she had no choice in the matter.

Maybe it would be better this way. She'd have an escort of a sort. Though he was her captor, he wouldn't allow anyone else to take her away. A secret part of her was excited. This was the adventure she'd been looking for. Aye, 'twas dangerous, the man was half-mad for certain, and his weapons were frightening. But, she'd be getting away from Dunrobin and her family. Setting out on her own—never mind she'd be with a deranged priest. There would be ample opportunity to escape, and if she ran into the men of the resistance camp along the way, all the better.

Because there was no way in hell she was going to end up wherever this wayward Highlander intended, or sliced up by his blade.

Chapter Two

Duncan regarded the lass with ill ease. She'd simply nodded. Hadn't uttered a word. Up until that moment, she'd been full of things to say. What had changed? Certainly not his threat to tie her up and gag her—hell, he'd threatened her more than once.

Heather Sutherland was up to something. Given who her family was, he wouldn't be in the least surprised. Sutherlands were all liars. They betrayed anyone who laid their trust in them, no matter how much they tried to appear good on the outside. Hadn't several of them married English wenches?

Heather's outward appearance wasn't exactly as he'd been informed. Although her attitude was precisely as he'd been warned. Headstrong, stubborn and spoiled.

Those who'd paid him to take her away had warned him of her wild beauty and lithe form. This lass *was* wildly beautiful with untamed blonde curls, peaches-and-cream skin, haughty arched brows and pouty pink lips. Her eyes were the color of heather—a fitting name for her. But lithe was not entirely correct. Though the line of her jaw, the length of her neck gave way to a trimmer body, she was poofy in the middle, with arms as thick as a squire's—only not as firm.

At first, he'd not been sure it was her. The chapel had been dark. The closer he'd gotten, the more his gut had told him it was she. When she'd opened her mouth, all doubt disappeared.

No matter. He couldn't care less what she looked like, as long as he completed his mission and delivered her into the hand of his employers and walked away with a pouch full of silver.

Typically, he actually liked a woman with sass. Meant she could hold her own. Had confidence. Wasn't afraid to put up a fight. The only exception to that rule was when he was attempting to abduct them. Then they needed to comply. Everyone was better off when they did what he told them. Cooperate and live, he often repeated. *Fight me and die.*

So why did her compliance bother him so much?

"Priest, will ye take me away?" She held out her arms, wrists together as though she expected him to cart her off to the dungeon.

"Aye." Duncan grabbed hold of her hand, soft and warm and petite. He tightened his grasp in an attempt to dull the sensations of holding her hand.

"When?" she asked, a brow raised.

Ballocks! He couldn't think around her.

"Didna I tell ye to keep your mouth closed?" he growled.

Heather shrugged and with exaggerated movements pressed her lips tightly together. Duncan had to keep himself from groaning. She was spirited to be sure. He shook his head. The woman who'd hired him to take her would have her hands full. And in two days' time, he'd be richer and free of the Sutherland chit.

Duncan led Heather past the priest's chambers, the door slightly ajar. He glanced inside to make sure the chaplain had not roused. The lass gasped, and he turned to see her peering over his shoulder. The man still lay collapsed on his back upon the small cot. Mouth open, he snored like a hundred hammers in a quarry.

"Did ye kill him?"

"Are ye serious?" He eyed her like she'd grown a second head. "He is snoring. I simply subdued him with a little tap on his temple."

Heather shrugged. "I...uh...hadn't noticed. Never mind that." She waved her hand in the air. "He's a kind man and did not deserve ye bashing him on the head."

"He'll wake with a headache. Nothing more."

She frowned at Duncan, her eyes squinting as she assessed him. Lord, her lashes were long. And why should he notice such a detail?

"Are ye a cruel man?"

"Some would say," his voice came out harsher than he'd intended, but all the better to keep him from getting distracted by the angles of her mesmerizing face. Besides, there was no use in lying to her. Those who died at the end of his sword would say he was cruel, unmerciful. But he always had a reason behind taking on each task he was hired to. And he never killed innocents. As a plus, he gave them all the last rites before he sliced into them.

"Are ye going to kill me?" It was the first time he'd sensed true fear in her. Candlelight flicked in her lavender gaze which was trained on his, and he had the distinct feeling she could read behind the lies in his eyes.

"Nay."

"Are *they* going to kill me?" she whispered.

Duncan hesitated and decided to tell her the truth. "I dinna know."

"Ye would abduct me and deliver me into evil's hands without knowing their plans?"

"I dinna care."

Heather looked stunned at his admission. 'Twas the truth he'd never cared about such things before. But for some reason, with her, there was a tiny flare of concern inching its way into his heart. He quashed it.

"Enough talking." The bells would soon toll for the family to come to morning Mass before they broke their fast. They needed to hurry, else his entire plan would go awry.

Duncan tugged a tripping Heather along the wall to the corner where a door led to a slim circular stairwell in the belfry tower. Up the stairs was a sleeping boy who'd soon wake to ring the bell. Down was the way out.

"Shh," he warned. If she woke that boy, he could toll out a warning and soldiers would meet them at the base of the stairwell.

Heather nodded, a little too compliant for his liking.

"Careful descending," Duncan warned, not that he needed to, but the stairs were especially narrow, and the lass seemed to be having trouble walking as it was.

"My skirts are giving me trouble," she grumbled.

"I'd be happy to remove them if it helps us to move with more speed," he offered.

She gasped, and he held in a laugh. "Ye would not dare!"

"Och, lass, dinna dare me to do anything. I'm always up for a challenge, and seeing a lass without her skirt would be a delight to a man in the morn." It was hard to tell what she would look like skirtless. There seemed to be a tremendous amount of cloth covering her lower extremities.

"Scoundrel."

Duncan chuckled. Teasing her about her skirts seemed to have distracted her enough that she made it down the stairs without incident.

He lifted the wooden bar slowly, making sure that he caused no sound to echo through the tower. Placing the bar on the ground, he opened the door an inch to stare outside. The door led to the gardens of the castle and, given that it was just now dawn, no one was about picking herbs or taking a stroll. He shoved the door all the way open and tugged her just outside into the darkened morning. He nudged the door quietly closed.

"Stay put," he murmured. Glancing around, he found a stone bench a few feet away. He lifted the heavy bench, upending it to hold the door in place.

"What are ye doing?" she whispered.

"Slowing down anyone who would try to rescue ye."

He didn't wait for her to respond, but instead walked right up to her, grabbed her about the waist and tossed her over his shoulder, surprised that she didn't weigh as much as she appeared to.

"Put me down! I can walk," she ground out breathlessly.

"Aye, but ye canna run as fast as I need ye to. And we've a need to make haste. Now hush else ye draw any of your precious brother's men to their death." He slapped her on the bottom and was rewarded with an outraged gasp.

Duncan ran with her to the end of the garden and stopped at the twenty-foot-high stone wall where he set her down. A cursory glance showed him that no one appeared to be watching them. The guards on the tower closest to them had their eyes on the sea. There had been four guards standing watch beyond this wall, but he'd taken care they would no longer be an issue when he'd climbed the wall just after three in the morning. No one had yet to miss them. Duncan was in the clear.

"Hold on to my back," he instructed, turning around and glancing at her over his shoulder. "Wrap your legs around my waist and your arms around my neck."

She gave him an incredulous look, which he ignored. Turning back toward the wall, he tested the rope he'd used to climb down. Still secure. Good.

"What?" she whispered harshly. "Ye canna possibly—"

He cut her off, flicked her another annoyed gaze over his shoulder. "I assure ye, 'tis possible, and I do intend to." Duncan again presented her with his back. "Grab hold. Now."

Heather didn't hesitate, thank goodness, but touched her hands to his shoulders and jumped, wrapping her legs around his waist and a death grip around his neck. Duncan swallowed and tugged at her arms. If he hadn't known better, he might have thought she was trying to kill him.

"Not so tight, else I lose my breath and we both fall."

Heather loosened her grip on his neck, but tightened her thighs around his hips. Duncan had to force himself not to groan. The lass had yanked up her skirts a little to allow enough flexibility in her clothing to grip him. A smooth calf brushed his elbow.

Mo chreach... he might just drop her. It had been much better when he'd imagined her legs to be as burly as his own.

"Where are the guards?" she asked.

"Gone." He didn't expound but began to climb.

Hand over hand, feet gripping the rope. He pulled them up at a steady pace, his muscles working with the added weight. Sweat trickled over his back, his arms. His palms grew damp but didn't hinder his progress. Heather clung tight to him. Whispered prayers, begged forgiveness for her sins, and wished not to die. Duncan held in his laughter, and at last they reached the ledge.

"Let go of my neck and pull yourself up onto the top." Pushing off the wall gently with his foot, he twisted his body around so Heather's back was against the stone.

"I dinna know if I can." Fear ebbed around the edges of her words.

"Aye, lass, ye can," Duncan spoke with knowing authority. "Go on. Do it now."

Heather blew out a breath, warm against his neck, then let go with one hand.

"That's it, Heather. Grip the wall." Letting go of the rope with one hand, he slid it under her thigh—gritting his teeth at the suppleness of her flesh. He didn't know which was more painful—holding up their weight on the rope with a single hand or touching the softness of her thigh. "I've got hold of ye. Ye can do it."

She seemed to gain some measure of safety from his grip on her thigh and took off her other hand, hoisting herself up onto the wall walk of the battlements.

Duncan made quick work of hoisting himself onto the stone floor and pulling up his rope. The sun was quickly rising. It wouldn't be long before guards came to relieve those Duncan had dispatched of. He tied off the rope on a crenellation, preparing for them to go down the other side.

"Get on." He crouched down, and Heather climbed onto his back again.

"Do ye make it a habit of having women ride ye?" she asked.

Duncan choked on his tongue. Holy Mother, did she realize what she'd just asked? With a wicked grin, he turned to glance over his shoulder. "Aye, lass, as often as I can."

Even in the dusky morning, he could see her face color red as a berry. Just to make her glow redder, he winked, satisfied when she let out a little gasp.

After making sure that the area below the wall was clear, he gripped the rope tight and climbed over the side. With measured movements, he walked them down the wall. The climb down was always easier than up. Once they were on solid ground, Heather dropped to her feet. He turned to see her smoothing out her skirts.

"Dinna be modest on my account, I've had your legs wrapped around me, your bare thigh under my fingers."

She let out an outraged snarl. "Only because if ye didna, I'd have ended up dead."

He snickered. "'Haps. Or maybe I just wanted the privilege."

"Ye're a brute."

Duncan bowed low. "I thank ye."

"'Twas not a compliment."

"Enough chatter. We must be away."

Dunrobin's beach was a hundred feet away, the waves lapping lazily at the shore, completely unaware that one of the ladies of its mighty castle had been so easily taken away.

"What will ye do? Sail away with me?" she quipped.

He shook his head and again tossed her onto his shoulder. "Nay, lass. Nothing so romantic as that."

Duncan ran toward the trees, careful to keep his eyes on the guards of Dunrobin. Once inside the cover of the forest, he found his horse, Blade, just where he'd left him, and set Heather on her feet.

"Where is my horse?" Heather asked.

"Och, such a spoiled lass ye are." Duncan gave her a pointed look. "This is an abduction, in case ye dinna recall. There will be no horse for ye. No way for ye to escape. Ye'll ride with me."

Heather crossed her arms over her chest, tilted her chin at a haughty angle and shook her head. "Nay. 'Tis indecent."

Duncan let out a surprised laugh. "Truly? Ye think I care for decency and your honor? I am abducting ye."

Was the lass daft? Did she not understand the concept of abduction? And for that matter, was he truly indulging her act? At that moment, he wished he had tied her up and stuffed her mouth with a rag. Then at least he wouldn't have to hear this nonsense. It was a stalling tactic. Had to be.

"I know," she said, her voice softer, as though she were thinking about something else entirely.

He glanced over at her, studying her. She was looking toward the ground, her hands wringing one another.

"What is it?" he asked harshly, disbelieving himself that he even asked. He wasn't supposed to care.

"Nothing," she said too quickly, glancing up at him with widened eyes.

"I doubt it," he mumbled. With the way she'd so openly run her mouth since the moment they'd met, she was certain to give him grief about something fairly soon.

But he wasn't going to wait to find out what it was. He was surprised that there weren't shouts coming from the castle already.

As if on cue, a loud whistle sounded from that direction. 'Haps the switching guards would have now found the bodies of the four he'd disposed of — or just found them missing. Didn't matter. He had little time now.

Heather heard the whistle, too. She whirled her head around sharply, staring back at the castle, her lower lip sucked into her mouth.

"Get on the horse," he ordered.

Heather turned away from the castle and approached Blade. Too easy.

"What are ye about, lass?" he asked, stepping closer, the air around them filled with tension. Would she bolt?

"Ye keep asking me that. There is nothing."

He doubted her. Narrowing his eyes, he studied her all the more. Her face was innocent enough, but lurking behind the beauty of her heather-colored eyes was a keen intelligence that had he seen it in a man it would have made him fearful.

Heather planted her hands on her hips and glared at him fiercely. "Maybe I should ask what's bothering ye? But ye're my captor, so I'm not supposed to ask ye questions."

How easily she'd taken the reins. "If ye must know, I think ye're up to something. No woman who's being abducted goes so willingly."

The lass had the audacity to shrug. "If ye want me to fight, I will. But I'd rather go without the bindings or a gag."

"Ye'd run if ye got the chance?"

"Should I nay want to?"

"Aye. But there's been many chances for ye to run, to scream, and ye've not used any of them."

"Maybe I want to leave Dunrobin."

That made him laugh. Hard. "A princess in her castle, spoiled rotten, the boss of everyone, and ye'd want to leave?"

"Believe it or not, I am more than a spoiled child as ye seem to think." Her words were spoken calmly, with a cool edge that made him pause.

"Run then. I should like to catch ye."

Heather didn't hesitate. She ran—but not back toward the castle. She ran in the opposite direction.

"What in bloody hell?" Duncan stammered.

The woman lifted her skirts, revealing creamy, sculpted calves—athletic legs—and hauled her arse up the densely foliaged hill.

Not at all what he'd expected. Grabbing hold of Blade's reins, he flung himself into the saddle and gave chase. He couldn't very well leave the horse, especially since she was running in the direction he wanted to go, and Sutherland warriors would be after them soon. Duncan leaned low over his warhorse's withers, gaining on the lass. She didn't look behind her, but kept a steady pace forward. A pace any normal male would have found daunting. She sprinted full force, without a falter in her footing, as though this were an action she enjoyed and practiced often.

No matter how well she raced, the lass was no competition for a horse. Blade nudged her in the middle of her back with his muzzle, and as she fell forward, Duncan swerved the horse to her left, bent low and lifted her around the waist, sitting her on his lap.

"Got ye."

Chapter Three

*H*eat flushed through Heather as though she'd been doused in boiling water. But it wasn't a painful burn. It made her wish for a fan to blow a cooling breeze over her face and neck. Made her want to curl into the hard, warm body of her captor.

Shameful, really.

The temperature was cooler beneath the trees where the sun had trouble reaching through the abundant leaves. Thank goodness for that, or she would have surely melted by now. They'd ridden for the better part of a half hour, her thighs pressed to his, her back held tight to his chest, her bottom touching…something long and hard. She preferred to think it was his weapon—and it was of a sorts, but this one made of all-male flesh.

The priest. A lie if ever she'd heard one.

Heather cleared her throat, wiggled forward, hoping to get away from his hardness, though it made her tingle in places she hadn't known could tingle. Made her yearn for… something.

Mostly, she wanted to get away from him. To shove his thick arm from her belly. To remove the tight grip he had on her hip. To hop off his massive horse and run away. Far away. To find the Scottish war camp. William Wallace. To be useful to her country and make her family proud. Her brother Ronan was there with his wife, Julianna—a warrior woman. If anyone, Julianna would see the merit in Heather's plans to fight for her country.

She'd not shun her or forbid it as her brothers Magnus, Blane and Ronan had done. They didn't think it was a woman's place. When Heather had brought up the fact that Julianna was the right hand of their future king, the men had all grumbled about her having been trained from birth and having the king's blood in her.

Well, with three older brothers, Heather had practically been trained from birth. Even her older sister, Lorna, and she had played warriors as children, fighting with pretend swords and shields in their shared bedchamber when their mother had put them to bed, and even later when their hired nurse had done the same.

Fighting was in her blood.

And she wasn't about to let the forbidden get in her way. Heather saw great things in her future. Great things for Scotland, and she knew she just had to be involved.

If she wasn't going to let the naysayings of her siblings get in her way, there was no way in hell she was going to allow a Highlander dressed as a priest obstruct her, either.

"Can we stop soon?" she asked, trying for meek, though it soured her belly. According to most men, a woman should know her place, and heavens knew, her family chaplain had preached it enough. 'Haps if she curbed her tongue, this devil priest would be more lenient, allowing her a chance to escape.

"Nay." Too serious. Had he guessed her intent?

"But I've need to…" God, her skin heated more at the mention of relieving herself than it had when he'd teased her about him giving women rides.

"Hold it," he instructed cruelly.

"But—"

"Lass, I'll nay be stopping. We're being followed."

"Followed?" That sent a chill cascading along her spine. She didn't want to be saved. Not yet, anyway. And if anyone was doing the saving, she wanted it to be William Wallace or Robert the Bruce.

Her adventure had only just begun.

"Aye. Now hush and hold on."

He spurred his horse onward, the poor animal covered in a lather of sweat as he'd been pushed faster and harder. Priest leaned forward, crushing her back with his muscled chest and forcing her to lean closer to the horse's neck. The hair from his mane flicked painfully onto her cheeks, and she squeezed her eyes shut to keep from watching the ground sweep by beneath their feet.

Heather wrapped her arms around the horse's neck and prayed they'd make it without either of them falling.

Priest veered sharply to the right. Seconds, and many slapping branches, later, they broke through the trees and raced across a rising and falling moor. The sun beamed down on them, feeling like it was burning the top of her head. Why, she asked herself for the hundredth time that day, had she chosen to wear so many darn layers?

They followed a winding, dirt-packed road. One Heather had ridden on the many occasions when she had visited her aunt and cousin Daniel at Blair Castle. She recognized the pattern of boulders that had been carved with various depictions of wildcat fights—some with each other, some with men, some with stags—hence the name, Wildcat Road.

Their pursuer had yet to make himself noticed, and Heather prayed he never did. This was her chance to catch a dream that manifested years ago, and only a few months ago had presented itself as viable a few months ago.

From what she'd overheard when Magnus spoke to his wife, Arbella, Robert the Bruce had betrayed Wallace at the Battle of Falkirk—and ever since, Wallace had lost his drive to fight, though last year he'd deployed to Europe to entreat France and Rome in gaining support for Scotland. There appeared to be some spark left in him after all. Magnus had spoken of Wallace returning to Scotland just last month, saying he was holed up in his home in Elderslie near Glasgow. Magnus and Arbella planned to visit Wallace on their way to Lorna's house in the fall for All Hallows Day. Heather was to attend in order to help their many children. She loved her nieces and nephews dearly, but watching them run around like chickens with their heads cut off, covered in muck like little piglets and yanking on her like puppies was not the way Heather envisioned herself spending the evening. She'd much rather enjoy the bonfires, delicious food and wine—and the dancing. Waiting several months before speaking to Wallace would be torture. She didn't have the patience for it.

Priest slowed the horse as they rounded a crag jutting with sharp-edged stones. He leaned to the left as they rounded right, pulling her along with him. Good God, she prayed she didn't fall from the horse. The fall would likely kill her. Blade was at least twenty hands high. The tallest she'd seen. Even more so than any of her brothers' horses. Apparently, stealing maidens was a lucrative business.

When they were again righted, her bladder screamed to be let down.

"Are we still being followed?" she asked, praying he said nay. "I may…um…make a mess of your horse." She squirmed for added measure.

The man grunted and sped the horse faster over the road, before at last stopping by a copse of barren trees apart from the forest. He jumped off the horse and tugged her down.

"Go. There." He pointed to one of the trees.

A sad excuse for foliage. The slim trunk would barely hide one side of her bottom.

"There is not enough coverage," she said.

"If ye piss on my robes, I'll beat ye within an inch of your life." He whirled his back on her.

An excellent opportunity to run. As if suspecting she might think that, he whipped back around, his billowing priest's robes like a cloud of black smoke.

"Dinna think of running. I'm sure your brother follows at a distance. He wouldn't want to be without his precious youngest sister."

Heather couldn't help herself. She stuck out her tongue at the man and then turned on her heel, marching straight for the trees. She wasn't brave enough to yank her skirts up, though, without first looking to see if the priest had turned around.

Thank goodness he had. She fairly danced with the need to relieve herself. Hiking up her skirts, she squatted and did her business. Either the man had a sixth sense or eyes in the back of his head, for when she was finished, skirts properly in place, he turned back toward her.

"Will ye toss me my satchel? There's water inside, and I'd like to wash my hands." An odd request, she knew, but necessary all the same. Living in a house full of males made her appreciate all the more being clean.

The priest gave her an odd look but did dig through her satchel for the waterskin. He handed it to her. But her hands shook, nerves getting the best of her. The waterskin slipped from her hands, splashing all over the ground.

"Careful," Priest said softly.

Heather glared up at him, certain that spilling all of her water was his fault. She tossed him the empty waterskin and he stuffed it back in her satchel.

"Catch."

She jerked her gaze up as he tossed her an apple.

Heather reached with one hand, catching the fruit easily enough. Thank goodness, her reflexes appeared to be back.

"Lucky," he said.

She smirked. Let him think so. Another thing she'd learn to appreciate with a castle full of men—besting them at their own games.

"Let us be on our way."

Heather climbed atop the horse, and her captor climbed up behind her. Thank goodness, she was no longer on his lap—but even still, his hard body touched hers in a way that made her want to faint.

"What is your name?" she asked, figuring that with such close proximity, and he knowing her first name, she might as well know his.

"Priest." His tone was dull and clipped. He didn't want her to ask any further questions.

But she didn't care. "Ye want me to call ye Priest? I'd rather call ye by your given name."

He only grunted and spurred the horse into a gallop—in the direction they'd come.

"What are ye doing? We're going the wrong way."

He grunted again.

"Are ye a savage? Speaking only in grunts and hisses?"

"I'm nay savage, but ye might think so after I gag ye with the hem of your skirt."

This time, Heather grunted. She took a bite of the crisp and juicy apple. It'd been hours since she'd woken, and it was the first thing she'd eaten since the day before. The juice of the apple and its sweet meat tantalized her tongue. Could have very well been the best apple she'd ever consumed. She was grateful to have brought them.

"Do ye want an apple?" she asked, realizing that he'd given her one but not taken one for himself.

"Nay. Not yet."

She tossed the thin core of her apple into the brush as they turned to head straight up the crag. Not exactly the way they'd come.

"Have ye lost your way?"

"I never lose my way."

"So, ye have a plan, then?"

"I always have a plan." The man sounded so sure of himself she was overcome with the need to punch him, or inflict some other sort of violence on him that he couldn't have possibly planned for. Show him that he wasn't as in control as he led her—and himself for that matter—to believe. "No more questions."

Heather did as he bade, afraid that, though he'd not done it so far, he'd be compelled to muzzle her.

The only problem with not thinking up questions to ask him was that she started to think of other things. Like how strong his chest was, and how nice it felt to have his strong arm around her waist. And how with the rhythm of the horse, their hips moved in unison, almost like a dance. How that dance made her body tingle, and she couldn't stop shifting.

And then her mind started wondering to other places, like what it would be like to have the priest kiss her, touch her again on her bare thigh, move with her like that when they were both—

Blasphemy!

She was doomed to hell for thinking such wicked, sinful thoughts about a man of the cloth.

Even if he was a fraud, it was unquestionably a sin to even think it. And she already had enough to confess. Adding lustful thoughts to the list was enough to launch Father Hurley over the edge. He might suggest to Magnus that instead of a visit to her aunt Fiona's—where she was always sent when her older brother thought she was starting to get out of hand—a trip to the nunnery might be better.

She wouldn't be able to live if they put her there, though! Sheer boredom and the need to rebel against every rule and structured hour would have the abbess bending Heather over her knee or taking a lash to her back, or whatever it was they did to punish nuns.

Heather was most certainly *not* nun material.

She closed her eyes and began begging forgiveness. Promising that from now on she'd try her best to be sin-free if only God would forgive her for her wicked thoughts.

Heather frowned. She was making promises she couldn't keep.

Forcing herself to forget about the hard heat molded to her body was difficult. Heather yawned, finding herself lulled by the rocking of the horse. At least if she fell asleep, she wouldn't have to deal with the tingling sensations that were cascading up and down her form. She could forget about it for a little while. Forget about *him.*

But as she started to let herself slip into sleep, a little voice in her head warned against it. If she fell asleep, she'd not be able to see where they were headed, nor would she be able to make contact with any Scottish rebellion warriors if they came across them. Sleep was out of the question.

Talking was the only way she knew how to keep herself awake. And so, she prepared yet another litany of questions for the priest.

"How much did they pay ye?"

"I told ye before 'tis not about the money."

"I heard ye when ye said it, but no man risks his life for free. Everyone has their price."

"Revenge." The word came out a harsh growl.

Heather swallowed down her fear, and squared her shoulders. "If it were completely about revenge, ye'd have taken me for yourself."

He grunted, and she hoped she hadn't just given him an idea. As if to taunt her, he canted his hips forward, pressing that intimate part of him to her bottom. She nearly drowned in her combination of cough and gasp.

"What harm will it be if ye tell me?" She scooted forward, away from him.

"There's a bit of silver in it."

"Silver. Hmm…"

"Dinna offer to double it. I will nay bargain for it." The priest tugged her backward, firmly planting her rump between his thighs. "Unless ye wanted to offer me another reward."

Please, God, let him not be offering up *that* in exchange for her freedom. "Not silver?"

"Mmm hmm." He nuzzled her hair, pressed his lips to the side of her ear, sending white-hot shivers all over her. What was he doing? Why was he doing it? Nay, why did *she* enjoy it? "What will ye give me that's better than silver?"

"I—I could not know what ye want," she stammered, pretending innocence, though his message was more than clear.

"Och, aye, ye know it." His hand gripped her hip hard, then skimmed upward just beneath her breast.

Heather gasped and jolted forward—a little too far. She gripped on to the horse's mane to steady herself from falling over the animal's head.

"I see ye understand."

"Aye. And I will not give ye *that*."

The man had the audacity to chuckle. Had he been teasing her this entire time?

"Ye blaspheme your profession." She should have been outraged, but instead she found herself intrigued by a man who was as much a fan of trickery as herself.

"Do I?"

"A man of the cloth with such lustful thoughts," she reproached.

"I am but a man, and ye a beautiful, supple lass." He squeezed her hip for emphasis.

Heather didn't know whether to be offended or flattered. Perhaps she was a bit of both. And that scared her most of all.

"Tell me this, lass, ye seem more concerned with what is to come rather than what has already occurred. Ye lack fear. Either ye are extremely dimwitted or exceedingly devious."

Heather's mouth dropped open, but before she could reply, he continued, "Given that ye pray in the chapel each morning before Mass begins, one would think ye might be a pious and virtuous lady. But I'm inclined to think ye go each morning, dutifully, to pay penance for your sins. What sins do ye have, lass?"

'Twas hard to close her mouth after it had fallen open. How in the devil did he know? She bit her lip to keep from retorting something truly unladylike, and instead replied, "Not nearly as many as ye, Priest."

His chest rumbled against her back as he laughed. "A pity we were not introduced under different circumstances."

"Because a priest and a wayward lass would have made such amiable dinner companions?" Heather said sarcastically.

"Nay, lass, not dinner companions," he said in low tones against her ear.

Her face heated again as a shiver passed over her. The man had a knack for turning her body heat up ten degrees with a few whispered words.

"I think I might have preferred the gag."

Priest laughed again.

Heather clamped her mouth closed, swearing she wouldn't speak again for...well, for how long she didn't know. But one thing was certain, she needed to stop entertaining the notion that there was more to this situation than a bad man stealing a noblewoman.

Chapter Four

*R*elief flooded Duncan as soon as they crossed through the narrow valley, and the abandoned castle crept into view. He'd been here before. Countless times.

The sun had begun to set behind the darkened clouds that gathered. They were in for a summer storm. He wouldn't be surprised if it hit before they had a chance to make camp within the crumbling castle's walls. But judging by the look of it, the rain would taper into a gentle mist.

"We are nearly there," he said, mostly out of courtesy to the lass. She'd been troubling him with talk since before dawn, but the last hour had remained silent, save for the grumble of her stomach.

"Oh." She cleared her throat and somehow managed to sit taller.

Lady Heather was more likely than not stiff as steel. She'd sat straight, prim and proper for the entire ride, and every time

The Highlander's Sin

he'd tugged her back against him, she'd inched slowly forward. If she sat any straighter, she'd snap in two.

The woman thought he was touching her indecently on purpose, and while that was partly true, it was also difficult to ride a horse when his companion was practically sitting on the mount's neck. Blade kept shaking his head with displeasure.

Thank the saints that in a few moments they would be off his poor mount's back and safely ensconced within the castle walls.

"Who lives there?" she asked.

He could tell she tried to sound strong, but beneath her haughty tone was a glimmer of fear. Her fear incited a feeling inside him he'd not experienced often—empathy. 'Twas unsettling.

"No one." At least none since he'd been born. It looked to have been laid siege to, not old enough to have crumbled on its own. One entire side of the keep was collapsed, the rest falling piece by piece as the years went by. But not so much that he thought it would be unsafe to sleep there.

"Then why are we making camp inside?"

"Because no one is there." Duncan tried to keep the exasperation from his voice. She still had yet to grasp the concept of his having abducted her and the need to keep a low profile because of it. "Did ye expect a feast filled with guests clamoring for your attention?"

Heather's elbow shot backward. Duncan leaned back just in time to avoid the jab. While she made a pretense of shifting in the saddle, he had the distinct impression she had, in fact, been trying to elbow him.

He had to clench his jaw to keep from laughing. The spirits of a dozen whiny wenches resided within the lass for certain.

"I expected no such thing." She paused a moment, her thoughts hanging nearly visible in the air. "I but wondered if this was where ye'd make the exchange for your pouch of silver."

And straight to the heart of the matter she went. "Ah, I see. Not this night. Tonight we make camp."

She nodded, her shoulders sagging a little in what he thought might be relief. "And on the morrow?"

Duncan shoved away that nagging feeling inside him. Forgetting who he was, what his purpose was, would only lead to trouble. Woman trouble was the last thing he needed. "We ride."

"South?"

He'd not tell her a damn thing. Else, she'd be able to concoct a plan for escape—an incident he was determined to avoid. "That, I'll nay be sharing with ye."

"To meet your overlord?"

Duncan frowned. The idea of anyone lording over him left a sour taste in his mouth. "I dinna have an overlord."

"Every man looks up to someone."

"I dinna."

"Not even God?"

His chest seized, pulling him back to a time when he had thought God might be on his side. But then all had been ripped from beneath him. Even those who'd taken him in had been little more than caretakers and teachers. Not family. Men of the cloth themselves. Duncan was alone. Though he wore the robes, he was anything but ecclesiastical. His higher power was the earth itself, the pleasures Mother Nature had to offer and the coin he could make with his skills as a fighter. "Not even God." The bitterness on his tongue could only be washed away with a few draughts of whisky and a willing wench straddling his thighs—and he was likely to only get one of those this night.

Duncan kept a keen eye out for anyone watching. They circled the walls. He found a few more stones fallen since the last time he'd been here and weeds growing tall around the edges — with a few matted circles in the grass where animals must have made a home.

When after walking Blade round the outskirts of the castle walls, it appeared they were alone, Duncan steered them back toward the spot where the once-wooden wall had rotted away. Probably the first problem the old lord of this place had suffered. He'd built his keep in stone first — and not the wall. Anyone could burn, chop or break down wood. It was more easily accessible than if the lord had born the patience to protect what was his before beautifying it.

Foolish.

A stone castle surrounded by a wooden wall was basically useless in Duncan's eyes. A waste of time and effort — the end result was an abandoned place that once must have boasted some beauty.

The courtyard possessed much of the same appearance as the outside, tall grasses growing up where he assumed a dirt-packed road had once been. Outbuildings had collapsed, some of them burned into crumbling ash. Abandoned broken wagons. Nothing much of use. Every person who came upon the castle took from it what they needed.

Duncan walked Blade right up the left side of the front stairs, the right having crumbled somehow — a stone from a trebuchet? He wasn't sure, but every time he visited, he did the same thing and rode his horse inside. No way was he going to leave his prized steed outside.

Inside was darker, though the arrow-slit windows and the partially missing roof did afford some light from the setting sun.

"Why—"

"Shh…" Duncan cut off the lass. Just because he didn't see anyone outside, did not mean there were no lurkers within.

He drew his sword, prepared to cut down anyone who attacked them. Gripping the hilt and scanning their surroundings, Duncan made their introductions. "Come out, ye rotten bastards."

Above, a few wings flapped hard as nesting birds let out panicked chirps in the broken silence. One poor creature must have been startled so much that its nest fell as it flapped away, spilling its eggs to the rotting floor. A rat to the right scurried over and under the decaying rushes, probably headed in the direction of the crushed eggs. A sorry-looking tapestry hung in drapes from only one corner, the opposite side having long since fallen.

There was no other noise. No rush of feet to hide or gasps of shock. No whistle of a sword being pulled from its scabbard. Only a few birds and rats were their company.

All the same, Duncan would use caution. Abandoned castles were excellent resting spots for anyone along the road. Not the safest of places with crumbling walls and the ability for nearly everyone to happen upon, but safer than the forest. Especially if it were to rain. A partial roof was better than no roof.

He slid his claymore back in place on his back and then dismounted, his boots crunching on debris littering the floor. Thank the saints, the odor of things rotting was muted, a slight musty smell, really, and that was all.

Heather looked down at him with wide, frightened eyes. A small, foreign twinge of guilt struck him. He'd taken her away from everything she knew, and while she'd put on a brave front, he knew the lass had to be terrified. She'd no inkling of what was in store for her, and honestly, he wasn't sure either. Lady Ross had insisted on the captive being Heather. No one else in the house would do, and the way the disgusting woman and her whelp of a husband had smiled and eyed each other with hungry interest every time they'd said the poor girl's name had turned Duncan's stomach.

Reaching up, he gripped Heather around her middle. Beneath layers, she had a tiny waist. Why she wore them, he hadn't a clue. Maybe to trick men like him into thinking she was larger. She sucked in a breath as he pulled her down, holding her against him a little too long. He gazed in her eyes, marveling at their color. Her hips pressed to his, and if he tugged her a couple of inches closer, her breasts would rub against his chest. Damn it. Why did *he* have to wear so many layers? He'd barely be able to feel the softness of her.

"Ye've beautiful eyes." The words were out before he could cease their stroll across his tongue. Now he was giving her compliments? Did he need to remind himself that this was an abduction and not a seduction?

Heather's lips parted, her pink tongue darting out over her lower lip and then rubbing over the upper, not in a sensual way, but nervously. Didn't matter, though, he found it entirely erotic.

"Thank ye," she said.

He grunted, wanting too much to kiss that enticing mouth and see if she tasted as sweet as she smelled. "I will not let any harm come to ye." A promise he couldn't keep if he turned her over to Lady Ross. "Not while ye're with me." Adding that disclaimer didn't make him feel any better.

Heather rested her hands on the backs of his forearms, her thumbs pressing gently to the insides of his elbows, making him aware that he still held her waist.

"Not a promise one might receive from a captor," she said, her voice hushed. Her face colored a little, and he noted that her chest heaved slightly — the lass's breath was quickening.

Did she like him touching her?

Hell, did she want him to kiss her as much as he wanted to?

Only one way to find out. Before Duncan could talk himself out of it, he lowered his lips slowly to hers. Soft, warm and supple. He slid his lips over hers, breathing in her flowery, feminine scent as his nose touched her cheek.

The lass resisted, shoving against his chest. But only for a few seconds. Then she leaned into him. He'd been right. She had wanted to kiss him as much as he'd wanted to kiss her. A thought he was uncomfortable with exploring. Heather slid her hands from his forearms to his upper arms, squeezing. He held his breath, still in a state of disbelief. Why was she kissing him back? And why did he care? He should simply take advantage of it while he could.

Duncan kept his hands firmly planted on her waist, not willing to explore anything further than her mouth. He wasn't sure if it was because he was too afraid of what touching her would do to him, or that it might scare her into breaking one of the sweetest kisses he'd ever known.

He nudged her lips open at the same time he asked himself what the hell he was doing. This was not at all part of the plan. Though it wasn't unheard of for abductors to rape their victims, Duncan was no rapist. Nay, he was enjoying this kiss, this play of his lips over hers, and he was going to kiss her till she went limp in his arms. He touched his tongue to her lip, getting just the reaction he'd hoped for—a shocked gasp that made his middle tighten and blood rush straight to his groin.

Duncan nibbled at her lips, not wanting to shock her too much with the thrust of his tongue into her sweet mouth. But Heather was a bold lass. She slid her arms up, around his neck, lacing her fingers into his hair, and tugged him closer, slanting her head to the side. A natural passion for kissing.

He was not going to disappoint her.

Driving his tongue between her lips, he melded it against the velvet of hers, rubbing, tasting, taking. With this kiss, he claimed her mouth, wished he could have claimed all of her. If not for the fact that she was simply a mission he was to complete, he might have found a spot within these broken castle walls where he could lay her down on his plaid and worship her from head to toe.

Heather was not the type of woman whom a man used to pleasure himself. With her feisty spirit, he was certain she would be overly entertaining in the bedchamber. Full of passion and life. She matched the tempo of his tongue, pressed her body against his. However many layers she wore, it wasn't enough to keep the heat of her from him, nor the suppleness of her curves.

Unable to help himself, Duncan slid his hands to her hips, squeezing as he massaged his way down to her buttocks. No amount of layers could hide the ripe roundness of her behind. As he gripped her rear in his hands, Heather gasped, for the first time breaking their kiss.

She leapt backward. Her hands untangled from his hair in a painful yank. The leather thong that had held his hair back trickled to the ground from her fingers. Wrenching her hand back, she tried to slap him, but Duncan caught her hand an inch before his face.

He made a *tsking* sound with his tongue. "For shame, lassie. Ye might have me thinking ye didna enjoy that kiss."

Fury filled her frown. If eyes could form daggers, she'd have shot half a dozen at him already. "I didna enjoy it."

Duncan snaked his arm around her middle and tugged her back against him. "I would beg to differ."

She panted with frustration and tried to wriggle free.

"Your eyes are darkened with desire. Lips swollen from kissing. Skin flushed." He pressed his hand above her breasts, feeling the quickened beat of her heart beneath his palm. "Your heart beats as fast as your breath." He scraped his stubbled jaw over her cheek and pressed his lips to her ear. "Your mouth can tell me ye hated it, but your body doesna lie."

Heather cried out in outrage and jumped away from him, her delicate little hands fisted at her sides. Duncan smiled wickedly in her direction and winked, loving how it appeared only to make her angrier.

"How dare ye speak to me like that? Do ye have any idea what ye've done? The extent to which ye've gone and the wrath my family will bring down upon your head?"

Duncan let out a short, bitter laugh. "Och, lass, ye dinna understand." He stepped closer to her, his smile disappearing as he stared into her heated, violet eyes. "I dinna give a fig about your family or what they'll do to me. Ye see, your family is the very reason behind what I'm doing. And for the record, I know damn well what I just did. This."

Without asking permission, nor waiting for her response, Duncan grasped Heather's upper arms in a vice-like grip and lifted her off her feet, crashing his mouth against hers at the very same moment. He took possession of her mouth, and he wasn't gentle like he'd been the first time. Nay, this kiss was a claiming, a show of power, a way for him to let his anger at her family channel through him and into her, all while knowing that she damned well liked it.

The wench struggled at first, wriggling in his grasp, kicking at his shins. But as soon as his tongue touched hers, all her struggles ceased, and she hungrily kissed him in return. Duncan slowly set her down, only to wrap his arms around her waist and lift her again, backing her up against a stone wall, where he held her captive. Nonetheless, as soon as her back hit and his hard body slammed against the welcoming planes of hers, he knew he had to stop.

This was only going to lead to a deed he was absolutely not ready for—one of a carnal nature. Hell, he could have kissed her all day. If she hadn't been a Sutherland, he'd have bedded her already. The fact remained, however, that Lady Heather was not his for the plucking, as much as he would have relished lifting her skirts to reveal the soft, wet petals of her femininity.

And, he wasn't a rapist. There was a big difference between him and other warriors for hire. Duncan had morals. Even if he had an empire full of sins.

"Damn it," he growled, shoving away from her warm and willing body.

Heather blanched, her face going about two shades lighter than the norm. "Get away from me," she managed to choke out.

The woman was just as affected by their kiss as he was. Duncan whirled away from her, not caring that she might be able to pull a concealed weapon from her person and attack him with it. His cock was rock hard and tenting the front of his robes in a way he knew would draw her attention—and vexation. His sexuality was his own enemy. A man of the cloth shouldn't feel the way he did, nor do the things he'd done.

Duncan had to admit the truth. He might have taken vows once, but he'd long since let them go.

Just like he needed to let go of this insane attraction he felt for his captive. His enemy's niece—Lady Heather Sutherland.

Chapter Five

"Time for bed," the priest said gruffly, swiping the leather thong she'd pulled from his hair off the floor. He threaded his hands through his hair, pulling it back and tying the leather in it once more.

Heather gaped at the warrior priest, still in a state of shock at being pressed up against a wall. Her mouth tantalized with his wicked tongue. The way he'd caressed her, sliding his body over hers... She was fairly certain now that his robes were a front for his true nature—a virgin-seducing warrior.

The few kisses she'd received in her life did not compare in the least to what had just happened between them. She could still feel his hard, hot body tucked so intimately to hers, his velvet tongue sliding roughly and then enticingly over hers. His hands gripping tight to her hips...her bottom. His scent—a masculine mix of the outdoors, horses and something spicy.

Good God, if he'd not pushed away from her when he had, she would have willingly lifted her skirts if only to find out if every touch was as exquisite as his kiss.

A realization that scared the wits out of her.

"Come over here." He walked to the far wall of the great hall, where the hearth still stood strong in the center. Broken furniture and discarded rubbish crowded the floor, and she had to pick her way carefully over it.

The castle had obviously long since been stripped of anything that held value.

"Sit."

Heather's heart skidded at his tone. Commanding, cruel, cold. No more of the passion that had ignited between them. A clue that what had happened affected her much more than it had him. If anything, he was angry about it. Not confused like she was. Confused about why she'd liked it so much and how to make her lips stop tingling. She pursed her lips, and then pressed them hard together, attempting to force herself to stop thinking about their kiss.

The warrior kicked away debris by the wall, clearing a space, and then pointed at the floor. Heather nodded and rushed forward, hating that she was so willing to comply with him. If he could be so cruel with a kiss, there was no telling to what extent he'd go if she riled him up enough. Her stomach growled.

"I'm hungry," she said quietly as she approached.

He stiffened. "Sit."

Heather frowned and followed his instructions, smoothing her skirts beneath her and praying no rats decided to nibble on her fingers and toes when complete darkness came and she'd no warning of their approach.

The man rummaged in a satchel, pulling out a few oatcakes and scraps of jerky. "Here."

"Thank ye." Why she thanked him, she didn't know. He didn't deserve that much, especially when he was tossing scraps at her like she was a dog.

He was rude, inconsiderate, had practically molested her—no matter that she'd liked it—and he'd taken her away from her family, intent on delivering her into the hands of some evil lord for a few coins. There hadn't been a chance to escape yet, but as soon as he was asleep, she was going to steal his horse and make a run for it.

Heather bit into the stale oatcake, hating how it sucked the moisture from her tongue. She choked it down and took another bite. Food was energy, and she was going to need it in a few hours.

She watched from hooded eyes as the priest wiped down his horse, fed the animal an apple and whispered in his ear. Treated his warhorse better than he did her. Not surprising. Most warriors did. Their horses were their constant companions. If they didn't treat them well, the animals were likely to rebel. A rebelling warhorse was dangerous, even potentially deadly to a warrior.

Mystery clouded her abductor. He wore priest's robes, the crucifix around his neck lent an air of religion, but the way he kissed was anything but saintly. Who was he? What was his story? Not that she should have an inkling of curiosity about him. He was, after all, trying to thwart her desire to meet up with William Wallace. But something about him compelled her interest.

With a frown she bit into the jerky—and practically cracked her teeth. It was so hard, she had to gnaw on it for a good minute before a small, mangled piece popped off. She shivered at the taste. Not good in the least. Tasted more like a slice of the priest's belt than dried venison flank. Heather actually pulled it back to make sure it wasn't a belt. Hmm. Nay. Definitely jerky. Just the very worst she'd ever had.

"Be happy I'm nay starving ye, princess."

Heather ripped off another chunk of venison and glared up at the warrior priest. How did he know she was so disgusted with her meal? He'd not even been watching her. That she knew of... He was sly as a fox, this one.

"Why dinna ye just take off those robes ye hide beneath and show your true colors?" she snapped.

He grinned in a way that was not quite filled with humor. "Would ye like that? For I wear nothing else."

"Ye disgust me." How could he just say the things he said? How could he make her feel the way she did? The man *was* dressed beneath his robes, she'd seen his warrior garb when he'd threatened her with the ax, but that didn't matter. It was the thought of him wearing nothing beneath the robes that sent chills racing up and down her arms. She wanted to run over to him and hit him repeatedly—until her fists cried out for mercy.

"Ye disgust yourself."

Heather let out a cry of outrage. "I dinna!"

"Huh." And that was all he said before he sat on a stool—or rather a chair that's back had been broken off. He bit effortlessly into his venison, making her wonder if he'd given her the worst pieces.

"What do ye mean by that?" she asked, unable to resist taking his bait.

"By what?" he asked nonchalantly as he munched.

Oh, she could feel the rage boiling in her blood. Instead of saying something she'd regret, Heather chomped down on another sawdust oatcake.

"Well? Are ye going to explain your question, or are ye in the habit of ignoring people?" The way he'd said it was as though he were trying to annoy her. On purpose.

"Ye are no person."

He lifted a brow and reached beneath his robes. Her heart thundered. What was he about? Had he somehow managed to strip nude and discard his clothes when she hadn't been looking? But when he pulled out only a small flask, she wasn't sure if she was relieved or disappointed he'd not made good on his threat to show her just what was beneath his robes. She'd felt *it*. Hard, thick and long. A woman of her age and status should have been afraid to feel such intimate parts of a man. But not Heather. She was intensely curious. Dangerously so. All in spite of hating him and the very ground he sat on.

"If I'm not a person, then what am I?"

"Good question."

She smirked, then licked her lips as he guzzled whatever was in the flask. Her tongue was dry, and she was suddenly overcome by an extreme thirst.

"And being an educated noblewoman from the house of Sutherland, ye've a good answer, I'm certain." Sarcasm laced his words.

The man was irritating. So much so she cringed. The corner of his lip curled as he observed her. Thick, kissable lips. Heather tossed the rest of her distasteful dinner a few feet away.

"Ye've just invited a slew of rats to feast on your leftovers and your luscious legs."

He thought her legs luscious? A twinge of heat roused between her thighs. God bless it, this man made her forget everything she wanted, needed. Made her forget her duty to Scotland and the very reason she'd left in the first place—because she was going to escape from him and find William Wallace.

"Ye're a cad. That's what ye are. And ye have no name."

"I have a name." He wiped a droplet of liquid from his lower lip with the pad of his thumb.

Heather crossed her arms over her breasts—partly in obstinance and partly to hide the fact that her nipples had hardened into achy, wanton buds. "Then tell me what it is."

He took another swig from his flask and observed her closely, seeming to study every angle of her face and form before he finally answered. "Duncan."

"Duncan," Heather repeated.

The Highlander's Sin

"Aye."

"Father Duncan?"

He nodded. "In the flesh."

"What about…" She trailed off, unable to form the words without having them trip over her tongue.

She wanted to ask him about their kiss. How a man of the cloth could hold such passion and wield it with such skill. Heather licked her lips and sat forward. "Mind sharing that drink?" Not the question she'd wanted to ask, but her thirst was becoming overwhelming.

Duncan strutted forward, handing her the flask. Their fingers brushed as she took it, and a tremor shook her. Dear God, how was it possible for him to have taken hold of her so easily? She was supposed to hate him. Thought she did. And yet, when he touched her—with the tips of his fingers—while passing a drink, a need for sustenance, she trembled.

"Thank ye," she muttered.

Heather touched the rim of the flask to her lips and tipped it back. Knowing it wasn't going to be water, she was still shocked by the burn that took hold as liquid fire poured onto her tongue.

She jerked the flask away and sprayed the liquid in front of her, followed by uncontrollable coughs. "What is this?" she managed.

"Whisky. And ye've wasted a lot of it." He snatched the flask from her and, with exaggerated movement, shoved the cork back in place. "I forget ye're but a bairn." Grabbing hold of a skin from where he'd placed his things, he tossed it to her.

Heather had good reflexes and had played catch enough that she easily reached out to snatch the tossed waterskin from the air. Duncan's eyes widened in surprise.

"Did ye hope I'd drop it?" she asked with a bit of snippiness. 'Haps he'd thought her catching the apple earlier that day had been chance.

Duncan chuckled. "Nay. I had hoped it would knock ye over."

"Hmph. Ye'll need a lot more than a waterskin to knock me over." She popped the cork and chugged the lukewarm, slightly scummy water. As unladylike as it was, she was once more spitting and swiping at her tongue and lips with the back of her hand. "Ugh, where did ye get this?"

Duncan shrugged. "I dinna drink water."

"How old is it?" she asked, eyes narrowing with concern, her stomach already roiling with the need to heave.

Again he shrugged.

Oh, God, if only she'd not spilled her own supply. Heather threw down the waterskin and made a run for the door, needing to expunge the slimy, who-knew-what water. But Duncan stopped her, his arm slinging around her waist.

"Where do ye think ye're going?" he asked.

This time his touch didn't send frissons of desire running through her, she was all too consumed with the need to purge.

"Let go of me!" she screeched, writhing in his hold. "I have to—" But before she could finish, it was already coming out. Soaked oatcake and jerky splattered inches from the only pair of shoes she had.

"Better?" he asked.

Oh, how she wanted to scream, to scratch his eyes out. No one had ever seen her upend herself before, and here he was asking how it felt. He had deliberately delayed her escape to somewhere private. Forget not hating him. She despised him with every fiber of her being.

"Ye're a bastard, whoreson," she growled, wiping her mouth with her sleeve.

Duncan stiffened behind her. "Ye've a nasty little mouth, my lady. Where did ye learn to speak like that? 'Haps I ought to issue ye a penance for speaking to a man of the cloth in such a way."

The Highlander's Sin

"Ye're no—" His coarse hand covered her mouth, stifling her words.

He tugged her back tight to his chest and leaned close to her ear. "That'll be a warning to ye. Next time ye speak to me like that, issue me names, I'll bend ye over my knee and whip your pretty little arse."

Heather gasped. No words came out of her. She was too shocked. No one had ever spoken to her that way before. No one. Literally. Not her parents before they'd died. Not her older brothers and sisters. Nor her aunts, uncles, and cousins. And never her own family chaplain. But this man. This priest... He took the fight right out of her, for she desperately did not want to be laid over his lap, her naked behind bared to his eyes while he whipped her. That would have been the ultimate in mortification. And she didn't doubt for second that he would do it.

"Shall I let go of ye? Think ye can behave, princess?"

Heather nodded, tears burning her eyes.

Duncan slowly removed his hand from her mouth and then his arm from around her waist. He backed away from her inch by inch, and as she felt his presence retreat, she stiffened upward, but couldn't turn around. The tears that had brimmed she couldn't hold back and now they slid in large rivulets down her cheeks. She was too embarrassed to swipe them away, or to face him, and so she stood there, facing the way out. Her escape.

Duncan didn't say anything to her, perhaps sensing somehow that he'd wounded her pride. No orders to return to her seat. She heard him moving around behind her. Her throat was tight, and her shoulders shook a little with the held-in tears. A quarter hour passed like that in silence, and she was well aware with the amount of time passing, that Duncan knew she'd cried. That he'd given her space, allowing her some semblance of privacy, the kindness of the gesture only made her wish she could hate him more.

"I'll nay be lighting a fire. Would draw attention, but with a plaid to cover ye, ye shouldna be too cold in here tonight."

Heather swallowed hard, discreetly swiped at her remaining teardrops and nodded. With a shuddering sigh, she composed herself.

"Come and lie down." It was not a request, but he said it softly, so that it felt like one.

Still unable to speak, afraid her voice would sound garbled from her cry, Heather bowed her head and turned, seeing that Duncan had spread a plaid wide on the ground and then another over top. Big enough for two. He'd made *them* a bed. Not her. *Them*. For a pillow, he'd rolled up his robe. There was nothing in her spot.

"Since ye've got on at least four gowns, I thought ye might spare one for a pillow."

Heather was stunned still—staring at the black robes carefully rolled up. She didn't dare look at him. He'd said before that he was naked beneath his robes. Was he now standing naked a few feet away and intending to sleep beside her in such a state.

"Here." He handed her a stick. "Chewing this will get the taste of your stomach out of your mouth."

Heather took the proffered stick with trembling fingers and tucked it into her mouth. Cinnamon burst in her mouth, not at all sweet like it was on rolls, but foul. Utter trickery, given its delicious scent.

"Next time we kiss, 'twill be doubly sweet."

Next time? Her stomach fluttered with excitement, and her breath hitched.

"I..." She couldn't finish.

"Take off a gown and lie down, Heather."

Oh dear heavens... There was no escaping this. Except... if he was nude, he might not run after her.

Heather whirled on her heel, prepared to make a break for it. But before she took three steps, his arm snaked around her waist, hauling her back.

"Dinna think about it."

She glanced down to see that his arm was covered in white linen. Not naked. He had on a shirt at least.

"Do I have to tie ye up while ye sleep?"

Heather shook her head, the thought of being held captive like that, terrifying.

"I thought lying beside ye would be enough of a deterrent to trying to escape, but I see that may not be the case after all. I've some rope I can use to bind ye."

She cleared her throat. "Nay. Nay, that won't be necessary." Miraculously her words came out strong and sober. "I will lay down."

"Do ye need me to help ye remove a gown?"

Heat filled her cheeks as the image of him behind her untying her and loosening the gown over her arms flooded her mind. "Ye'd probably like that, but nay."

"I will nay lie to ye, lass. The idea is enticing. But I merely asked to be practical."

"Nay, thank ye." Heather made a move to step away from him and was shocked when he didn't hold her back. Keeping her back to him, she reached behind her and untied the knots at her back—knots she'd somehow managed to do herself after wriggling into the gown, a feat in and of itself without the help of a maid.

Once she'd taken off the gown, she felt instantly lighter. Two other gowns and three chemises made up her ensemble.

"Ye might consider wearing only one outfit on the morrow. Must be infernally hot."

Heather whirled to face Duncan, intending to issue him some reprimand, but his threat of a whipping and the sight of him in a plaid and leine shirt took the words from her tongue. Gone was the leather jerkin and wicked ax.

There was no trace of a priest left, but a brawny, devastatingly handsome warrior who stole her breath and made her heart leap into her throat.

Chapter Six

A roar, foreign to him, rushed through Duncan's ears.

He'd been frozen, watching as the lass reached behind her and tugged at the ribbons of her gown. Though he'd known she was covered in infinite layers, the thought of her undressing before his eyes had been enough to make him want to get down on his knees and beg her for more. Beg her to peel away each and every gown and chemise.

And Duncan never begged for anything.

In just a few short hours, Heather Sutherland had him undone. She turned around, his emotions mirrored in her expression as she studied him without his priest's robes. He stood before her clothed, just as she was, but the idea of one less layer seemed doubly powerful. They were both intoxicated by it. A realization that made his blood rush harder through his body. Together, they were toxic.

The gown she'd been wearing was a muted evergreen of lightweight wool. This one was more of a sage color. Both were loose, and he was unsure if that was intentional for layering or if they were even her own clothes. They were certainly not the fashionable gowns he would have seen on a wealthy woman.

"Ye dinna dress like a sister to an earl." His voice was lowered, and he gazed at her with hooded lids.

"Worried ye have the wrong lass?" She cocked her head, toying with him, evidence of her spirit pushing through despite his threats to punish her.

He took a step closer. "Nay. I know who ye are."

"How?" Heather seemed to hesitate a moment before taking a step back.

He didn't want to answer. Lady Ross had described Heather to him in detail. When he'd sneaked on to the castle grounds to research his entrance and escape routes, he thought he'd spied her. Pretending to be older and crippled with a hood pulled up over most of his face, he'd looked out for her but wasn't sure if the lass he'd seen was in fact Heather. She'd worn an *arisaid* tucked up around her middle filled with apples, and several young lads and lassies were plucking the fruit from her makeshift basket.

She stood up straighter, jutting her chin forward. "How?" This time there was some force behind her question.

"Ye sass more than a lady should." He tried to frown.

"What would ye know of how a lady should act?" Feminine hands planted on her rounded hips.

"More than ye."

That got her goad up. Heather huffed a breath and stormed toward the makeshift bed he'd created for the two of them. She crumpled up her gown in a ball and tossed it down, where it landed in a heap of fabric that resembled nothing of a pillow.

"Let us be clear on one thing, Duncan. Ye may think ye know me, but in truth ye've not a clue. Nobody knows the real me, and I'll be damned if I let some heathen tell me how I should and should not behave."

The woman had the uncanny skill of making his skin bristle with irritation. At the same time he wanted to wrap his arms around her, he also wanted to shake some sense into her. "I thought I made it clear ye were nay to insult me?"

She frowned, covering the tremble in her lower lip. But he saw it. A lot of bravado she had, and he had to give her credit for that. He liked a woman with a backbone—when he *wasn't* abducting her.

"Will ye make good on the insults? Bend me over your wretched knee and violate me?" Fear showed in her eyes, even if her lips were curled into a sneer.

Duncan groaned, rolling his eyes. "If ye were nay a lady, I might have suggested joining a traveling play group. Your theatrics are extraordinary."

He might have threatened to pummel her arse—and, boy, would he have enjoyed the view—but he would not violate her in such a way, no matter how angry she made him.

"Go to bed afore I change my mind," he growled.

Without a second passing, Heather leapt between the plaids he'd laid out, tucking the blankets beneath her armpits. She crossed her uncovered arms over her middle so that a hand rested on either opposite forearm and closed her eyes. She looked like a corpse lying like that. 'Twas disturbing.

He frowned at her, willing her to open her eyes, but she didn't. He caught himself staring at her chest to see if it rose and fell as she breathed. It did. "I need to inspect the grounds. Make sure we are still alone."

Heather nodded but still did not open her eyes. Was she purposefully avoiding him?

"Ye've got Blade for protection."

She chuckled but did open her eyes and look over at him. "Lot of good a horse will do."

"Dinna underestimate him. Blade is well-trained."

She giggled some more, staring at him like he'd grown a tail. He frowned, wondering if she'd somehow managed to become foxed on the few droplets of whisky that may have made it into her system. Blade may not have been a guard dog, but his horse would not think twice about lifting onto his hind legs and pummeling an intruder with his front hooves. "I'll be back."

"Wait!" she called out in a high-pitched whisper.

Duncan turned around with a raised brow. She'd sat up and held out a hand imploringly. "Aye, princess?"

She rolled her eyes, a sudden change in her alarmed expression. "I do wish ye'd stop calling me that."

Ah, at least now he knew how to change her moods. "And I wish ye'd stop acting like one."

Heather waved away his insult. "Let us say that your magnificent steed is not able to protect me in the event someone more nefarious than ye should happen upon me. How am I to protect myself?"

"Scream." Duncan turned back toward the entrance to the great hall. He'd check each level of the castle first and then outside—

"Scream? Are ye jesting with me?" The woman sounded like he'd told her to go jump into the nearest loch and hand-catch them some fish for dinner.

Duncan whirled, ready to gag her for certain this time. Enough threats. "Devil take it, woman, what do ye want of me? Should I give ye my sword?"

She nodded, serious. "Aye, that would be good."

Exasperation did not begin to describe the burning emotions pummeling his insides. "Lass, ye canna handle my sword." And he meant that in more ways than one.

Heather pursed her lips, scrunched up her pert nose. "I've handled a sword before."

"And I've heard that line more than a dozen times."

Her face colored. Either she understood the double entendre or she might genuinely know how to handle a blade and was getting angry at him for doubting her. And he was seriously leaning more toward the former.

"I'm serious."

Damn, it *was* the latter.

"I'm not giving ye a weapon." He turned back, deciding he would ignore any more interruptions. He had to scout their camp before all light was lost. These were dangerous times they lived in. He wasn't going to get caught unawares and with a woman holding him back.

"Do ye truly think the Earl of Sutherland would allow his sister to go untrained in protecting herself?" she called after him.

Duncan responded over his shoulder, not bothering to slow his pace. "Ye're here, aren't ye? Let that answer your question."

He was pretty sure whatever it was that she grumbled behind his back was worse than bastard, whoreson or heathen. Duncan smiled, had to stop himself from whistling. There was something about the lass that really got his blood rolling. He was either burning with rage, hot with desire or laughing his arse off.

It'd be rough when he had to drop her off with Lady Ross. The part of him that was starting to doubt this mission was only growing stronger.

"Not a chance," he mumbled. He was not going to let that impish twit wiggle her way inside his head. Letting her change his mind would be his downfall.

Duncan was a loner. And he'd remain that way until he met his end, preferably a death worthy of a warrior.

Exiting the great hall, Duncan was careful to step quietly over the stones and scattered debris. If anyone had chosen to make camp in the courtyard in the time they'd been inside, he need not let them know he was here. In all his days of coming to the ruins, not many dared to camp inside. The castle was rumored to be filled with restless spirits and demons. He'd never run into any ghosts, and the only demons he was aware of were his own.

Stepping silently, he crept to the main doorway. Two large wooden, iron-studded doors used to fill the space, but one had long since fallen and rotted into the ground. The other hung on a hinge. The only reason he'd never repaired them was that doing so would have called attention to his being there. And would have invited unwanted guests to try to slumber there as well.

A cursory glance around the courtyard showed it to be quiet. There appeared to be no one approaching from where he could see through the broken-down gate, but that didn't mean they were safe from the rear. This castle had been built upon a motte, and so it looked down into the surrounding valleys, but it was not protected by a loch or the sea, nor a cliff. Completely exposed in the open wilderness, it was no wonder that it had been easily overtaken.

The sun was fast setting, and the storm that had been brewing in the skies above appeared to have picked up speed. Not a simple drizzle, as he'd first thought. Mother Nature was not working well with him on this mission. But he refused to believe in superstition, which told him everything he was doing here was wrong. Dark clouds made the already setting sun dimmer, and a fierce gust of wind blew, bending the grass and weeds that grew over abundantly in what had to once have been a neatly kept courtyard. Nay, he would still not change his mind.

And he needed to secure the premises.

Storms meant there was more of a chance someone would seek shelter here, despite any ghosts or demons. Duncan jogged down the stairs, making his way around the perimeter of the castle, not seeing any sign of an intruder nor one who might be returning. The valleys beyond looked clear of stragglers. There was a good chance they wouldn't be bothered here.

Duncan made his way back into the castle from the kitchen doorway, and began to carefully check every room, storage area, nook, alcove and hidden door that he knew of. By the time he'd made it to the third floor, he was confident they would spend at least the next foreseeable minutes in peace.

Then Heather screamed.

A bloodcurdling sound that sent every hair of his on end, and prompted him to bolt to the nearest stair, taking them three at a time, hands pressed against the crumbling stone walls as he made the circular dissent. Upon the bottom stair, he drew his sword.

By the time Duncan made it to the great hall, Blade was in full pursuit of the intruder and Heather had managed to climb up onto the makeshift stool he'd sat on earlier, a broken chair leg in her hands as she turned in a frantic circle.

"What the bloody hell is going on here?" Duncan roared.

Heather blathered on, pointing with her free hand at the ground where Blade stomped with fury.

"Speak, woman," he ordered.

"A…a…"

A rat the size of a cat leapt, hissing, from beneath a pile of rotted rushes. Its front paws extended, tiny white razor claws ready to tear into flesh, but Blade was on the animal like green on grass. He stomped three times, the third time finally crunching the vicious animal beneath his hoof with a bone-chilling crack.

"I was about to tear into ye for having screamed about a bloody rat, but that was no normal rat."

Heather shook her head, trembling from fear so much he could see her shake. "'Twas a demon rodent."

"That it was." Duncan took wide steps over to her and gently pried the chair leg from her death-like grip. Tossing the leg away with a clatter, he wrapped his arms around her and pulled her from the broken chair.

He would have put her down, but she sank against him, wrapped her arms tight around his neck and trembled like a leaf in a storm. Duncan found himself stroking her back and whispering words of comfort in her ear.

"'Tis all right, lass. The thing is dead."

"But there…there might be others." She shuddered.

"None that we canna handle."

"Dinna leave me alone again." Heather pressed her forehead to his shoulder and drew in a few quaking breaths.

"I will not." It wasn't a promise he was certain he could keep—in fact, it was one he knew he would ultimately break. "Come, now, let us get some rest. There's a storm brewing, which will likely make our journey tomorrow all the more difficult. We'll need our energy."

Heather nodded her agreement and allowed Duncan to put her on her feet. He took hold of her hands, tugging them from around his neck, and led her over to their makeshift bed, now a jumble of woolen plaids, a gown and a robe. The looks of a love nest if he'd been a stranger observing. But there were no nude bodies here, nor any lovers. And he wasn't a stranger observing, but the man actually living through this odd sequence of events.

"Can ye please light a fire? Or a torch or something? I dinna think I'll be able to sleep in the dark."

Duncan straightened out the plaids and rolled her gown back up into a plump pillow. "Lass, if I light a fire, the smoke and light will draw in every predator on two legs within viewing distance. A torch may do the same."

"A candle?" Her eyes pleaded with him.

Even now the room was becoming gray. The only reason it wasn't completely black was the full moon shining through the gaping hole in the roof above them.

"I will light a candle." That much he could do for her. As soon as she was asleep, he'd blow it out to save the precious wax.

Seeming satisfied, Heather knelt on the plaid before rolling onto her side and curling up into a ball, facing away from him.

Duncan rummaged through his sack for a candle and flint. He lit the wick and set it in a makeshift holder he fashioned with a piece of wood.

"Thank ye," she said meekly.

"Ye're welcome." He studied the way she lay so vulnerable, shoulders sunken in. All the fight had gone out of the poor lass.

Poor lass. Here he was, the one who'd stolen her away, and he was feeling sorry for her, empathizing with her plight. But it wasn't just that he felt sorry for her. She'd hit something deep inside him. He'd never reacted the way he did to her with any other captive. Heather was not the first beautiful, feisty woman he'd been paid to abduct.

There was something different about her, though. The quirk of her brow or the way her lips curled mischievously when she smiled. The spark of fire in her unusually colored eyes. How she was willing to fight with him, despite his threats, and even how she seemed to take his abducting her as a bit of adventure.

Odd, truly, that she would interpret it that way. But it only made him admire her more.

Duncan shook himself out of staring at her and lay down on top of the plaid, elbows bent and his hands behind his head. He stared up into the rafters, watching the way the small amount of flame from the candle made large slow-moving shadows on the old wood. Within a year's time, what was left of the roof would likely fall.

There were char marks on the walls, and he guessed it was from a fire, though he could never be certain whether it was from the siege laid to this place or a campfire gone wild. He'd been drawn here since he was an adolescent. He'd been on a week-long hunt-and-gather with the other monks of Pluscarden when he'd happened upon it. They'd often gone on these journeys, looking for new plant life and animals that didn't live in the vicinity of their abbey.

The prior had been inquisitive, scientific even, although he believed wholeheartedly in God being the almighty healer in all things—he'd also believed the Lord had given them everything within their reach to see his potential grow and will be done.

But the prior had not adventured with them that time. A younger, more adventurous monk had taken them out, and his excitement at finding these ruins had been addictive. From that moment on, whenever they'd left the abbey, Duncan had tried to make his way back here. When others had found it foreboding, he'd found comfort in its walls.

Almost like it were home. But that was impossible. His home was far north of here.

Beside him, Heather's breathing slowed and grew even. Falling asleep had not taken her long. He was surprised. Most of his captives stayed up all night worrying themselves sick over what would happen when the morning came.

Heather must have been extremely exhausted—or she trusted him to keep her safe. A jest if there ever was one. How could she trust him when he was her enemy?

Duncan leaned up on his elbow and blew out the candle. The scent of the snuffed-out wick surrounding them. He yanked off his shirt, leaving his plaid in place. When he lay back down, Heather murmured something in her sleep and rolled toward him, flinging a warm leg over his thighs and an arm across his chest, her fingers stroking lightly across his nipple.

He jerked with her touch, but she only murmured something else unintelligible, then sighed. This wasn't a jest. She was well and truly asleep.

Ballocks. It was going to be a long, *long* night.

Chapter Seven

*H*eather woke with a start, trembling from a nightmare—a rat jumping like a crazed loon straight for her throat. Sweat dripped over her temples, soaking the tresses that framed her face.

But what she actually woke to was even scarier than a heathen rat. She was cocooned in warmth and hard, male flesh. She was lying on her side, her legs entangled with Duncan's muscled thighs—crisp hairs tickling her calf and the bottom of her foot. And her arm was draped so casually over his bare chest, as though it belonged there, palm flat over his steadily beating heart.

Pushing up on her elbow, she saw that Duncan was wide awake, gazing at her with an odd expression she couldn't decipher. Watching her. How long had he known they lay like this, and why hadn't he attempted to remove her?

"Ye're finally awake," he muttered, his voice tight.

"Aye," Heather breathed, carefully removing herself from his amazing form. She gazed at him, nude from the waist up and only the plaid blanket covering his lower half. "Ye were dressed before." Her heart kicked up a notch.

"I'm still dressed." He tugged down the blanket, showing he wore his own tartan wrapped around his waist.

Thank goodness for at least being partially clothed. She cleared her throat. "Where is your shirt?"

He raised a brow and picked it up from beside him. "Right here. I was hot. Have ye never seen a man's chest?"

None that had ever made her stare, nor feel such tingly heat... Broad shoulders. Thick, corded muscles. Dark, swirling chest hair.

"Of course I have," she retorted. "I do have three brothers."

Duncan rolled up, displaying a wicked crunch of abdominal muscles. If she'd had a fan, the accoutrement would have been put to full use. Heather found her mouth suddenly dry, her heart pounding as though she'd faced the rat again. But this was no rat by far, but something infinitely more sinister—she was starting to *like* her captor.

To anticipate... What? A kiss?

Heather leapt up from her makeshift bed and planted her hands on her hips. "Why were ye touching me?" She didn't bother to curb the accusation.

Duncan shook his head and grinned at her like she was a silly child. "Och, lass, did ye not see that ye were the one touching me? I but lay there enjoying your attention."

"And *allowed* it." She narrowed her eyes until they were little slits and she could barely see, hoping he would finally take heed of the seriousness of the situation.

Duncan laughed. "Ye look like a fool when ye try to glare too hard."

Heather gasped and removed her hands from her hips, crossing them instead over her chest, as though to protect herself from his assault on her pride. The man was full of rubbish and an imbecile to boot. She sniffed. "I am not a fool."

"Then admit it." His lopsided grin was starting to irritate her immensely.

"Admit what? I just told ye I'm no fool."

Duncan stood up, his muscles unfolding in such a display of raw male power, Heather was stunned speechless. Arms fell from their crossed position. It seemed like every breath she took hinged on watching the display of masculinity. Her eyes roved over the breadth of his chest, the corded muscles of his shoulders and arms. She dared not look lower, because there was a tempting line of hair and muscle that seemed to arrow just beneath his plaid. Instinctively, she knew if she looked *there*, it would only lead to something more. The details of what *something* was, she wasn't sure, but it most likely involved kissing, and that, they'd both decided, was not a good idea to repeat.

"Admit ye were touching me."

Heather looked up toward the rafters, in part because she was praying for patience, but also because she had to take her eyes off of his chest. "Put a shirt on," she snapped.

"Admit it first."

She flung her arms out in exasperation. "Fine! I was the one touching ye. But I will not admit that I did it on purpose. I must have rolled over in my sleep and touched ye by accident."

"If ye say so. I say ye cuddled next to me and purred all the night through." He winked. Slowly.

Just that little blip of eyelid movement sent a tremor of excitement through her, followed whiplash fast by a sweeping anger. "Ye're a cad!"

"Ah, ah, ah!" he warned, advancing toward her with two predatory steps. "Do ye recall what I said would happen if ye called me such things?"

Heather growled out her frustration and leapt backward, careful not to fall on any of the mess that surrounded them. "I dinna like ye very much, Priest."

He only chuckled, but he did stop coming toward her. "Well, princess, that makes two of us."

Pain squeezed inside her chest. Why did she care what he thought, and why did it hurt to hear he didn't like her? Heather gritted her teeth. It shouldn't matter. They seemed to be at a standoff, both of them glaring each other down as if in the next second or two they might attack each other.

"Let us pack up then, so ye can be sure to quickly dispose of me. I've a need to get away from ye just as much as ye appear to need to get away from me." She snatched her makeshift pillow and unraveled it, tugging it over her head and instantly feeling the temperature rise in the room. Taking his advice about reducing her layers would have meant defeat. "Besides, are ye nay just chomping to get your hands on a bit more silver?"

Duncan picked up his shirt from where it lay crumpled near his feet. "'Tis not the silver I'm looking forward to. Truth of the matter is, I have plenty to get by on. But the look on your brother's face when he realizes I've got ye, now that will be priceless."

"But ye will not have me. The person who hired ye will," she pointed out.

He smiled cruelly, sending a shiver of dread racing along her limbs. "Trust me, ye'll wish it was me that had taken ye."

"Trust *me*, that will be the last thought that crosses my mind."

Duncan growled and yanked on his shirt, stuffing it roughly into his plaid and then slamming his arms into his billowing black robes. Hardly the vision one had of a priest, and she was sad to see all his skin once more covered. She'd rather liked the view.

Heather chewed her lip as she bent to roll up their bedding. She tried to ignore her hurt feelings, but they just kept nagging at her. 'Twas ridiculous that she'd let a man like Duncan get to her, that every harsh word stung and every kind word made her heart flutter.

She hated him at the same time that she did not. A confusing mix of emotions swirled inside her mind with him in the dead center of it. How was she supposed to cope with that? Was coping possible?

Having the bedding rolled, she turned to find Duncan readying his horse for departure. With nimble steps, mostly in hopes of avoiding another rat, but also because her brothers had taught her not to rush a bear, she approached and handed him the blankets.

"Thank ye," he grumbled.

Heather was a little taken aback that he'd thanked her. She'd half expected him to grab the cloth from her hands and shove it onto the horse before tossing her up on the animal's back. Beneath his hard exterior, there was definitely a man with heart. If they hadn't been in the situation they found themselves in, she might have thought she was the woman to help him expose that beating organ.

As it was, she was most definitely, absolutely, positively *not* the woman for him, nor he the man for her.

"Ye're welcome," Heather said begrudgingly, hating that her aunt had drilled manners into her and that she felt the need to impart them on this devil.

How funny that such a mundane exchange of words meant so much more. They were both giving in, both being cordial when in their situation niceties were the last thing she'd expect.

Niceties would be coming to an end soon, though, for Heather was certain of one thing—she'd not be present for the exchange of her person to whatever vile villain had paid for her. Though she was loath to admit it, there were a multitude of demons worse than a seductive warrior. She was mostly sure she'd be able to escape, but there was the remote possibility that she wouldn't. Ending up in the hands of people who would be cruel to her...was frightening. No matter. She just wouldn't let it happen.

"Is there going to be a need for me to tie ye up?"

Heather swallowed, feeling exposed, as though Duncan had read her mind. Keeping her eyes trained on him, she shook her head. She was half telling the truth. There would be no need for him to tie her up, for that would only delay her ability to run away, the sooner the better.

"Good. Wait here, while I check that the courtyard is clear." Duncan took a step toward the doors of the great hall that led to the main entryway.

Heather hurried forward, walking beside him. "I'm coming, too. Ye did say ye'd not leave me alone here. And besides...I've a need for privacy." She wasn't going to try to find an old chamber pot that no one would empty. Nature was her best resource at this point. As a woman of a war camp, she'd have to get used to it.

Duncan grunted, but at least he was giving in. He sped forward, as though trying to shake her, but Heather wasn't going to be left behind. It may have taken her two steps for every one of his, and he may have only been walking while she practically ran, but she stayed beside him, or mostly beside him, anyway.

"Stubborn chit," he grumbled.

The comment only made Heather smile, and a little homesick. How many times had she heard the same thing from her older brothers?

Whenever she'd become too much of a handful for Magnus, he'd shipped her off to Aunt Fiona and had begged her to learn a thing or two from their stoic relation. He'd lamented that she'd needed a woman to ground her, not just her older brothers. Things had changed slightly, though, when he'd married beautiful Arbella. The English noblewoman had welcomed Heather with open arms—despite her heritage.

Heather surmised Arbella must have been Scottish at heart, for how else could her brother have fallen for her? Having Arbella's approval had also helped Heather get over the fact that she was of the enemy's blood. Arbella was sweet-natured, kind, intelligent and had a humorous side that Heather found infectious.

She'd quickly become a mother figure, and the only times Heather'd been sent to Aunt Fiona after that had been when Arbella was too sick from being with child to intervene. But those visits had never been long, because as soon as Arbella had realized Magnus sent her away, she'd made him bring her back—and buy her something pretty, like a new pair of embroidered hose or a hair comb.

Family belonged together. At home. That was what Arbella said. That Heather shouldn't be sent away when she got the better of him, but that she should learn to behave better—in the company of her family. Aunt Fiona was family, but she wasn't responsible for rearing Heather like Magnus was.

But talk had started to change in the recent months since she'd turned nineteen. Talk of marriage. Talk of building Heather's future as mistress of her own home.

Talk that had made her nauseated.

The very idea of it had spurred her into action. She'd been looking for an excuse to leave home, and learning about the marriage talks and Wallace's return to Scotland had been all the push she'd needed to plan her destiny.

And then in had stepped Father Duncan, or whatever his real name was. Too good to be true, her plans to use him as an escort were backfiring.

They crept through the entryway of the castle, still and quiet, their breath seeming to echo in the massive ruins. Duncan peered through the gaping hole where a door used to be attached, then turned back to her and nodded. She was struck by how his nearness, his attention to her, made her shiver.

"All is clear, go about your business."

Creeping down the stairs, she sauntered around to the side of the castle, away from his view, and was about to crouch when he rounded the corner.

"What are ye doing?" she asked, exasperated, dropping her skirts and standing.

"I canna leave ye alone. Remember?"

Heather frowned at him, letting out a frustrated growl. "Turn around then."

Duncan chuckled but complied. When she'd finished, he said, "Now ye turn around."

"Why?"

He raised a brow, and she felt heat flood her cheeks. "Oh!" she gasped, and leapt into a half circle, facing away from him.

"All's clear," he said when finished.

Heather nodded, pressing her lips tightly together, hoping to numb the sudden tingling she felt on their surface—a memory of his kiss.

"Then let us not delay in delivering me into the hands of the evil lady who hired ye."

Duncan grinned. "Such dramatics. Did ye have a tutor teach ye that or is it all natural Heather Sutherland?"

She frowned up at him. "Nothing about me is dramatic, and I guarantee I put forth nothing but my true nature."

He let out a short chuckle. "Your husband will have his work cut out for him."

The mention of a husband was only a fist to the gut for more than one reason. "In case ye forgot, ye're taking me to people who will most likely kill me. If they dinna kill me, my reputation will be sullied enough that the only man willing to marry me after this fiasco will be some older, blind and mutilated man my brothers pay to take me off their hands." She backed away from him, feeling for the first time the pain of what her future would entail. "That is what ye've given me. So

The Highlander's Sin

ye're correct. My husband, if I ever have one, will have his work cut out for him, for I am certain to be one of the most unhappy brides this kingdom has ever seen."

Tears burned the backs of her eyes. At least if she made it to Wallace, she might have glory to back her name, and perhaps a strong warrior would marry her when she decided it was time to marry. But if Duncan succeeded in his mission, misery was the only fate she could look forward to.

She'd take her own life before she let that be her fate—and she didn't really like the idea of dying.

There was only one way to solve this issue, well two really. Her escape had to be successful, or she had to kill Duncan. Killing a man of the cloth was sure to doom her to hell—another fate she'd rather not see come to fruition.

Heather squared her shoulders.

She had to escape from him.

Today.

There was much strength buried beneath layers of a spoiled princess. Duncan would give Heather that much.

He didn't like the determined set of her shoulders. Nor the way her lips had become strained and flat, not their usual plump and kissable appearance. *Ballocks.* Thinking about her plush lips brought him the vision of her creamy legs as she'd hoisted her skirts up around her hips. Dear Lord, it had been an image he'd burned to memory the moment he caught sight of her...

And he ought to forget it. She was not the woman for him. Not in this lifetime, nor the next.

What exactly was she thinking? Planning? He assumed he'd not find out from her own lips, but if anything, he believed she would attempt an escape.

And, ironically, he couldn't blame her. Part of him wanted her to be able to succeed in such an attempt. She didn't deserve the fate in store for her. No more than any innocent did. Her family was his enemy, and she a means to exact his revenge.

Not entirely fair, he admitted, but since when did he care about fairness? Today, apparently.

Duncan gripped her upper arm, not so gently, and started to steer her back to his horse. He was a little surprised when she didn't balk at him or try to pull away. The lass was definitely up to something. She'd not been this compliant since the moment he'd seen her on her knees in the chapel.

"Up ye go." He circled her waist with his hands, holding his breath while touching her, and hoisted her onto the horse. Without a pause, he mounted behind her.

He'd have welcomed a grand winter snow right about now, to cool him from the combination of summer heat, too many layers of clothes and the warm, supple body of his captive. The way they melded together in the saddle had her rounded behind centered right on his cock, and he was already hard.

They would have both probably been more comfortable with her riding behind him, but he wasn't about to risk a stab in the back, or her falling from the horse on purpose and getting a head start running away. He had no doubt he'd catch her should she run, but it would only delay the inevitable.

"How long?" she asked, her voice a purr, softly caressing his nerves. Cunning, she was.

"Another day." A day that would likely last an eternity.

She nodded but said no more. Duncan narrowed his eyes, staring at the back of her head. What was she up to?

Whatever her intentions, he was going to be on high alert. Heather Sutherland would never escape him—else he'd quit his livelihood. If he failed in this, he would never be hired again. A fate that would damn him in so many ways. One of which meant he'd have to face his past.

And the past was best left buried.

Chapter Eight

*T*hey stopped at midday, at the base of a ravine, safely hidden in an alcove cut out of the mountainside by a waterfall.

Rushing water splattered into the burn below, before rushing toward its ultimate end at a loch somewhere nearby. Droplets of water bounced from the stone into the small alcove, wetting the hem of Heather's skirts and the tips of her shoes.

She stared at the water as it fell, the way the sun reflected off of it in a myriad of colors. Reaching out, she touched her finger to the rushing falls, feeling the power behind the water's push.

"Ye'll get yourself soaked," Duncan said, his voice more surly than ever.

He'd been silent as they'd ridden away from the ruins, and every once in a while he'd jerked her back against him as she'd tried to lean as far away from him as possible.

"I'm a grown woman. I think I can handle a little water," she bit back.

No use in hiding her temper with the man. They wouldn't know each other much longer now anyway.

Duncan grunted. "Here." He thrust an apple toward her that had seen better days.

Visible bruising marred its once-smooth, green flesh, a few gashes were slashed across its skin. "Nay, thank ye," she muttered.

"Eat it."

Heather grabbed the apple from his hand. "Can I have my dagger back?" She'd yet to see the blade since he'd confiscated it, and darn it if she wasn't going to at least attempt to slice off the rotten parts of the apple.

Duncan grabbed the apple back from her and within seconds had sliced away the gashes and bruises, leaving a misshapen white and green sorry excuse for an apple. But all the same, it was a kindness he'd showed her.

"Thank ye," she muttered, biting into the fruit.

Despite how it had appeared, the apple's taste was quite pleasant.

"'Twasn't a rotten apple, lass. Simply banged up in my satchel. I'm not so cruel that I would feed ye spoiled food."

She swallowed her bite, unable to resist a retort. "Nay, ye'd just feed me to evildoers."

He didn't respond, but he did glare daggers at her as he peeled and sliced his own apple. She had a feeling he wished it were her head beneath his blade.

Heather leaned her head to the side, exposing her neck. "Why dinna ye cut me now and be done with it?"

"Enough theatrics," Duncan growled. "Eat this, too."

He tossed her a leather pouch.

"What is it?" She imagined poisoned mushrooms or deadly herbs hidden inside the pouch. Instead of slicing her, he'd see her bleed from the inside.

"Almonds."

Heather loved almonds, but it seemed a trick to her. "Why would ye give me your almonds?"

Duncan glowered at her. "Because I would not have ye say I mistreated ye."

"Then ye should let me go. I dinna want your kindness in the form of food." She tossed the pouch back at him and Duncan seized it in midair.

He caught her off guard when he threw it back.

Not expecting him to do that, she missed it completely, and it hit her just above her left breast with a dull thud.

"Ouch!"

She looked at him sharply, gripping the pouch where it had fallen in her lap. It hadn't really hurt, but it had surprised her enough that her pride was injured.

He was trying not to laugh. "I didna mean to hit ye with it."

She flung it back toward his head. "Well, ye did."

Duncan ducked, reaching up and catching the pouch where his head had been.

Heather was sorry to have missed. How good it would have felt for the pouch to hit him square in the forehead. To leave a red imprint that would have eventually turned into a bruise.

Duncan held out the pouch between them. "Truce?"

"Does that mean ye will let me go?" she asked with a raised brow and a sarcastic smile.

He shook his head, sadness entering his eyes that she'd not seen before. "Not this time."

This time... As if there would be another time?

"Well, I'll not have ye fattening me up with your almonds just so I'm juicier to those monsters that'd eat me whole." Heather crossed her arms over her chest, letting her eyes drift around the small alcove.

Bravado kept her from cracking, though on the inside she felt herself starting to break. Lord, she had been naïve to have thought this could go her way at all.

Likely they wouldn't be here long. She could risk jumping through the falls and into the water. There was no telling how deep it was, but she could swim, and that might give her a head start in escaping, even if he jumped in behind her. She frowned. There was one major issue with that escape plan—she was still wearing multiple layers. The fabric would swiftly wick up the water and weigh her down. She'd be lucky to move her limbs at all before she drowned.

Jumping through the falls wasn't going to work. Anything having to do with water needed to be crossed off her list. Unless...

Unless she knocked *him* into the falls. She'd have plenty of time to run with him sputtering in the water, his robes filled with moisture.

"What plan are ye concocting now?" Duncan asked.

Heather jerked her gaze toward him. Why did he have to be so darn handsome? He leaned against the wall, one leg stretched out and the other bent at the knee, an arm resting on it, the dreaded pouch of almonds dangling from his long, masculine fingers.

"What?" she asked.

"I asked ye what ye were scheming about in your mind. Ye disappeared for a few minutes, staring into the water."

Heather shook her head and waved away his accusations. "I wasn't scheming anything, ye—" She stopped herself from name-calling, in case he made good on one of his threats to spank her or tie her up. "I was simply lost in memory..." She made a point of trailing off, as though the memory were something sweet she'd savor. Knocking Duncan through the falls would definitely be a memory she would savor as soon as she got the deed done.

Hopping to her feet, Heather swiped at her skirts, brushing off the bits of leaves and dust that had gathered from sitting on the cavern floor. "Shall we be on our way?"

Duncan looked up at her with his eyes narrowed. He roved over her form in a way that made her blush and bluster. She crossed her arms over her chest, wishing he wouldn't look at her like that.

"Well?" she asked, not bothering to hide the annoyance in her tone.

"Why the sudden hurry?" The infuriating man pulled the strings on the pouch and dumped a few almonds into his palm.

The nuts looked good. Fresh. He popped them into his mouth and stared at her, waiting for her reply.

"Why the sudden need to relax? Thus far ye've had urgency on your side."

Duncan chuckled, a low grumble in his chest that gave her gooseflesh and set her nerves afire with the need to press her chest to his and feel that rumble. Why, she had no idea, and she certainly found it irritating.

"I had a feeling we were being followed. Best to stay out of sight for a short while."

"Followed. Still?" She whirled, half expecting their little hiding spot to be stormed. Throughout their ride today she'd not heard anyone, seen anyone. How was it possible they'd been followed? She peeked outside, studying the forest but seeing no one.

"Aye."

"By who? And won't they see your horse?"

Duncan shrugged and dumped more almonds into his hand. "I dinna know who, and if they see my horse, they will see that he is abandoned."

Heather gaped at him in disbelief. He sounded so mundane, as if they discussed the various colors of summer flowers and not the safety of his prized horse. "Surely they will steal him then."

"They can try." A confident grin curled his lips.

Heather put her hands on her hips. "What makes ye so confident?"

"There are many reasons."

The man was exasperating. Heather stared hard at him, willing him to look away from the almonds in his palm. "Care to share them?"

"Not particularly." He glanced up at her briefly and then returned his attention to the almonds.

"Arrogance is a sin."

"I, more than most, am well aware."

She crossed her arms over her chest. "A priest should not be arrogant."

Duncan looked up at her in earnest, but not for curiosity's sake. She could see that in his eyes. The man was observing her, studying her reactions as much as he was studying her words. "Why not?"

"Because 'tis a sin," she said, exasperated.

His eyes danced with merriment. "Not in my case."

"And what makes ye so special?"

"We are all special in His eyes."

Heather grunted her disgust. Talking to the man was like dancing on a thin rope. One was easily swayed to fall any way the wind shifted.

"Ye're impossible." She turned her back on him, glancing through the short walkway they'd traveled to get to this spot. It'd been scary, walking on the thin ledge and clutching the side of the mountain. The only other option had been to swim up to it, and neither of them had wanted to get wet. The same truth held for the return to shore.

"That may be true, lass, but ye're stuck with me all the same."

Heather didn't know why, but his statement sent her from bordering on irritation to boiling rage. She whirled, and stalked toward him, kicking the sole of his boot. "Not of my own choosing." Her voice didn't echo but sounded strangely silent, the falls deadening her shout.

Duncan *tsk-tsked* her. "Noise like that is likely to bring our guests knocking on our doorstep." He didn't make a move, simply stared up at her, his eyes hooded. "And likely to get yourself gagged."

She swallowed back her retort. That was the last thing she needed. Her vow to be good so he wouldn't tie and gag her had slipped her mind when rage had taken over, but she allowed reason back in. Escape was her number one priority, and shouting at her captor was only going to annoy him. She didn't need Duncan annoyed. She needed him relaxed. Too relaxed.

"Have any more of that whisky?" she asked, adding some sweetness back into her tone.

"Want to get me drunk?"

Heather shook her head, forced her face into a docile expression—difficult since she was anything but passive. "Nay, Duncan." She allowed his name to roll slowly off her tongue, hoping to entice him the way she had other men. "Just thirsty."

The change in him was immediate, and Heather forced herself to remain unchanged by it. He stood, eyes darkening as he studied her. No more care for his almonds. Oh, nay, all of his attention was on her.

"What are ye up to?" He was suspicious. She wasn't surprised.

Heather gazed up at him through her lashes. "Nothing. I give up."

"Give up? Ye?"

She nodded. "Now, if ye would, the whisky please." If he'd known how much she hated the sour, bitter, stinging taste of whisky, he might have appreciated the limits she was willing to go to.

Duncan shook his head slowly, eyeing her with distrust. "One thing the lady who hired me said was that ye were cunning. Not to underestimate ye."

Heather stiffened. Who knew her? Who could tell him all about her? Who had betrayed the Sutherlands?

"A compliment, to be sure, but I swear," she crossed herself, "that I am not trying to pull the wool over your eyes."

How easily she was capable of lying. Father Hurley would see her punished for a fortnight at this rate. Abducted or not.

Duncan leaned close, his scent enveloping her. Instinctively, she wanted to lean in closer, but in her mind she knew it was a bad idea. Heather leaned back, but inch by inch he drew nearer, until she had to brace a hand behind her on the stone wall to hold herself up.

"Ye're a pretty little liar," he crooned, his voice as silk-edged as her own had been. "But I give ye credit for trying. Now I just have to figure out how—"

An ear-piercing whistle sounded through the falls, causing both Heather and Duncan to still. She swallowed hard, afraid to breathe. Her stomach twisted into knots. They'd been found.

She stared at Duncan, eyes so wide they hurt, but he didn't look at her, no matter how much she willed him to do so. His attention was outside the falls. Body stiff, he seemed made of stone.

Another whistle sounded, this one different. Two people? More than two? How in the world were they to know? God, would they have any warning before someone was upon them, before swords thrust through the diamond falls and into their hearts?

Heather jerked her gaze to the falling water, half expecting to see the flash of metal as their enemy stabbed into their hiding spot.

Her heart leapt with sudden hope. What if it wasn't an enemy, but her brothers? Or better yet, men of the resistance?

What if they saved her? She tried to bring the sounds of the whistles back into her mind, but they were lost on her, not sounding in the least familiar. That didn't mean all hope was lost, though. The sound of the falls could have altered the tone of the whistles, making it harder for her to decipher them.

Even with those thoughts, her stomach started to sink. She was fairly certain her brothers, her hope for salvation, were not on the other side of the water.

"Dinna make a sound," Duncan whispered.

He waited for her to nod, then he nodded in return.

He slowly withdrew his sword. She barely heard him move. He was stealthy, as he should have been, and as he had been when sneaking into Dunrobin Castle.

As Duncan edged closer to the visible opening of their secluded spot, Heather pushed herself up against the wall. If need be, she could run through the waterfall, yanking at her gowns as she went.

Duncan was in the perfect position for her to shove him through the water and attempt to make her escape, but that would only call attention from whoever stood on the other side. And she didn't want to do that. Here was another opportunity for escape wasted.

Oh, how she wanted to curse the fates for what they'd served her, but there was no time to feel sorry for herself.

Where was her dagger? She had to at least protect herself. Duncan's satchels were a few feet away. No hint of her knife, but she thought she'd seen him shove it back inside the sack.

She inched along the wall toward the satchels, while Duncan made slow-moving steps toward the ledge they'd walked in on. He paid her no attention, the entirety of his focus on the outside of their spot.

When she reached their satchels, she eyed the insides, careful not to move, in case he turned around to see her. Glinting on top of the various paraphernalia was her knife—the same gilded handle. Had to be hers. Keeping her eyes on Duncan, she bent down, grabbed the knife and then straightened, holding the hilt in her hand.

The metal was cool and comforting against her overheated palm. If nothing came of this moment, at least she had her knife back. Heather inched her way back to the spot she'd stood before, keeping her eyes glued to Duncan's back. *Dinna turn around*, she repeated inside her head, willing him to obey her silent demands. Luck was on her side. She angled the knife up her sleeve, keeping it in place with a couple of her fingers. She needed a hiding spot for the weapon. Her boot seemed the most likely good spot. Careful not to direct his attention back on her, she lifted her leg and shoved the knife in her boot, making a pretense to scratch her calf.

She'd been paying so much attention to her task, she'd lost track of whether there were any more calls from outside. Duncan stood still by the entrance, but he no longer looked rigid and ready to do battle.

"Is it safe?" she whispered.

He glanced back toward her and frowned, putting a finger to his lips in a silent gesture for her to be quiet.

She guessed it wasn't quite safe yet.

Chapter Nine

The bastards were waiting.

Duncan could no longer hear their whistles or hurried steps, but he could sense them, feel their excitement as they waited for him to come out from behind the falls.

A warm, gentle breeze blew, shifting blades of tall grass and cattails on the banks of the water. The men were not in sight.

They'd probably seen Blade's quality and guessed that a horse such as he would not have been left alone to wander. They'd also expect that the owner of such a horse would have a nice pouch, thick with coin.

Damn. He should have thought of a better way to conceal his horse, smeared mud on him to hide the shine of his coat. He'd taken off his saddle, and all the tackle, but apparently that had not been good enough. Blade's regal stance spoke volumes about his breeding and cost.

The men who waited beyond knew horse flesh, but had also established a way to communicate through whistles. It meant they were either professional criminals or warriors. He prayed the latter was false, and that it wasn't Heather's family come to find her.

The sinking sensation in his gut when he thought of them taking her away was not a good sign. Duncan couldn't, *shouldn't*, care about her. Not even a little bit. He felt better thinking the sudden onslaught of emotion was because, if the Sutherlands caught him, they'd kill him.

Death didn't scare him. The Sutherlands didn't scare him.

Dying without seeking revenge on those who'd destroyed him gave him cause to worry. The last twenty years of his life had been devoted to planning the day he'd finally avenge his family. With Heather in his custody, it was all coming to fruition, and he wasn't about to let some greedy outlaws ruin all that.

Heather pressed to his back, practically draping herself over him. He sensed it was from fear. A slight tremble shook her. She was afraid of whoever was out there — or she was afraid of what he'd do to them.

"I dinna think it is my brother," she murmured.

Why would she tell him that?

"Reason?" He kept his eyes trained outside the cave, waiting for any sudden movement.

"I didna recognize the calls." She curled her fingers into his back, a subconscious move he was sure she wasn't aware of.

"That doesn't mean 'tis not them," Duncan pointed out the obvious. Her brother could have changed his call on a whim, not that it would have behooved him to do so, unless his other calls had been recognized. Understanding that, he didn't push the idea of her brothers attacking completely off the table. They could have changed their call so Heather wouldn't identify it and warn him.

A dainty movement against his back could have been her shrugging her shoulders. She didn't embellish on her thoughts.

Duncan dragged in a breath and crept a little closer to the opening, hoping he might catch a flash of movement where the water thinned.

Heather trailed along with him. He hadn't the heart to tell her to back off—mostly he liked feeling her. Found comfort in her closeness. Wanted to protect her.

A loud whiz sounded, and a sharp waft of air touched his cheek. Heather shrieked just as an arrow cracked against the stone six inches from his face and clattered to the ground in front of them.

Duncan reached back and gripped on to the first place he could grab, which happened to be her hip. Supple, rounded. Not now! Now they were being attacked. "Back up!" he called.

Heather leapt out of his reach and scurried back into the alcove.

The water parted as another arrow came through the center of the falls but fell before hitting anything, its momentum deadened by the heavy, falling water.

"Recognize the arrows?" he asked. He doubted she would. They were crudely made, looked to be carved with a knife minutes before they were shot. Instead of steel points, chipped rocks were tied to the ends with hide. They'd cut skin, do some damage, but there was always the hope that an arrow so badly made would bounce off a man's body rather than go through it, stunning a man instead of killing him.

Heather's face had gone pale, and she stared down at the shaft, shaking her head. "Nay."

"Damn." Outlaws were upon them. Outlaws were the worst of them. Vicious, desperate, they killed for an apple or a crust of bread, but before they soothed their harried bellies, they'd fill their lustful appetites with the treasure that lay buried between Heather's thighs. That thought made a rage hotter than hell burn through Duncan's blood. He grabbed

Heather's arm and yanked her to the farthest point of their tiny cave. "Stay here. Crouch down."

Heather was quick to do as he demanded, sinking to her rear and hugging her knees to her chest. "Will they come in here?" Though her voice quivered, she sounded strong.

"I dinna know, lass. Stay at my back, and I will keep ye safe."

She nodded. He wished he could do more to comfort her, soothe her fear. But he couldn't. Duncan wasn't going to lie to her and tell her everything would be all right, when, in fact, they could both die today for whatever meager contents the bandits stole from his satchels. That just wasn't who he was. He might have been a mercenary, but at least he was an honest one — well, for the most part.

Heather lifted her gaze to his, her eyes wide as she studied him. "I know ye would only save me because if ye didna ye would not get your coin, but I want ye to know all the same that I appreciate it."

What a punch to his gut. He was a bastard, and she'd just told him as much.

Duncan pressed his lips in a firm line and reached toward her, stroking an errant strand of hair away from her face. He rubbed his thumb over her cheek, marveling at the softness of her flesh. "I'd have saved ye no matter what. I'm not as much of a whoreson as ye think I am."

And he wasn't lying. He would have protected her, because there was something growing between them that even though he fought against it, that little part would never let him see her harmed. A little part that Duncan sensed would become a bigger problem with those who had hired him if he got them out of this mess. Regret was beginning to weave its way into his conscience. Abducting Heather was his mission, but damn, if some fraction of him wasn't considering keeping her for himself.

"Prove it," she challenged, gaze locked steadily on his. There was some of that fight in her he'd seen before. The ferocious tigress that was willing to stand up to a dangerous mercenary and issue ultimatums.

Duncan hadn't realized until then how much he hated to see her cowed. His blood surged with renewed vigor.

"I will."

With no more arrows flying through the water just yet, he crept back toward the side of the cave with the ledge that they had walked in on. One of the outlaws was hugging the wall and sliding his feet a few inches a minute. The bastard looked scared out of his mind. His clothes were dingy, his hair stringy, greasy, hands and all other exposed flesh, in dire need of washing.

Duncan grinned.

Outlaws he could handle. They weren't trained like he was.

"Good afternoon to ye," Duncan said to the man.

The sound of Duncan's voice must have startled the outlaw so badly, he barely glanced at Duncan as he jerked backward and then grappled unsuccessfully for purchase on the slippery wall. Fingers dug against the walls, toes teetered on the edge.

"Wish we could have spoken further," Duncan tormented the imbecile, who promptly fell backward. Arms and legs flailing wildly, he yelped as his body hit the water, where he was swiftly swept away by the current.

But he wasn't alone. Shouts sounded from the bank. Two outlaws jumped from their hiding spaces among the water weeds, running after their friend, neither willing to jump in to save him. While two rushed after their drowning friend, several others stalked toward the damp ledge their counterpart had just fallen from.

"Be careful," Duncan warned, lip curled in a cruel smile. "'Tis slippery."

"Ye'll pay for murdering Hamish," one shouted. His plaid was not as dirty as the previous intruder's, nor was his skin as filthy. A leader perhaps. Duncan wondered if that meant he would be wiser or just as dumb.

"Gladly, if ye can reach me." Duncan sheathed his sword, leaned his shoulder casually against the stone wall, crossed his arms over his chest and watched the man mount the narrow ledge.

Duncan had traversed the slim path many times, more than he could count. He'd easily led Heather across its path, only having to grip her arm once when she'd slipped. What these idiots didn't realize was that above their heads, Duncan had chiseled out handholds when he'd realized it was a spot he might seek refuge often with his targets.

This would be the last time he came here, though, now that he'd been found.

The man made it about three feet before he slipped, but his balance was better than the last guy, and he hugged the wall, his back rising and falling rapidly with his breath.

"Good catch," Duncan remarked. "Ye might just make it."

The man growled in response. From the shore, his comrades shouted their own encouragement, but the brute simply turned his head toward them and shouted for them to shut their mouths.

Duncan snickered. The man's nerves were spooked. All the better for him to fall.

"What is happening?" Heather hissed from behind him. "Who are ye talking to? Is he close? What will ye do?"

Duncan didn't turn around. He wasn't going to take his eyes off these fools for a moment. "Hush," was all he said to her.

From behind came a disgruntled garble. Most likely she'd called him some heinous name, but he'd forgive her this time.

"Was Hamish your bowman?" Duncan asked, the fact that no other arrows had come their way a telling clue.

The man bared his teeth, spittle foaming as he growled. He slid ever closer, arms outstretched and his body planted chest-first, to the wall. "Do ye think we'd send in our only bowman?"

Duncan shrugged. "Nay sure."

The man was only a few feet away now. At this rate, he'd likely make it. Duncan took out his sword again and pressed the point of his sword into the cave's floor. With two fingers on the hilt, he spun it, making an eerie scraping noise as the steel ground against the stone. The noise drew his opponent's attention, and he stopped walking.

"Ye're just going to stab me when I reach ye," the outlaw stated.

Again, Duncan shrugged. "Did ye want me to take a step back and allow ye to gain your footing before I stab ye?"

"How gallant of ye." The man's tone was filled with sarcasm.

Duncan grinned. "I do try." He tilted his neck to one side, popping it, and then the other. "What will it be? Do ye prefer to be sliced where ye stand or shall I allow ye to come closer before I send ye to your death?"

Heather gasped behind him, and Duncan tried to ignore her, but the maggot must have heard. His eyes widened, and lust replaced the fear in his gaze.

"I think I'd like to gain my ground."

Duncan could guess why. The bastard actually thought he might have a shot at killing Duncan and raping Heather. He shook his head and frowned at the man, giving him a look that said his sad fate had been sealed.

"I would not have advised it, but if ye insist," Duncan said with a shrug.

"I insist." The outlaw scrambled the last few feet, lunging into the alcove toward Duncan.

An easy step to the right put Duncan away from the brute, who had expected the impact of their bodies to break his fall.

Instead he lurched forward, tripping over his feet and falling forward onto his hands and knees.

"Oh...not a lucky start," Duncan harassed. "Shall I wait for ye to rise at least?"

The man growled and shoved himself to his feet. He whirled in a circle, his hungry gaze roving over Heather before he turned back to Duncan with a snarl. He practically tore his crude sword from the loop at his hip. Holding it pointed out in front of him, he waved it at Duncan.

"I'm the best sword fighter in my crew. Prepare to say goodbye to the lassie." The outlaw nodded emphatically, truly believing his own words.

"Well, I canna say that anyone has called me the best at sword fighting, but I've never walked away the loser." Duncan twirled his sword one more time before lifting it and tapping the tip to the outlaw's.

That made the outlaw grit his teeth, but despite this outward anger, the man couldn't hide the tremble in his hands, his true feelings and weakness.

Duncan pushed the tip of his sword on the ground and with his free hand waved the man forward. They circled one another. As Duncan came round to seeing the ledge in view again, he saw the other men of the outlaw's camp crossing. No way in hell was he going to put his back to them again. He lunged forward, lifting his sword up and smacking it against the other man's dull blade.

The blow jarred the man. Perhaps he hadn't thought it would be coming so soon or with such force. All the same, he parried. Duncan pushed him backward toward the ledge and his friends. He didn't even have to use half his skill to take down the witless sop.

Once the other man's feet teetered on the edge of the ledge, Duncan grinned cruelly and pushed. The man flew backward, tunneling into his comrades, three of them tumbling into the water below.

One clung on for life.

"All your friends are gone, mate. Ye might consider running." Duncan rested the blade of his sword casually on his shoulder.

The rotter quivered in his flimsy boots but still shook his head.

"Truly? I'm only going to toss ye into the water."

The man looked at Duncan, then flicked his jittery gaze to the water below. With a shocking move, he leapt into the current.

"What the hell?" Duncan muttered, watching the man drift down toward his friends.

"What happened?" Heather asked.

"The bastard jumped." Duncan's voice was filled with confusion and amazement that the man had jumped to his death rather than deal with Duncan head-on.

She giggled, nervously, sounding near on the verge of hysteria. "I guess fighting the current was a better option than fighting ye."

"I suppose he was only being intelligent. Might have been the smartest of the whole damn group."

Duncan stared after the disappearing crew for a few moments longer and then turned back around to face Heather. She stood against the wall, still pale in the face but her eyes no longer filled with fear.

"Thank ye," she said, her lashes fluttering as she looked toward the ground and then back up at him.

Duncan's stomach tightened. He liked her a little too much. Time to get that out of his mind.

"I was only saving my own arse," he growled.

Heather startled, the small curve of smile that had formed on her kissable lips fading into an angry frown. Good. When

The Highlander's Sin

he'd started considering keeping her for himself rather than handing her over, Duncan had known he was creating a mess of things, known his need for revenge would not be completed.

"The proper response when one is thanked is, *ye're welcome*," she retorted.

Duncan stormed forward. Inches from her, he lowered his face so their eyes were locked, an intimidating stance he saved for those he wished to frighten into submission. Heather only straightened taller, squaring her damn shoulders.

"I'm not the proper kind," he bit out.

"I noticed." Heather's voice was a little breathy, like she couldn't quite catch it.

Her gaze roved to his lips and he had a good idea of why she was losing her breath. When he stared at her lips, he could only think of one thing—kissing. Only sheer force of will kept his eyes glued to hers.

"Och, will ye attempt to seduce me?" His own voice lowered a notch, all the pent-up battle rage rushing through his blood. He wanted to pin her up against the wall and take it out on her, punish her with a kiss, and more. How far was this feisty little lass willing to let him go?

Heather backed away, 'haps seeing the need darken his eyes.

Duncan tugged her back where she belonged—flush against him. "Ye can pay me for protecting ye, with a kiss."

"I'm no tart. I will not pay for your services with my body." Her words said one thing, but her body said another as she sank against him.

"Fine, then gift me with a kiss in appreciation for saving ye."

The only response he got was the tilt of her head, a curious glance, and then her lips brushed his.

She was kissing *him*.

Aye, he wanted it, but he would have bet his life she'd never do it. He stiffened, unsure what to do. Normally the aggressor, he wasn't used to a woman's advances. Heather sank further into him, her trembling hands pressed to his chest, curling into the fabric of his robes. Could she feel the erratic beat of his heart?

And still he couldn't kiss her back. 'Twas almost like he'd never been kissed by a female in his life, the virgin priest he was supposed to be.

But before she pulled away, he snapped out of whatever shock she'd put him in. He circled his arms around her waist, splayed a hand on her back and lifted her into the air. Duncan pressed his lips firmly to hers, nudging her to tilt her head and part her lips. He claimed her mouth then, showing her what a true kiss was.

His tongue slid over hers, tasting the apple she'd eaten. She was sweeter than fruit, and delicious as hell. He wasn't sure he'd ever be able to quit kissing her. Raw and powerful, their passion was genuine. No other woman had kissed him with such wild abandon. Heather gave all of herself in a kiss, and he was more than willing to give her everything, too. But kisses like this one only led to one thing—and before he pinned her to the floor and hiked up her gown, Duncan pulled away.

Panting, they gazed intently into each other's eyes for the span of several heartbeats.

"A sinful kiss for a virtuous man of the cloth," Heather murmured.

Duncan chuckled. "A wicked wanton ye are, nay the virtuous virgin I was promised."

"'Haps a little bit of both."

"As a priest, I take that as a confession. Now for your penance."

Chapter Ten

*H*eather's lungs ceased to function, unable to draw breath for at least a hundred heartbeats. Or so it seemed. She'd lost count of how many times the erratic organ beat within. The sound of her blood rushed full through her body, and every nerve tingled.

She'd kissed *him.*

Not the other way around. This time she'd been the one seeking out his lips. Her only consolation was that it had been his idea to begin with.

His threat loomed large in the forefront of her mind. *As a priest, I take that as a confession. Now for your penance.* An atonement was the last thing she needed to worry about.

Lungs burning, she finally sucked in a gulp of refreshing air.

"I think it conceivable that since ye're a priest and ye've also sinned, that we call it even." Heather took a step back, wondering just how he would take her bold words.

Duncan grinned. Not at all what she'd expected.

"Tell me this, lass, did ye enjoy it?"

She scoffed, backed up another step and crossed her arms over her breasts, flattening them and hiding the evidence of her perky nipples. "Hardly."

Duncan's grin widened, a dimple forming in his stubbled cheek. What the hell did he find so funny?

"Then perhaps ye'd allow me to do it again. If we are going to sin, then it had best be pleasurable for us both. No point in sinning if it doesn't feel good."

"What kind of priest are ye?"

"Not a very good one." He winked.

That small movement sent a shiver of anticipation rattling through her bones. For shame! Her brothers had warned she'd get herself in trouble…and here she was, flirting with a priest. Nay—worse! Kissing a priest and wishing he'd touch her in inappropriate ways.

Dear God… She was worse than her older sister, Lorna. Heather winced. That wasn't very nice of her to think. Lorna was a wonderful, intelligent person. It wasn't her fault that she'd been seduced by Laird Montgomery when he'd come to buy sheep from their clan. It wasn't her fault that the devil laird had planted his seed and from it a bairn had been conceived.

Heather would not let the priest plant his seed in her. She shook her head, and Duncan raised a curious brow. The internal monologue she was brewing must have shown partially on her face.

"Quelling the demons?" he asked, an edge of teasing in his tone.

"There is only one demon here, and 'tis ye."

The man had the audacity to tilt his head back and laugh uproariously. He clutched his middle as if what she'd said was the funniest thing he'd heard in all his devil life.

"'Tis not that funny," Heather grumbled. But her statement only seemed to make him laugh more. "Stop that." Her voice was filled with the same tone of command she'd heard the nursemaids use on her nieces and nephews.

Duncan only laughed harder, swiping at tears that actually gathered in the corners of his dark eyes.

Anger boiled within Heather. She hated when people laughed at her. But this was worse than someone laughing when she tripped, or teasing her over the latest hair foible. This was him laughing *at* her.

Blinded by her rage, she reacted on impulse, thrusting her hands out and shoving him backward with all her might. Only thing was, she met with solid muscle, and her arms jammed backward, making her entire body rock off balance.

"Oh," she cried out, stumbling back.

Too late, Duncan seemed to see what was happening. A collision course no one could avoid, and it was all her fault. He lunged forward as her head ducked under the pounding falls, the water plunging swiftly down on her, demanding that she fall into the choppy waters below. Heather reached out, grappling for anything, feeling the tips of Duncan's fingers, but he wasn't fast enough. Her feet skidded, never regaining purchase. What felt like an eternity later, she fell through the air, water sprinkling over her, and then a giant splash as she pounded into the river.

The current took issue with her clothing, sucking her under the cold, watery depths. She flailed her arms, trying desperately to break the surface, but the water nymphs demanded her attention at the bottom of the burn. It was deeper than Heather had surmised. Her feet had yet to touch the bottom, though her face was fully submerged.

What sounded like an explosion came from her left. Duncan? Was that the sound of him plunging into the current?

Fear propelled her to paddle harder. Her lungs burned as though someone had lit a fire within her. *Dinna breathe. Dinna suck in the water.*

Heather blinked under the water, hoping somehow by doing so the murkiness would clear and she'd be able to see if it was in fact Duncan who'd fallen or just the sound of water crashing against the rocks.

A strong kick up, and her head broke the surface. She gulped in a breath of air before the current grabbed hold of her skirts and yanked her back down.

This was what drowning was like. This was what it felt like to die. The water was cool against her skin, soothing, and yet its vicious tug and swirl made her limbs grow weak and exhausted. Another break through the surface. A second gasp for air, and back down under.

Losing her clothes was the only way she'd be able to save herself.

With frenzied tugs, she yanked at the ties at her back. Just when she thought she had a firm grip, the ties slipped loose of her slowly, numbing fingers.

She clawed at her chest, hoping to rip the gown from her body, but the waterlogged fabric formed some sort of bond, making it unbreakable. Everything she tried failed. Overcoming this seemed far from reach, impossible.

Heather wanted to scream out her frustration, but doing so would only mean choking down more water.

Dinna give up.

But it seemed hopeless. Heather couldn't beat the current. Her numerous gowns were dragging her down. Her stubbornness was drowning her.

Dinna give up!

Not yet... Not until she was dead. Heather kicked again, flung out her arms once more and just barely broke the surface. But instead of being dragged back under, she was hauled into Duncan's embrace.

"Good God, lass," he said, his voice filled with fear and relief.

"Duncan," she croaked, her voice weak, throat raw. She coughed. Her lungs were so tight. Coughs racked her body, water spilling from her lips as her lungs forced out the unwanted invasion.

"If we've a chance of making it to shore, I've got to take off at least one of your gowns. Ye'll drown us both in the kingdom's supply ye've got on."

Heather managed a weak smile at his humor. But water sloshing into her mouth prevented her response. Duncan's powerful legs swirled in the water behind her, an arm anchored around her middle, and he went to work on her ties.

"I've got to cut it. Too wet to untie."

Heather nodded, no longer caring, simply wanting to get out of this wretched water. She was tired…so tired.

Duncan shifted behind her, and then she felt tugging along her back as he cut the gown. She didn't fear he'd slice her skin, only that his blade wasn't sharp enough to get the deed done.

Beneath his breath, he cursed her gown, grumbling obscenities that would normally make her laugh, but she was too exhausted to enjoy them. Yawns kept widening her mouth and allowing water to splash inside.

The cutting must have worked though, because now he was tugging at her sleeve, yanking and jerking. She held her arm out, hoping it would help, but the limb felt so heavy, it was a great feat to lift it a few inches in the water. Duncan barely noticed her weakened state. He went about his mission as though she were as dry as air and weighed no more than a feather.

One gown removed, she felt instantly lighter.

"I'm taking off another."

His words broached no argument, which was fine with her, because she didn't care if she came out of this raging burn naked. As long as she came out.

Overhead, the clouds rumbled, darkening, perhaps angry that Duncan was going to free her. Was God angry she'd not yet drowned? Was he punishing her for being ungrateful? For leaving her family? For her stubbornness?

"Storm," she whispered.

"Dinna worry over it." Once more she was lightened. Duncan, having developed a rhythm in cutting away her wet gowns, was quicker this time. "That ought to do it."

Thank goodness. She'd only one gown and three chemises left. She only saw one of her gowns drifting a few feet away, and then it was snatched under the water, disappearing from view, as though the angry current would devour the wool instead of her body.

"Lean back against me."

Heather did as Duncan instructed, resting her head on his shoulder. He kicked up until they were both no longer straight up and down in the water, but at an angle.

"Kick your feet, slow and steady."

Heather willed her legs into action, matching Duncan's kicks. He held her around the middle with one arm and used the other to paddle toward the shore.

It seemed like every foot of progress they made, the water hauled them back a few inches. The shore was so close. Maybe six feet away, and yet it felt as though they'd never arrive, doomed to repeat this motion forever.

"Come now, princess, ye've got it. Keep your faith alive."

Heather prayed silently or aloud, she wasn't sure. All she knew was she was asking God to please, please not let them drown. She clutched Duncan's arm around her waist, holding on for dear life.

At last they reached the shoreline, but it was at least a foot or two up. They'd have to climb. Not such a big deal normally, but the water was still quite deep, and Heather was so exhausted. Duncan grasped ahold of an exposed tree root, holding them still in the water.

"I need ye to be strong, lass. Grab hold of the root."

Heather swallowed around the burning in her throat and nodded. Slowly unraveling her fingers from his arm, she turned in his embrace and gripped the root with both hands. Duncan stared down at her, his brow wrinkled with worry and concentration.

"I'm going to push ye up from your legs. Brace your feet on the sides of the embankment. Hold on to the root and walk your fingers up its length, and your feet up the side, until ye feel comfortable pulling yourself over the side."

Comfortable? She was certain that was not how she'd feel at all. Determined, aye.

Water dripped from his hair, over his temples, and even from the tip of his nose. Was there anything Duncan couldn't do?

"Did ye hear me, Heather?"

His voice jarred her from staring. "Aye."

"Do it now."

Heather braced her feet on the sides of the bank, praying no snakes were making their homes in burrows dug out in the dirt around the root. It they were there, she willed them to ignore the need to retaliate at her invasion.

Duncan slid his arm from around her waist, and she cried out in fear.

"Climb." He shoved against her rear, his palm flat on her buttocks—enough to make her scurry into action.

The root was slippery, but she willed herself to hang on, to keep pushing forward. To not think about snakes, or pain, or the warm hand shoving against her nether region.

"Almost there." Duncan's voice sounded strained.

The woods came into view, and for a moment she panicked, expecting to see a horde of enemies waiting there to lop off their heads, but the woods were empty, save for a few squirrels and birds. Heather took a deep, unwavering breath and let go of the root with one hand to grab at the dry knots of the tree's roots upon the ground.

"I've got hold of a tree root," she called.

"Good. Lift your knee over the edge, and I will give ye a push."

Heather tried to lift her knee, but it was twisted and weighed down by her gown. "I canna!"

"Aye, lass, ye can. Do it."

Heather gritted her teeth and, with all of her might, willed her knee up and over the edge. Every muscle in her body screamed from it. Her lungs burst, and she gasped, pushing off that solid knee and rolling the rest of the way onto the bank.

She'd made it. She wasn't dead. As she lay there, catching her breath, she'd almost forgotten — Duncan!

Heather glanced over the edge, and nearly bumped her head against his. Apparently climbing up wasn't as big a feat for him as it had been for her.

He lay on the ground beside her, his chest heaving. Rolling his head toward hers, he smiled. "I think your gowns weigh four stone each."

A short gust of a laugh escaped Heather. "Ye might be right about that." Their eyes locked, and they were both silent, serious as they observed one another. "I'm sorry."

"For what?"

"For shoving ye. This is all my fault. I could have killed us both."

Duncan reached up, touched her forehead with his index finger and said, "Ye're forgiven."

Heather shoved his hand aside. "I dinna want ye to absolve me of my sins, Duncan. I wanted to apologize to *ye*."

He frowned. "Me?"

Heather rolled her eyes. "Aye. I nearly killed ye."

"Was that your intention?"

She shook her head, exasperated. "Nay, ye buffoon." But as soon as the words were out, she felt contrite. "I'm sorry for calling ye that."

"We all get angry, lass. And aye, 'twas extremely stupid what ye did, but ye had no intentions of falling backward, nor of me saving ye. I shall now be aware in the future that ye are an impetuous, senseless princess."

Heather's mouth fell open with shock. Had he truly just insulted her? *After* she'd apologized? "I suppose I deserve that," she grumbled. He was right, after all. Were his words not unlike many she'd heard before? Hadn't she just admitted as much?

Heather glanced up at the tops of the trees crowding out the sky, flopped an arm over her forehead and tried to still her racing heart and breath. "I thank ye all the same for saving my life."

Duncan grunted.

An answer she took to mean he hadn't saved her for anything other than his own personal gain.

Through the trees, the sky still looked gray. A crack of thunder was followed by a flash of lightning.

"We'd best find Blade and then make a new shelter afore the storm truly hits," Duncan said.

"'Tis already hitting."

"Aye, but from the look of black coming from over there, it's going to be a rough one."

Heather glanced toward where Duncan pointed over the swirling deathly waters. The sky was swiftly turning black with storm clouds, likely to kick up winds that could carry away people and sheep.

Duncan stood beside her and reached out a hand. She grasped onto it, feeling the strength of him as he pulled her up. Her legs shook from the effort of standing. Every muscle was sore, exhausted. What she wouldn't have given for a nice hot bath and the comfort of her bed at Dunrobin.

It was then she noticed Duncan's attire—or lack thereof. He wore only his soaked leine shirt. The light-colored fabric was nearly transparent, showing the dark crisp hair of his chest and every contour of muscle.

Heather swallowed, willing herself not to look below his chest.

"Where are your clothes?" she asked.

"I took them off afore I jumped in. No need for us both to be dragged under." The way he spoke, so nonchalant, as though he regularly walked around nearly nude.

She turned her gaze toward the sky, forcing herself not to admire the raw, sheer masculinity of him. "Then I suppose we'd best find your things before we get the horse."

"Why is that?" A teasing edge lined his words.

The man loved to torment her in any way he could. "Ye're indecent."

"Ye're not much better."

Heather glanced down at herself. The three chemises and gown did nothing to hide the outline of her body. Her soaked dress clung to her like a second skin, and her nipples were visible, pushing like two tiny hard stones against the fabric.

She cleared her throat, realizing he, too, was staring at her breasts. "Thank ye, for saving me," she said again, perhaps this time hoping for a better response, or mayhap she needed a distraction from her turgid nipples.

"Ye're welcome."

Chapter Eleven

Duncan gripped tight to Heather's small hand. Her fingers were cold and not likely to get any warmer. Gusts of wind took the heat of summer, and he could feel her shiver with each blow.

They had to hurry to find shelter, and he wouldn't make the mistake hiding out behind the falls again. Too much chance that their previous attackers had been able to make it safely to the shore as well and would backtrack to seek revenge.

Duncan put two fingers in his mouth and blew. The ear-piercing sound rippled through the forest and brought out an answering whinny in the distance. Thank God for his amazing horse. The animal was cantankerous to anyone but Duncan. Blade was more likely to get put down than mounted by another rider.

"My horse is safe. We're almost there," Duncan said, looking behind him at his beautifully haggard captive.

"All right," she said, barely more than a whisper.

Heather was growing weaker. Her lips were blue, face pale as a Highland snow and her eyes were drooping. She shivered constantly, and if he'd had anything other than a wet shirt he would have given it to her. As it was, he doubted heartily she'd welcome the wet shirt off his back for comfort, or the sight of his naked rear.

Fat drops of rain started to plop against the foliage, splattering to the ground and upon their heads and shoulders. The last thing they needed was more water.

Duncan expected to hear Heather groan, but she didn't make a sound. The lass was trying with all of her might to be brave, to power through their ordeal—hers, really. They'd nearly drowned, but at least she was not being delivered to strangers on a polished platter—yet.

Guilt riddled him. The part of him that didn't want to give her up was growing stronger with every second. When he'd seen her tumble through the falls, there hadn't been a question of letting her fend for herself. And he'd not jumped in because of the pouch of silver, either. He'd willingly dived into danger to save her, because deep down, Duncan actually liked the fiery woman. Immensely.

Ballocks! How had this happened?

He was not free to fall for anyone, to like a woman. He was, for all intents and purposes, not his own man—he belonged to the church, to the clan who didn't know he existed, and to those who paid him. Most of all, he belonged to the devil in hell for all the many sins he'd committed, no matter how many times he'd been absolved.

Duncan glanced back at Heather again. There was no expected rush of hate for who her family was. Nor a need to toss her to the wolves, but instead an intense desire to wrap her in his arms and never let go.

Yet again, Fate intervened when he sought to meet out his revenge on the cursed Sutherlands.

Yet again, Fate had intervened when he'd sought to mete out his revenge on the cursed Sutherlands.

A few years before, he'd been at the kirk, waiting for the Sutherlands to arrive so he could kill them. He'd not expected to marry two of them. To wish them joy and happiness. When he'd given them his blessings, he'd wanted to stab them in the hearts. But, instead, he'd let them go. Coward that he was. Another chance had taken up residence. When he'd sneaked into the castle of Magnus' cousin—Brandon Sinclair—again to seek out his revenge, he'd been unable to do it. The man's wife, Lady Mariana, had sat with two beautiful babes in her arms, innocent lives that he could not take.

Duncan believed that Fate played a hand in most things. Not being able to seek out revenge on the Sutherlands on those two occasions had been partially because the woman—Mariana—had not been to blame, nor part of his issue with that damnable family. And also, because Fate had wanted him to wait until now, when he'd found Heather.

Oh, Fate cursed him. Fate played tricks with his mind. How could she torment him so? To fall for his enemy…

Duncan shook his head. Such a thing would be committing treason against the memory of his family, against his whole life. Impossible.

Pounding upon the ground before them startled Duncan from his thoughts. Damn it. He wasn't normally so muddleheaded, but the lass was messing with his mind.

He tugged her behind a tree, pressing her spine against it, and covering her front with his own back.

"Dinna make a sound."

There was no telling if the approaching horse had a rider, or if it was Blade. He prayed it was his mount. It would be difficult to fight without his sword, and only a shirt on for protection. He didn't even have his shoes on, for heaven's sake. *Mo chreach*, nor his sword. The weight of the weapon would have only dragged them down into the water. At least he still had the knife tucked into the sheath at his wrist that he'd used to cut Heather's gowns.

Duncan reached for the knife now, preparing for the worst and praying for the best. The angry snort sounded like Blade. He took a chance and glanced around the side of the tree, watching his horse approach with a rolling mist chasing at his heels. Indeed, the coming storm was going to be brutal.

"Thank the saints," he muttered. Checking the immediate surroundings to be sure his mount had not been followed, he surmised that all was clear. "Our ride has arrived."

Heather pressed two little hands against his shoulders, peering around him. "Thank the saints, indeed."

"Let us hurry to gather the things I left at the falls and then we'll be on our way. I know of a cave nearby where we can make camp until the storm subsides."

Duncan lifted Heather onto his horse and climbed up behind her, wincing as his cold limbs hit the heat of his horse. He'd been so preoccupied about Heather, he'd not realized how his own flesh had chilled.

He urged the horse forward, his fingers curling around the mane. Thick, wiry hair sliced into his pruned fingers like sword edges. The ride through the forest was jarring, his wet flesh rubbed raw against the bare back of the horse.

They'd drifted farther down than he'd realized. By the time they reached the falls, rain fell in earnest droves, pummeling them, and black clouds blocked out the majority of sunlight.

Duncan shaded Heather's face from the pelting droves with his arm, but he feared he did little as rainwater soaked her hair.

"Wait here on Blade," he said, when they reached the ledge by the falls leading to their tiny, private alcove.

"Be careful. 'Tis bound to be more slick in the storm," she said.

Their words were drowned out by the storm, slipping from their mouths silently and coming back on the wind.

Duncan nodded. He patted his horse on the neck and leaned in, whispering, "Take care of the lady."

Blade nodded his head, shook it. Could have been in answer or it could have been that he sought to flush the water from his eyes.

Duncan wasted no time. There was no point in waiting to see if the rain would subside. It likely wouldn't, and they were out in the open now on the edge of the forest. He bolted toward the ledge, his toes sinking deep into mud and popping out with each step he took. Mud-covered feet would not make his approach to the alcove any safer.

He glanced up at the sky, praying for safety and strength as water pelted his face, and then he took his first step up, wavering as he centered his weight. Duncan leaned against the wet stone, sensing how slick it was around his hands and his feet. He took a tentative step forward, measuring the extent of the ledge's slipperiness. Not as bad as he'd thought.

Taking it slow, he inched to the side, his chest pressed to the stone wall, back to the angry current below. He blocked out all noise of his surroundings, zeroing in on his breath, his heartbeat and the measured steps it would take to get to the alcove, where he could gather his things before having to make the treacherous walk again.

Duncan blew out a breath when the alcove was within leaping distance. He jumped to safety, skidding a little as his wet, muddy feet hit the dry alcove floor.

He gathered their things, stripped off his wet leine, pleated his plaid, rolled it around his hips and pulled his black robe over his shoulders, securing it at the neck. Back in costume he felt safer, calmer. Hidden.

One last order of business. He stuck the backs of his feet briefly under the falls, washing away the muck before slipping his feet back into his hose and boots.

Ready to make the walk again, he checked first on Heather, raising his arm to her. She raised hers in return before ducking her head away from the storm. They'd be lucky if she didn't get sick from this. Duncan was used to being out in the elements, but he doubted Heather was. Ladies normally ran for shelter at the first shift in the wind, safe from harm before a drop of rain could even fall.

Even as the thought went through his mind, doubt crept in. She struck him as more adventurous than that. Perhaps the lass stayed behind to dance in wanton circles as Mother Earth's nourishment fell all around. 'Twas a fact he'd yet to hear her complain.

But it could have been that she was so frozen she couldn't speak, a thought that sent a most unsettling feeling through him. He had to get her to shelter straightaway.

With Heather as his sole thought, he made it over the ledge and back to her side before he realized he'd stepped foot on the dangerous stone shelf. The woman was taking him out of himself. Dangerous. Just being near her put him on treacherous ground.

He made quick work of pulling her down, putting the saddle and bridle on Blade, and then getting them both settled back onto the horse's back. He would not have normally gone to the trouble in a storm, but carrying the saddle and satchels on their laps would have been a bit much. He expected to hear some witty comment about how he was finally dressed, but she said nothing, simply leaned back against him, shivering.

The exact opposite of what she'd done every other time they'd ridden together. The lass was unquestionably ailing.

The storm showed no sign of relenting, only the warning of worse things yet to come. Duncan kicked Blade's flank, urging his mount into a gallop through the soggy mud and torrential downpour.

"Just a short ride away," he said, comforting Heather, the horse and himself.

Every passing minute found Heather sagging heavier and heavier against him. She was definitely not herself. The Heather he knew would have been nearly over the top of the horse in her haste to get away from him. Damn it! She couldn't catch a fever on him! Duncan wouldn't allow it.

The cave loomed into view, or rather its surroundings did. The entrance was hidden behind an overgrowth of gorse bushes that he'd made sure to plant and a very tall oak that had been there for a century at least.

Duncan wasn't the only one to have found the cave. Occasionally when he came upon it, there were remnants of passers-through, but he'd never run into one. Today may prove to be different, given the weather.

"Dinna make a sound," he whispered, though she'd not spoken thus far.

He slowed Blade to a painful walk as what felt like buckets full of water fell from thick leaves that had filled up, and rain that had managed to avoid the trees altogether pelted against their cheeks.

There was no way to ascertain if one or more people had taken shelter within the cave. He wasn't about to call out a greeting.

No prints remained indented in the muck, the rain heavy enough to wash away all evidence that anyone had ever stepped here. No horses roamed the vicinity. But that didn't prove anything. Duncan himself planned to bring Blade into the cave so the animal could dry off and remain warm.

Only one way to find out, and there was no use standing outside to figure out another course of action. Heather needed warmth and a roof immediately.

He urged Blade forward, around the wide oak and bushes to the narrow path that sat between them and the cave entrance. There was no scent of smoke or sound of people talking. They might just get lucky.

Before they reached the entrance, Duncan stilled his horse and gave Heather the reins. She opened her mouth to protest, but he put two fingers to his lip. With her nod, he dismounted. He pulled his claymore from the sheath at his back and gripped it in two hands as he crept forward. Either not having alerted those who resided inside to his presence, or he and Heather were truly alone, no one popped their heads out to see him. Positioning himself to the side of the entrance, he called out, "*Feasgar math.*"

When he was greeted with silence and no one came out to investigate his presence, he peered around the corner. Darkness filled the cave. Thank the saints, it was empty.

A deep sigh of relief escaped him. He gripped Blade's bridle and tugged the horse and his charge into the cave. Instantly, the roar of the storm dulled, almost as though they'd stepped into a different realm. The sounds of the rain and wind were calming now that the storm no longer assaulted their bodies.

Duncan held out his arms to Heather, who barely seemed to notice him. She practically fell on to him as she slid from the saddle. He wrapped his arms around her and carried her over to the side of the cave. Duncan settled her against a wall and knelt in front of her.

"Are ye all right, lass?"

Even in the dim light, he could see how pale she was. Hair a mess, it stuck to her cheeks and neck. Water dripped in rivulets over her forehead, nose, chin. She rolled her gaze toward his and nodded.

But the glassy of her eyes said otherwise.

Duncan frowned, patted her awkwardly on the shoulder and then stood. He took all the satchels off his mount and then removed the saddle and bridle, sure to give Blade an apple before he went about anything else. The horse had done a great duty bringing them here, suffering more than the both of them in the process.

"As long as no heathens came and took my supply, I've got a stack of wood in the back of the cave. I'll light a fire to warm ye up."

Heather grunted.

Duncan pulled the jug of whisky from one of the satchels and handed it to her. "Drink a few sips of this while I gather the wood." He forced a laugh, trying to lighten the mood and his fear. "Try not to spit it out this time."

Heather barely cracked a smile as she held up a limp, cold hand, grabbing the jug from him and letting it fall heavily into her lap without taking a sip.

"Do ye need me to hold it to your lips?"

"Nay," she croaked.

Duncan watched until she'd uncorked the jug and took a healthy sip, eyes closed as she did. But she let it fall a little too easily back to her lap, making him nervous she'd spill it all over herself. He re-corked it and gave her a once-over. Pale. Blue lips. Glassy eyes. Soaking wet. Shivering.

The lass was bound to be ill with fever inside the next hour if he didn't get her warmed up and dry soon.

He slid his hands along the familiar walls of the cave until he reached the far back left corner, where he'd spent nearly an entire day carving a nook in the wall to store wood that would be easily concealed from any outsiders seeking shelter. His fingertips hit wood. Blessed be. Appeared only a couple of pieces of wood had been removed. Whoever had shared this shelter with him had been kind enough to re-stock it.

Filling his arms with several logs and kindling, he carried them back to the center of the cave. He stacked the wood in a crisscross pattern and then pulled a flint from his pouch. It only took four sparks to light the kindling. A warm blaze took root, and instant heat reached his fingertips.

"Come here, lass."

Heather remained seated. Her eyes were closed.

Duncan trudged toward her, lifted her into his arms, feeling the length of her slight form against his. She opened her eyes, staring lifelessly up at him.

"Ye need to get warm," he said.

Heather nodded, and he carried her to the fire, setting her down before it. Her eyes fixed on the jumping orange and yellow flames.

"Feels nice, does it not?"

She nodded and held her shaking hands near the heat. Even her fingertips had gone blue.

Despite the warmth of the fire, they were not going to get dry quickly by sitting in front of it. Nor would her body heat be restored.

"I'm afraid I'm going to have to ask ye to remove the only gown ye've got left and any undergarments ye're wearing." He hated saying the words. How lecherous they sounded in his own ears.

Heather glanced up at him, and even in her haze, he could see a flash of fury in her eyes.

"Not in this lifetime, Priest."

Chapter Twelve

Remove her clothes?

Heather was already freezing. It took all her effort not to let her teeth chatter. Her skin was covered in gooseflesh, and her fingers trembled, her toes numb, knees knocking as soon as she stopped concentrating on keeping them pressed firmly together. Keeping her legs bent toward her chest seemed to hold in whatever warmth she had. Taking off the only garments she had was hardly her idea of getting warm. She stuck her hands farther toward the blaze, then yanked them back as one of her fingers felt the singe of heat a bit too closely.

"My lady, I swear upon it, I am not trying anything untoward. We need to lay your clothes flat so that they dry, and right now, sopping wet as they are, they are bound to make ye sick." Duncan's voice was calm, full of reason.

She glanced away from him. Looking at him made her want to believe that what he spoke was true, but she knew it couldn't be. All the *my ladies* in the world wouldn't change her mind. No man had ever seen her naked—save her brothers and father when she had been a wee bairn. Only her maids had seen her nude as a full-grown woman. Father Duncan was not going to be the first grown male to see her without clothes. That privilege was saved for her husband—of which she had none and no plans for in the future.

"Nay," she said, pleased that her voice came out strong, no matter how weak she felt at the moment.

"Heather."

The sound of her name spoken from his lips jolted her, and she jerked her gaze back to his.

"Duncan."

"Dinna mock me, lass. I'm deadly serious."

"And so am I. Ye'll have to wrestle me to the ground and rip the clothes from my *cold*, limp body."

"Dinna make me do it."

A chill swept through her—not from the cold. His gaze was stern and gave her no doubt that he would indeed lay her flat and rip the fabric from her body like he'd done in the water.

"Please, Priest. Dinna make me take off my clothes." Her lower lip trembled. She was starting to break. The utter humiliation of being abducted, almost dying and now getting nude... Heather had always thought herself strong, but in this she was suddenly sure she was as weak as a bairn.

Duncan turned around and rummaged through one of his satchels, pulling out one of the plaid blankets they'd used at the castle ruins.

"I'm not a monster," he said, holding out the blanket. "'Tis dry. Now get undressed and wrap it around yourself."

Guilt simmered, but she squashed it. She'd had every right to react the way she had. If she'd not, 'haps he wouldn't have offered her the blanket.

"Thank ye." She took the proffered fabric, feeling its soft warmth in her grasp. A surge of energy filled her.

Outside their cave, the storm raged on, threatening any living thing in its path—plant, animal or human form. But braving the summer tempest suddenly seemed better than dropping her clothes—the only protection she had—in front of a man. Especially this man. She was more worried about her own reaction than his. Every time he looked at her, some portion of her body fluttered and sang.

"Ye're welc—"

Before he could finish, she dropped the blanket and bolted around him, skirting the fire, the horse, his dropped satchel. Her muscles screamed from exhaustion, but she did not give in to their protest. She had to get away from the only man who seemed able to elicit a response from her, a need to change who she was, what she was, and what she wanted out of life. He made her see life differently, and she wasn't about to give up on her dreams of helping her country. Not for all the good, warm rush of feelings in the world.

Surprise registered on Duncan's face, and he lunged toward her, grabbing onto the fabric of her sleeve. Heather didn't stop, didn't care when she heard the wrenching sound of fabric tearing.

Her last gown.

She kept running. The dull roar of the storm turned on full force as she ducked out of the cave and was immediately pelted by rain, blasts of wind whipping her hair painfully into her face.

"Stop!" she heard Duncan call faintly.

She was sure he'd bellowed it, but the storm deadened the sound. The last thing she was going to do was stop. Hands out in front of her, she pushed past the gorse bushes and slipped in the mud, falling to her hands and knees on the soggy ground. She scrambled to her feet, muck-covered hands gripping tight to her skirts.

Not familiar with the area, Heather had to guess which way the road would be. And even when she reached it, there was no telling if she should go right or left. *Dinna let such thoughts slow ye down,* she cautioned herself. Picking up speed was difficult as the rain turned stable ground into mudslides.

And then, Duncan caught her around the waist, tumbling them both to the ground. She fought against him, rolling back and forth, kicking, hitting. But all she succeeded in doing was getting them both thoroughly covered in mud. Duncan managed to get hold of her wrists, pinning them to the ground above her head. His huge body straddled hers, thighs pinning hers together.

"Get off of me," she said, her voice weak from screaming.

Fury showed on Duncan's face and laced his words. "Are ye daft? Will ye get us both killed?"

"Nay," she whimpered. "I simply want to be away from ye."

"Every wolf in the area has heard your mewling death cries and will be coming in for the kill. And should any outlaws have heard your screams, they'll be racing toward the sound to catch a bit of what ye have left over to offer."

Heather refused to let his words frighten her, though her heart did cinch at the thought of being eaten alive by animal or man. Instead, she focused on something positive. "And should anyone be looking for me, I've just alerted them to my whereabouts."

"Ye're so proud of yourself." A fierce frown marred his brow.

"Aye," she said smugly.

He leaned down close, his nose touching hers. "And yet, here we are, and I've got ye at my mercy."

A realization she'd been trying to avoid. "Will ye ravish me like the outlaws would?"

Oh, God, why did the thought send tingles racing along her skin? Suddenly, her thighs felt the pressure of his, her hips felt the weight of his body, and she had to threaten them to remain rooted in place, not fall open, searching for his heat, the way she wanted. Her chest heaved as her breath quickened.

"'Haps ye'd like that," Duncan said. He moved a knee from the side of her and pressed it between her thighs, gently pushing her legs apart.

And her shameful thighs complied.

Duncan slid his body between her legs, and a hot rush of need flared from the juncture of her thighs. For all she was aware, the raging storm could have subsided.

"'Haps I'd like it, too," he murmured, leaning close enough for her to feel his breath on her neck. He flicked out his tongue, tracing the shell of her ear. At the same time, he rolled his hips against hers.

White heat shot from that wanton spot on her body. Something hard, something long, rubbed tantalizingly at the most secret part of her.

"Get off me," she said meekly, too meekly. She shoved feebly at his shoulders.

Duncan only rubbed his body harder against her. He moved both of her pinned wrists to one hand, and with the other gripped her hip and massaged. Of its own accord, her knee bent, came up around his hip, tucking him closer to the sensitive parts of her that he'd forced awake.

"Do ye truly want me to stop?" he asked.

Lifting his mouth from her ear, he locked his gaze with hers. Mud streaked over his nose and forehead. He looked endearingly charming and dangerous all at once.

A weighty question. Did she truly want him to—nay, nay she didn't. But was it necessary? Aye. Most definitely aye.

"Please, help me up." She shivered, mostly because she'd shifted and that hard part of him stroked over her, but also from fear and the chill of being completely soaked by pelting rain.

In a swift, purely masculine move, he leapt to his feet and held out his hand to her. "I'd never hurt ye, lass," he said.

Heather ignored his hand and tried to push herself up to standing, but her limbs were weak and sore from her *swim* and trying to run away and from having lain in the muck, ready to shed her clothes and offer herself up to him. Before she could ask, Duncan was beside her, his hand on her elbow, infinite warmth shooting from the spot. He drew her to her feet. But he didn't stop there. With one behind her back and another sliding beneath her knees, he lifted her up, holding her tightly against him.

He jogged back to the cave with her in his arms, as though she weighed no more than his jug of whisky. By the time they'd gotten inside, most of the mud had been washed away from their skin, though her gown, so light in color, was thoroughly ruined.

Duncan set her on her feet and gave her a stern look as he handed her the blanket she'd discarded before. "Now ye need to get undressed."

"I'll be fine."

"I will give ye to the count of three before I start unlacing ye myself."

Heather glared at him, weighing her options. She could make a run for it again, but he was only likely to catch her once more. It'd been stupid to run the first time, downright witless to do so the second. Gritting her teeth, she stomped a foot and turned her back to him, trying desperately to reach for the gown's ties.

"Do ye need me to help ye untie it?"

"Nay," she spat, but it was evident in the few minutes she tried to do so herself that her fingers would not cooperate. "Aye."

Duncan didn't say a word, didn't mock her for dismissing him and then pulling him back. He simply untied the dress and waited to see if she wanted any more help. Again, she was struck by the realization that beneath his harsh exterior shell,

The Highlander's Sin

the man was true and genuine. She supposed he would have had to be as a priest. Precisely why she should not let him kiss her and make other scandalous advances—even if they felt amazing.

Keeping her back to Duncan, Heather slid the gown off of one shoulder and then the other, peeling it down her arms and then dropping the heavy, soaked garment at her feet. He drew in a sharp breath, and she whipped around, covering herself, though she was still essentially clothed in three chemises. But they were wet, and just as his leine shirt had been sheer, she was sure her chemises were, too, despite the multiple layers.

His eyes darkened as their gazes locked. His mouth was pressed into a firm line, a haunted stripe of lips, as if he couldn't make up his mind how to react. Heather felt the familiar chills of heat centering in her sensitive parts. The way she'd felt when he'd kissed her, touched her thigh. Why was she having them now when he looked at her?

"Turn around," she ordered him, though it came out more like a plea. She licked her lips, wishing it were he touching her in such an intimate way.

Duncan slowly turned. The heels of his boots echoed in the cave as he shifted his feet until his back was all she saw. For a split second, she wished he was back in that wet shirt, so she could examine his body the way she wanted to, without him being wise to it.

"Hurry, lass."

Why did he want her to hurry? Was he also curious? Did he feel the sparks of heat that seemed to be taking over her entire being?

Heather tugged at the ribbons of all three chemises at her throat and, as one, peeled them down her body, stepping out of the white pool of fabric.

She stood upright, shivering all the more—and she wasn't sure if it was from cold, because the fire had surely heated their little cave, or because a few feet away stood a man she found entirely too enticing and she wore nothing but her skin.

Her nipples hardened, pink, upturned buds, almost like they reached out for him, wanting him to… What? Touch them? God, what would it be like for him to…kiss them?

Heather coughed, choking on her own breath. Duncan leapt around. Heather screamed, flung an arm across her naked breasts and moved her other hand down to cover the curls nestled between her thighs.

"Turn around! What are ye doing?" she cried.

"I thought—" But he didn't finish his own sentence, just stared at her, devouring her length in a way that made her nipples ache and sweet twinges of desire flicker beneath her triangle of curls.

"Turn around." For her sake, she prayed he'd listen, for her voice had clearly lost its urgency.

Duncan didn't turn around. He took a step forward. Her eyes widened. He opened his mouth, but no words came out. Instead, he whirled back around. Heather bent quickly to pick up the plaid blanket and wrapped it around herself until she was sure not a smidgen of skin showed—including the tips of her toes.

"I'm covered," she murmured.

"Thank God," he answered.

Heather couldn't help herself. She laughed. She laughed so hard she could barely stay on her feet. Drunken giddiness took over—but she was hardly sotted. She'd had a tiny sip of whisky and had barely felt its heat in her belly. She was drunk on something else entirely—relief, stress, something.

"Have ye gone mad?" Duncan asked.

The expression on his face only made her laugh harder. He looked truly stricken.

"Ye might need to take a seat." His frown deepened as he spoke to her and pointed at the ground. He stomped forward and pressed the back of his hand to her forehead. "Ye've not caught a fever yet. What's the matter with ye?"

"Have ye never heard anyone laugh before?"

"Aye, I've heard plenty of people laugh. But never one in such a state as yourself. What have ye to laugh about?"

"Have ye been in this situation so often, then?" Her laughter stilled. How many others had he abducted and brought here? How many others had he stripped naked in the rain?

Duncan stroked a finger over her chin, making her tremble. "Make no mistake, Lady Heather, I've *never* been in this situation before."

All laughter ceased as their gazes once more locked. She searched his eyes for the meaning behind his words, but all she found was a bottomless pool she wanted to dip into. She swallowed, licked her lower lip nervously.

"If ye've never been in a situation such as we find ourselves, then how do ye know we shouldn't be laughing? We are alive, are we not? Dinna ye find humor in it?"

"Nay." His gaze was firmly on her lips.

"Not even a tiny bit?"

He shook his head.

"What do ye see?" she asked.

"A beautiful woman."

Heather gasped, not having expected that to be his response.

"Ye're not allowed to say that."

"Why? Because I'm a priest or because I'm your captor?" Duncan's voice had taken on a gravelly, low edge that made her toes curl into the cave floor.

She bit the inside of her cheek and mumbled, "Both."

"Maybe I dinna want to be either."

"What?" She didn't understand what he was saying. How could he not be either?

He stroked his palm over her cheek, warm and coarse. Heather bit her lip to avoid the sigh poised to escape. Toying with her wet tendrils, he curled an end around his finger.

"Ye make a man forget what he is." Duncan's tone deepened.

She watched her darkened, damp hair form a slow circle around his index finger. A thousand butterflies danced in her belly. "How can ye forget who ye are?"

"I'm forgetting who I'm not."

"Ye speak in riddles." She met his heady gaze, again trying to see the man beneath the mystery.

Duncan's lip curled slightly on one side, forming a dimple in his cheek. How desperately she wanted to kiss the spot.

"With ye… I want to be someone else. Someone I buried."

"A man ye killed?" A chill snaked up her spine.

He shrugged. "In a matter of speaking. He was me."

"Why did ye…do away with him?"

Duncan shook his head, dropped the curl from his finger. The hint of smile left his face, replaced by a dark, brooding frown. "I didna. Someone else did, leaving me to pick up the pieces and form a new life. This life." Bitterness dripped from his words as he held his arms out to the side, palms up, and looked around the cave.

Duncan was a broken man. One Heather felt a sudden urge to heal. She reached an arm through the blanket and touched his chest, feeling the slight bump of his heart beneath her fingertips.

"Who is inside here?"

"No one." He stepped away from her, telling her without words that he didn't want her to pry.

But Heather wasn't going to allow him to back away. She stepped forward, filling the space between them. She touched her palm to his stubbled cheek and spoke softly. "Tomorrow, or the day after that, ye're going to give me up to people who will likely kill me, and if they dinna, I'm as good as dead besides. At least tell me who ye really are."

He studied her face for the span of several heartbeats, his lips in a firm line, brows crinkled together. "I'm Duncan. Of Clan MacKay."

"MacKay?" The clan was a familiar one. Many tales centered around them—and a few within her own family. One. namely, Uncle Nicholas, had gone against her father's wishes and had slaughtered Laird MacKay, his entire family and many in his clan. A faction of the clan had since returned to their holding and begun anew. Was Duncan's family amongst those her relation had murdered?

"Ye've not heard of us?"

Heather shook her head and glanced toward the ground, feeling shame at what her uncle had done to the clan. "I've heard."

"I am your enemy," he said.

She glanced back up at him, frowning. "Nay. Not my enemy at all."

Duncan's face grew darker as he glowered down at her. "Not your enemy?" he repeated.

"Nay."

He groaned, whirled away from her and found the jug of whisky he'd discarded before. Popping the cork, he took a long swig. Without a glance her way, he held it out to her. Heather took hold of the jug and drew in a small sip. This time, she did feel it burn a path down her throat, and she shuddered.

When she handed it back, their fingers brushed, giving her the urge to grab hold of his hand—an urge she did not give in to.

Duncan took the whisky, and, between sips, unhooked his priest's robes, revealing an inch of tan, muscled flesh at a time. Riveted, she could not turn away. He tossed the billowing black fabric into a corner. Heather's eyes widened, her mouth dry. He wore only his plaid at his hips—no shirt.

What she'd glimpsed beneath his wet leine was nothing compared to viewing his flesh uncovered. Broad, muscled shoulders led to sinewy arms that bunched and lengthened with each of his movements. His chest was…breathtaking. She swallowed, unable to truly focus on much else. A sprinkling of dark hair curled over rippling muscles and an abdomen that resembled stacked stones. He was a powerhouse. His own fortress.

Heather had seen plenty of strong men before. Her brothers, cousins, clan warriors… But none compared. None had made her feel the way Duncan did. None had made her weak in the knees just from staring at his naked torso.

So engrossed in staring, she'd nearly forgotten what they'd been speaking about until he said it again—"Not your enemy, lass? If I'm not your enemy, then who am I? Do enlighten me, for I've lived the last twenty years as though your family were demons and I the devil who would put them down."

Heather wet her lips, hoping her voice didn't come out a croak. Her mouth was so dry, her chest tight. She didn't want to have this serious conversation. She just wanted to touch his muscles, to see if they were as hard as they looked, or if his skin was rough or soft. Shallow of her, aye, the man was ripping open his chest and showing her what lay inside. But maybe that was just it. By revealing himself, he was trusting her, pulling her in, though they really should have been pushing each other away.

"I don't know," she whispered.

"Have ye gone daft? I stole ye away from your family."

She nodded. "Aye, ye did that, but then ye saved me when I fell in the water. Am I to still call ye my enemy when ye saved my life?"

The Highlander's Sin

He stalked toward her. She backed away. Aye, she wanted to touch him, but the closer he got, the closer that wish came to being a reality.

Duncan continued to advance on her. Coming closer. Closer still. And then her back was hitting the stone wall of the cave. She clutched at the blanket surrounding her like a lifeline. A memory of her sister-by-marriage, Arbella, came to mind. A conversation they'd had in which Heather had proclaimed that she would choose her own husband, and if he didn't want to be her man, she'd take him.

Lord, if the circumstances had been different... She might just have made Duncan hers forever, wrapping her arms around his neck for a kiss and helping to heal the brokenness blackening his insides.

But in this current situation, she trembled at the knees and tightened the cocoon of wool around herself, because that was the only barrier between him and her—the only shred of decency she felt she had left.

Duncan pressed his free hand on the wall above her head, pinned her to the stone with his hips. A hard bulge of something pressed between her thighs—his sword? His...shaft?

She chewed her bottom lip.

He took a long draw of whisky. "Why do ye play games with my mind?" he said in a low growl. Pressing his nose to her wet hair, he breathed deeply. "I had a duty."

"I'm not playing games," she whispered. "I'm not keeping ye from your duty."

"Aye, but ye see," he took another swig, "ye are."

"How?"

He fingered the blanket around her neck. "By being so tempting."

"I'm only wearing this because my clothes were wet."

"Wet..." He nodded, his eyes boring into hers. Duncan pressed his forehead to hers, the tips of their noses touching.

Would he kiss her again?
God, she wanted him to kiss her.

Chapter Thirteen

*L*ips as tempting as a cherry tart.

Duncan breathed in Heather's scent, trying to grasp some shred of control. She was his captive. She was a virgin. She was so damned tempting.

His cock raged with the need to drive between her thighs, and every inch of him screamed to peel the blanket from her clutching fingers and reveal the beauty of her body to his eyes. He'd caught a glimpse when she'd stripped off her wet clothes—long legs with tight, lithe thighs. Rounded hips. Plush breasts.

Enough to make him forget who they both were. Enough to make him want to change the course of his destiny.

"Let me kiss ye," he said.

His cock was pressed tight to the juncture of her thighs, and he wanted more than anything to rip away his plaid and her blanket so that he could feel the damp curls of her sex part on his shaft.

"I canna," she whispered.

"Why?" Their lips were only an inch apart. All he had to do was sink against her.

"'Tis wrong."

She had a point, even if she didn't sound completely convinced of it herself. But that wasn't going to stop him from desiring her.

"There is one thing ye must know about me," he said, dragging his lips along her jawline. Soft skin…

"What?" Her voice shook.

"I was forced into those robes. The church is not my destiny."

Her throat bobbed against his lips when she swallowed.

"What is?"

Duncan pulled at the blanket enough to reveal the crook between her shoulder and neck. He pressed his lips to the rapid beat of her pulse, suckling gently at the tender flesh. Heather let out a short gasp. When he looked up at her, she'd sucked her lower lip into her mouth, silencing her reaction.

"I'm not sure anymore," he answered honestly. This time he was the one swallowing hard. "I became a mercenary in order to train for the day I met up with my enemies, so I could exact vengeance." He shook his head. "Not sure about that so much anymore, either." He gave her a pointed stare, wondering if she'd realize, see in his eyes, how much she'd changed him.

Shooting a pale hand from inside the clutches of her blanket, Heather took the whisky jug and held it to her lips. 'Haps she did see. Duncan stroked a hand through his hair. It was drying quite a bit quicker than hers.

"I had a plan," she blurted out.

Duncan raised a brow. "A plan to escape?"

She shook her head, then stilled it, crinkling her nose. "Well, aye, ye canna expect me to simply allow ye to hand me over to the heathens who paid for me. But that is not what I meant."

"What did ye mean?" He traced a finger along the column of her neck, following his touch with a path of kisses.

She took another long pull of whisky. Duncan took the jug away from her, corked it and tossed it through the cave, where it landed perfectly on his discarded robe, unbroken.

"Enough drink. Tell me what ye meant." He tugged at her earlobe with his teeth.

Heather's breath hitched. "I had a plan before ye came to Dunrobin. Ye ruined my plan."

"And what was that?" He grinned, toying with the ends of her hair again. "To plait your hair and weave a crown of gillyflowers?"

Heather rolled her eyes. "What ye must think of me," she drawled out.

"The same I think of any princess."

"I'm not a princess."

"Might as well be. Now tell me about your plan."

She pursed her lips. "Never mind."

"Ah, but ye see, I do mind. I'm very interested to hear the workings of your mind and your grand scheme." He rubbed the edges of the blanket were it lay near her collarbone, itching to tug it away.

"How do ye know it was grand?"

"Everything ye do is grand."

She tilted her head to the side and smiled. "Ye have a point."

He was glad to see cheer returning to her, to see that she was no longer shivering. Her eyes were clear of haze, and whatever illness she'd been on the brink of receiving had dissipated.

He plucked gently at the blanket. "If ye dinna tell me—"

"Och, dinna threaten me, Highlander. What leverage do ye have? This blanket?" She pinched it at her neck and tugged. "Ye've already seen me naked."

That he had... And the mention of it only brought the sweet memory to the forefront of his mind.

"Dinna talk about the blanket," he said. His gaze roved to where her breasts were. Beneath the wool he was sure her arms covered them, for her hands peeked out from the middle of her chest. He could simply part the folds and reveal...so much.

"Fine. I shall tell ye of my plan, but ye mustn't laugh at me."

"I canna promise not to laugh." He winked.

"Then I won't tell ye."

"Then I'll be forced to rip this bit of plaid from where ye stand and toss it into the burning fire. Besides, ye laughed like a banshee not a quarter hour ago, 'haps now 'tis my turn."

Heather pouted prettily, pushing her pink lips out. Lord, he wanted to sink his teeth into her, to lap at every inch of skin on her body and then do it all over again. His cock was already rock solid and leapt at the idea, pressing itself further against her.

Her eyes widened. She was obviously aware of his arousal, though she said nothing and remained perfectly still.

"I want to find William Wallace."

He couldn't help it. The laugh escaped him in a short burst and then grew into the same maniacal cackle she'd had before. "Find Wallace? Whatever for?" he asked between chuckles.

Heather's cheeks had brightened into two flames. "Ye're impossible!" She swatted at him, which only made her blanket dip low on one creamy shoulder. "This is why I didna want to tell ye."

But Duncan had stopped laughing, because he'd seen that shoulder, and she'd yet to realize that it was still showing. One freckle sat dead center in it. He fell forward, pressing his lips to the tiny beauty mark and inhaling the scent of her skin. Heather gasped and pushed against him weakly.

"Dinna," she whispered.

Duncan pulled his mouth from her skin. Not because he wanted to, but because he didn't want to scare her away.

"Wallace is not an easy man to find," he said.

"Aye. I know it. But my brothers said he was back in Glasgow."

"We are nay going to Glasgow."

"I know."

"Is that why ye came so willingly with me? Because ye thought I might take ye closer to Wallace?" A spear of jealously drove through his gut. "Are ye in love with him?" He couldn't help the hint of disgust. Wallace was a great and powerful man, no doubt. Brave and hearty, what this country needed in its war against the English. But Duncan would have had the same reaction toward the thought of her loving any other man.

Besides him.

Devil take it! Duncan wanted Heather to love him.

Ballocks!

She crinkled up her pert little nose and shook her head, her eyes narrowing. "Nay, of course not. How could ye think such a thing?"

"Then why do ye need to find him?"

"Because I want to fight, of course."

Duncan swallowed, the breath taken from his lungs. His relief at hearing her say she wasn't in love with Wallace was strong, and yet his shock at hearing she wanted to get herself killed rocked him to the core. "Fight?" He prayed he hadn't heard her correctly.

"Aye. I want to fight for our freedom. I want to convince Wallace to reconcile himself to our cause again. To ask for his position as Guardian of Scotland back. We were never so strong as we were with him."

Duncan took a step away from her, somehow able to keep himself balanced, even though she'd shaken him. "Ye're a political little chit are ye, nay?"

She tugged the blanket tighter around her and shrugged. "I'd not thought of myself that way particularly, but I guess ye could say that."

"Ye'd not last a day."

Heather lifted her chin, jutting it forward in a show of obstinacy. "How dare ye say such a thing?"

"'Tis the truth. The men would eat ye alive."

"There are plenty of women who've come before me that have held positions in politics. My brother Ronan's wife, Julianna, for one."

"The Bruce's sister? Have ye met her?" The woman scared him.

"Of course I have, she's a gem."

"A gem?" Duncan snorted. "A black diamond, sharpened into a blade and thrust within a man's gut."

Heather's reaction was swift, fierce, and he didn't even see it coming. She closed the distance between them and socked him in the gut.

"Like that?" she ground out.

He barely doubled over. Though her blow had stung a little, she'd hardly the momentum to cause damage with all the blankets holding her arms back.

"Why not shed the blanket and show me a real punch?"

"I'd not give ye the pleasure."

Duncan gripped her arms and lifted her a few inches off her feet. "I could crush ye, lass. Crumble ye to dust with one hand. Dinna tempt me to punish ye."

"Do it, I dare ye."

He was not normally one to toss a challenge like that aside. But knocking her out was not what he wanted to do. Nay, Duncan wanted to kiss the breath from her. He hauled her against him and did just that, crushing his lips to hers. Punishing her for all she stood for and all the pain he'd endured

The Highlander's Sin

over the years. He assaulted her mouth in a fiery kiss that left them both panting and breathless.

Heather grappled with the blanket with one hand while the other managed to snake out enough to wrap around his ribs. Her breasts were flattened to his chest with dizzying effect. He'd never been so taken with a woman, so crippled by the need to have her. Every nerve was afire with desire, demanding he slake that need.

But Heather wasn't a woman a man rutted. She was a woman he cherished, took his time with.

And realizing that, he slowed the kiss, stroking his tongue over hers, melding his body against her, feeling every curve. He set her on her feet, mostly so he could grip a round buttock in one hand and her damp hair with the other.

This was wrong. So wrong. Knowing that didn't stop him from doing it. He couldn't stop, couldn't get enough of her.

"Och, Heather," he crooned against her lips.

She answered with a soft whimper.

"We must stop," he said. The voice of reason reminded him she wore only a blanket, and with just a few more seconds of his mouth on hers he was bound to shred the fabric from her body and lay it on the ground where he'd make sweet love to her for the duration of the storm outside.

"Aye," she agreed. Trembling in his arms, she held tight to him as though he could keep her from falling. But he wasn't so sure he could hold himself up properly, not with the spell she'd put him under. "Why do ye bother to be a gentleman when ye're only going to turn me over to someone else?" She bit her lip and glanced up at him with eyes clouded by desire and curiosity. "Why not show me what pleasure is before ye doom me to a life in hell?"

Guilt rocked him. He was dooming her to that. But it was necessary. Or at least it had been. Now he wasn't so sure.

"Nay," he answered, refusing to take what she offered. He didn't deserve it.

Her face colored a shade darker. "Am I so vile, so wanton? Or was that part of what was paid for?"

Duncan shook his head. "Nay."

"Nay, what?"

"Ye're not vile or wanton."

"But my virginity was paid for."

"'Twas recommended ye arrive intact."

"But ye can kiss me all ye want? Look your fill?" Anger filled her eyes, and her lips drew into a grimace. "Well, look then." Heather tossed the blanket aside, revealing her body in all its naked splendor. But, for some reason, when she showed him like this, he refused to look. "For this will never be yours, Priest."

She turned her back on him and stalked toward the opening of the cave.

A pain centered in his chest, spreading outward, making him feel like someone had stabbed a sword straight through his heart. What was that feeling? Guilt? Not entirely. 'Twas more like heartbreak.

How could his heart break when it had never been in one piece? He gazed at her backside, her long hair curling and waving down to the tops of her buttocks. Locks that were a mixture of damp and dry, tickling the spot he'd just clutched. Her buttocks formed a perfect heart shape. She hooked a foot behind her ankle and leaned against the opening.

Did she contemplate running naked in the rain in her haste to escape him?

He was worse than a cad. Worse than the most vile of men. Teasing her. Taunting her. Mocking her. She'd never know how much he truly wished he could have seen their fates changed. But wishes were merely that, and not truths. He'd barely been able to piece his own life together, still running without having gone to accept his own true destiny. Hiding beneath the shroud of his priest's robes.

Duncan picked up her blanket and walked slowly toward her. He slid the warm wool over her shoulders, and she accepted it without a word.

"I'm sorry, lass," he murmured. "I'm a broken man, forcing the shards of my darkness on to ye."

Heather didn't turn around, but spoke to the howling winds. "We are all broken in our own way. Ye can only find yourself if ye're willing to pick up the shards."

He'd never heard wiser words. Not even the prior or priests at Pluscarden had been able to give him better advice. They'd only advised that he pray, that he attempt to move on. Not until he'd met this wisp of a woman had anyone ever told him he ought to deal with his destruction. To face it head-on.

"Ye're right."

Heather turned around, her eyes pleading. "Take me to Wallace. I will never tell anyone that ye stole me. Please, just let me fulfill my destiny, and ye can go about fulfilling yours."

Duncan gazed down at the woman he'd abducted, the woman who'd made him question everything in his own life, and yet he'd barely known her for more than a couple of days.

He shook his head. "I canna."

Anger stabbed from her eyes. "I see. Then ye are not willing to make a change. Ye will always be an evil coward. Ye're not fit to wear those black robes." She bumped past him and went to sit before the fire.

Her words sliced through him easier than any blade. He'd not realized how much she'd come to mean to him, how much her opinion mattered. He didn't want her to think he was evil. Nor a coward. He was willing to do what it took to protect her. But one man wasn't strong enough to save her from an entire brooding clan. "'Tis not like that, lass. If I dinna deliver ye, they will only go after your family."

"An empty threat meant to force me to your will," she muttered.

"I speak the truth," Duncan said. "Those who've paid me want your family dead. All of them. This is just the beginning. A call to war."

"Tell me who they are."

What could it hurt now? By this time tomorrow, storm willing, they'd be at the inn where he would say goodbye to her. "Lady Ina Ross."

All the color drained from Heather's face as though she'd seen a ghost and knew her life was over. "God save me."

Chapter Fourteen

*H*eather knew that it'd be a miracle if the good Lord reached down from the sky and altered the events that were playing out before her. The slim chances of that happening meant she had to rely on three alternatives.

One, she could pray mightily hard that her brothers were able to track them through the storm and find this cave. But, in that case, they would most likely kill Duncan. His death was not something she prayed for. If anything, she wished to give him a hard slap of sense. To help him set his path straight, whatever it might be, and oh, how she wished that future might have had something to do with her — another impossibility.

The second alternative was even more unlikely than the first, and that was that she'd somehow persuade Duncan to forget this harebrained plan and let her go. The Rosses were a force to be reckoned with. She didn't doubt that. Ina Ross, daughter to the late laird, had been no doubt planning the demise of the Sutherland clan ever since they'd killed her father. And her husband — ironically an English noble, Sir Marmaduke

Stewart—had also been biding his time. He'd been betrothed to Magnus' wife, Arbella. But Magnus had swept in and stolen her away. That hadn't sat well with the prideful lout. He'd married Ina because in her there had been a kindred spirit, but not the healthy kind. The two of them had been stewing for the past several years, causing little disturbances here and there, but Duncan had been right when he'd said they were planning a war.

Her fate with them would be death. There was no doubt in her mind. She might as well give her confession now and pray it was quick.

That left only the third option, which seemed her best shot—herself.

"Ye know of Lady Ross and her English husband, then?"

Heather gave him a questioning glance. "Where have ye been, Duncan?"

He seemed startled by her question, but he didn't reply.

"They are our clan's worst enemy. All of the Highlands knows it, even the Bruce. The late Laird Ross ran Wallace and his men ragged with his schemes alongside the English king. We killed him three years or so ago, and then his idiotic daughter and stupid Sassenach husband became our problem."

"I do seem to remember some issue with the Ross clan a few years back."

Heather rolled her eyes and asked again, "Where have ye been?"

"Busy."

"So busy that ye didna notice what was going on in the world around ye? Did ye nay have to bless any warriors or give last rites to the dead?"

"I bless few."

"And I'm sure many thank ye for that."

"What do ye mean by that?"

"How good is the blessing of a sinner?"

Duncan's face fell for an instant before he recovered himself, and she felt instantly sorry for her harsh words.

"I'm sorry," she said.

"When I was a boy, my family was massacred by an enemy clan, my priest cut down right before my eyes. My home burned, and the only refuge I had from our enemies was within the church. And my only solace was accepting mercenary missions with the intent of gaining strength for the time I met with my enemies. I dinna need your pity, nor do I care to hear more of your offending words."

Heather swallowed. The way he glared daggers at her made her wish she could sink into the stone. It was sinister, angry, and yet the edges were rimmed with something that didn't quite match such emotions—regret. "What is the name of the enemy clan?"

She almost hated to hear the answer. Though she must know, he'd nearly said it before. He'd been so adamant on taking her and it not being for coin—there was only one other reason it could be.

"Sutherland."

Heather's heart skipped a beat. Her vision wavered. Before he'd answered, she'd thought he might say it. But there'd been just a small amount of hope that he would say someone else's name, that he'd not blame her family for the destruction of his, even if the facts were clear. No matter how much she felt a strong pull toward him, it could not be reciprocated. Even his kisses... What had they meant?

She pulled her knees in tight to her chest, as if they could be a shield to the damaging information he'd just relayed. "Ye must be mistaken," she answered.

Duncan glared at her and slowly shook his head. "Ye would deny me the truth?"

"What truth?" She raised her shoulders in a partial shrug and met his gaze. "What should I know? What should I be telling ye?"

He studied her, and she could practically see him mulling his answer over his tongue before he spoke. Duncan had a good straight face—one that hid every thought—but the emotions that must have been rolling through him at that moment were not allowing him to hide from her.

"Duncan, I'm sorry for whatever was done to your family. But I," she shook her head, "I wasn't a part of that. Please dinna hold it against me."

"There are casualties in every war."

His response chilled her. "Am I to be a causality?" Images of him choking the life from her, slitting her throat with his threatening blade—all of it came to mind.

As if in answer, the blade she'd shoved into her boot came to mind. If only she could reach it. She could pull it out, put it to good use. At least she'd be able to put up some fight against him. If she could get to it. He'd no doubt win whether she had a blade or nay. Not that she wouldn't try her damnedest to send him to the devil if it came to it. The thing was…she studied his muscles, the way they clenched and bunched. Pure strength. She wasn't built to fight against a power like his. Her mind had always been her first defense.

"Answer me." She was proud when her voice came out strong, fortified. Letting him get to her was out of the question.

"I canna."

"Ye're a coward."

Duncan shifted suddenly closer, his arm so close to the flames she was sure his flesh would ignite. "One thing I'm not is a *coward*."

But she could see the doubt flicker in his eyes. He wasn't as confident as he would have her believe.

"Do ye have a soul in the world?" She hadn't meant to ask it, to remind him that he was all alone. The thought had spun in her mind and shot out of her mouth before she had had a chance to temper it.

Duncan sat back heavily. "What is that supposed to mean?"

"Is there anyone ye can count on, truly?"

"I have the monks at Pluscarden. The prior."

Heather shook her head. "But ye're an outcast. Not truly one of them."

The muscle of his jaw flexed, and he ran a hand over his face, tracing the outline of his chin. "Ye've a sassy mouth, wench, and I've a likely need to stuff it."

Heather gasped, recalling how real his threat to gag her had been. She was lucky not to have been bound and silenced already. A small jab of pain centered in her gut. She supposed a part of her had thought he was starting to take a liking to her… Their kisses had been so passionate, so genuine and had made her start to question things she'd long since thought to have laid to rest. The idea that Duncan was only mocking her, never truly wanting anything more than to exact revenge on her family, cut her to the core. "Ye're a barbarian."

Duncan laughed bitterly. "And ye're a spoiled child."

She resisted the urge to stick out her tongue at him, knowing that would only strengthen his observation of her, however false it was. Spoiled… Hardly. Heather had always made certain she was an active part of her family. She earned her keep and never sat up in her chamber whiling the day away with talk of gowns and the latest hairstyle.

"Ye know nothing about me, other than what ye heard from Ina Ross, and she's as reliable a source as the squirrels rummaging around in the trees."

"Tell me, then, lass, what makes ye think ye're not spoiled? Do ye have a nice hot meal every morning to break your fast, at the nooning and again afore ye go to bed between your soft sheets with a fire built up to keep ye warm?"

"Having food to eat and a warm bed does not make me spoiled."

"It does when I grew up with a crust of bread and water and a bed so cold I woke up with an icicle on my nose every morn in winter."

Heather shuddered. "Ye lie."

Duncan bared his teeth. "I never lie."

"Lying is a sin."

"Aye."

"And ye're no sinner?"

"Not in that way."

Heather grunted, wanting nothing more to do with this conversation. She couldn't help it that her brother was a powerful laird, willing to keep her basic needs met in a way that was superior to Duncan's upbringing. But what more could she say? She couldn't change his mind. And she wasn't really willing to try.

The rain still fell in horrid droves outside, and the wind howled. Lucky for them, the trees and shrubs kept the wind from tunneling inside their warm cave. But as soon as it was over, Duncan would likely make them leave.

Her stomach growled, but she ignored it. She wasn't going to ask him for mercy on her belly. Her sopping wet gown and chemises still lay crumpled where she'd left them. Darn. If she didn't lay them out now, they'd still be wet by the time he chose for them to leave, and she didn't want to risk the chance of him making her leave naked. Lord knew, he might do just that. Escaping naked was most definitely not part of the plan.

Heather managed to sit up on her knees. Her back to Duncan, she tucked the ends of the blanket beneath her arms to hold it in place, and then gingerly went about laying her clothes flat to dry.

When she finished the last chemise, the side of the cave looked like it had a carpet of tarnished white linen and ribbons. The white pattern was marred only by the dirtiness of her once-lavender gown, now more of a dingy-looking gray.

She turned back to the fire, her fingers cold from having handled the wet fabric. Duncan seemed to be waiting for her.

"Sit," he ordered.

As soon as she'd plopped down, he handed her a strip of jerky and an oatcake. She eyed the offering with disdain, remembering the last meal consisting of these same items—extremely unpleasant.

"Eat."

Heather rolled her eyes, ignoring the way he spoke to her in one-syllable words. If he wanted to act like a brute, she need not get her goad up about it. She was already well aware the man had a rough side. Staying away from it was how she'd survive the short time they had left with each other.

But thinking about being separated from Duncan, even though she despised him, made her stomach plummet. She didn't really want to be away from him. If anything, she wished he'd shake off that brooding exterior and kiss her again. When he kissed her, she felt like she was soaring, as though she could do anything in the world. It was powerful, intoxicating, and she hated to admit that she wanted more. As much as he made fire rage through her blood, he tempted other, deeper emotions, too. Emotions she wasn't sure she could ignore much longer.

Across the fire, Duncan attacked his jerky with vigor. He fairly gnashed his teeth, but all the while he kept flicking his gaze at her. What in all of the world was he thinking?

Stubborn herself, Heather refused to ask. Instead, she, too, bit down on the jerky as though she'd perish without it. When she finished her piece, another was flung into her hands. By the end of the second piece, when Duncan tossed her a third, she simply flung it back.

"I wouldn't eat another piece of jerky if my life depended on it," she snapped.

"Well, then, suppose 'tis a good thing ye're not going off to find Wallace. Men in a war camp live for days off jerky and nothing else."

"'Tis vile."

"Like your attitude," he ground out.

"Hateful man."

"Spiteful wench."

Heather stifled a cry of outrage, leapt to her feet and whirled in a circle, searching for something, anything, she could use as a weapon. She wanted to hit him, to club him over the head with a thick piece of wood. But there was no spare wood to be had, and if she trekked to the back of the cave to find his stash, he would know what she was doing. With a huff, she sat back down.

"As I said. Spoiled."

Anger burned inside her. "And, as I said, ye're the worst sort of man I've ever met in my life."

He winced but caught it quickly, replacing that moment of vulnerability with a hardened stare. "A good thing ye'll soon be out of my hands."

Heather curled her hands into fists, her nails biting into the sensitive flesh of her palms. How did the man have the power to affect her so much? Tears burned the backs of her eyes, and she blinked rapidly to keep them at bay. She would not cry in front him. Would *not*. Could *not*.

The tears, however, couldn't care less about how she felt. They gathered until they blurred her vision and then started to spill in fat drops on to her cheeks. She ducked her head, glancing toward her lap in hopes of keeping her utterly feminine, child-like reaction hidden. No need to hear him tell her once more what a spoiled brat she was. Here she was, so frustrated she'd been unable to control herself, and now she cried like a bairn.

But darn it! She had a good excuse. Not only had she been abducted, half starved, nearly drowned, and denied enough sleep in the last few days, but her feelings were thoroughly hurt and her dreams of a promising future had been all but burned away like the embers in the fire.

"Are ye crying?" Duncan's voice was softer, not the harsh tones she'd become used to.

She ignored him. He didn't need to know if she was crying or not. Even if it was fairly obvious. Her shoulders shook, nose ran, eyes burned. She swiped angrily at her face with the blanket.

Scuffing boots echoed in the quiet hollow, and then he was beside her, his body heat warming that side of her.

He didn't say anything, didn't touch her, just sat beside her. Heather didn't know what to do, how to react. If he'd been her brother Magnus, she'd have leaned against his shoulder and let her sobs come out as loud as they needed to be. If it'd been her brother Blane, she would have begged him to retaliate against whoever had done this to her. Her brother Ronan would have let her punch him until her tears were no more, and her sister, Lorna, would have given her the best advice. But her family wasn't sitting beside her.

Nay, the one sitting beside her was the one who'd caused her to cry in the first place. And because of that she didn't know what to do besides sob quietly into her lap, all the while begging herself to let it stop. It was humiliating to let him see how much he'd affected her, hurt her.

Confusing, too, since he said nothing. All the more befuddling was how she gained a sense of comfort from his nearness.

When her tears began to subside, and she could find her voice again, she said, "Let me go."

Duncan had been nice to her, and here she was crying her eyes out. The Ross clan would not be so nice to her, and to show such weakness in front of them would be more humiliating than showing Duncan.

"I canna," he said quietly, and she sensed the regret in his words.

"Why?" Heather turned her head slightly, leaning a cheek against her knees. "Why canna ye?"

Chapter Fifteen

Guilt soured Duncan's stomach.

"My family will triple the coin the Rosses would give ye. They can take care of themselves. We'd welcome the war. I promise ye." Tremors left over from Heather's cry laced her words.

Duncan shook his head and locked eyes with hers, which were rimmed red and a brighter blue than purple at that moment. He resisted the urge to wipe the wetness from her cheeks.

"'Tis not the coin that holds me." He'd plenty buried in the stone walls of the abbey.

"I've told ye I had nothing to do with your family's slaughter, though if I could have, I would have tried to stop it."

"Ye were barely old enough, if even born yet." He supposed he ought to tell her his weakness. Where Lady Ross had him, strictly by the ballocks. "Ye see, if I dinna deliver ye, they will burn my abbey, and all those who reside inside it."

Heather gasped. "How can they? That will certainly condemn them all to hell."

Duncan shrugged. "They dinna seem to care about that. They are fueled by rage and care not for the path they will follow in the afterlife, but only for the life of now."

"And ye were the perfect man to see it done. Levelheaded, well-trained, and wanting revenge on my family."

He shrugged again. She had the right of it. 'Twas the reason he'd agreed, but not the reason for carrying it out. Though the monks and prior angered him sometimes, he would never see them suffer. They'd taken him in when he'd had no one. They'd raised him, fed him, sheltered him, clothed him, educated him. Duncan was not sore enough about cold winter nights and stale bread to wish them harm. Never. If anything, he owed the church his life. They had toughened him up. He'd have perished with the rest of his family if not for them.

"We all do things for those we love that canna often be explained," he answered.

"Love," Heather said, biting her lip and looking away. "Something I'll never know if ye give me up to those monsters. I'll be lucky to see the morning." She laughed bitterly. "Ye see, as soon as ye leave, they will slit my throat. Ye'll deliver the message to my family that they have me, because ye would know nothing otherwise, and ye're a priest they can trust. All the while, I'll be rotting in a shallow grave, if they even give me that much, while they sharpen their blades in preparation for murdering my family. Shall I issue ye my thanks now, or would ye prefer it upon my deliverance?"

With each word she uttered, Duncan grew colder and colder until a numbness surrounded him. Visions of her lying in a grave, staring up at him, lifeless, made him shudder. "One life for the lives of hundreds," he muttered, hating himself.

"I'm to be a sacrifice."

He swallowed, cursing himself. "Are the hundred men of the cloth at Pluscarden to go in your stead? They will not abandon their abbey."

Shadows covered her eyes, and she flicked her gaze away. "I dinna know."

"Death comes to us all, princess." The words sounded cold even to his own ears, and he was disgusted to have uttered them.

"Ye're cruel," she said, and rightly so. Heather leaned away from him, closer to the fire, as if she'd prefer to be burned than sit beside him.

Hell, he'd rather be burned than ever have to say what he'd just said again. He wasn't a cruel man, wasn't the sort to let an innocent go to her death. And here he was, doing just that.

Empathy bade him to beg her forgiveness, but his pride kept his tongue motionless. If he could have, he would have saved her from the fate he'd led her toward. But, truly, how could he save the abbey from destruction and not give her up to her enemy's hands?

There was only one way. And it meant that Duncan had to forgive the family who'd destroyed his own. That meant giving up everything he'd stood for practically the whole of his life. It meant approaching his own enemies and begging for help.

Duncan wasn't a beggar, and he wasn't sure he could change who he was, even to save her life.

"Get some sleep. On the morrow we ride, rain or none."

Heather nodded, avoiding eye contact. He tossed her the remaining blanket as a pillow and watched her lay her head down, her back facing him as she curled into a little ball. Her shoulders shook. She was crying again.

He hated himself at that moment, seeing her so vulnerable on the floor, a shadow of the woman he'd met in the Sutherland chapel. He'd done that. Broken her.

Duncan had to force himself to look away, to hide from himself the damage he'd done. Dragging his feet to the cave opening, he leaned against the wall, crossed his arms over his chest and looked out into the woods. Wind pelted the rain with force into the trees, but the leaves acted as tiny shields, trying their damnedest to protect the forest. But the wind was strong, bending some smaller, weaker trees nearly in half.

Blade sauntered forward, nudged Duncan's arm with his muzzle. The horse blew out a disgusted breath, his nostrils flaring. Was he upset with the storm, or did he, too, think Duncan was a cruel man?

"What would ye have me do?" Duncan asked under his breath. "Marry the chit and declare war on the Ross clan? Side with my enemy and call them brother when I've done nothing over the past two decades but imagine their blood on my hands?"

Blade snorted again and nudged his shoulder a little harder, this time causing Duncan to shift on his feet.

He glowered at the animal, disbelieving he was actually having to explain himself to the beast. "I'll nay do it. 'Tis a duty I have for the sake of my family's souls. My father would roll over in his grave."

Duncan glanced over his shoulder. Heather lay still, her tears either having subsided or sleep rescuing her from the pain Duncan had caused. Just imagining the emotional torture he'd put her through sent a fresh shaft of guilt into his heart. He'd been surprised by the welcome warmth her company had brought—and not at all surprised by her feisty tongue. But how much he enjoyed sparring with her had jarred him. When Lady Ross had debriefed him, he'd expected to hate this mission, to want to murder the lass before turning her over, but it'd been the exact opposite of that.

Aye, he'd threatened her plenty of times, but mostly because he liked to see her reaction, not because he intended to actually go through with whatever punishment had come to mind.

Disappointment took hold, tightening a rope around his middle. He was discontent with the idea of letting her go, with what the evil couple would do with her. He was disenchanted with the idea of burying his revenge. But the notion of marrying Heather... A seed had been planted in his mind and began to grow roots, extending through his head, down his neck and growing stronger by the minute.

He turned away from her. The longer he stared at her, the likelier it was he'd ask her what she thought of the idea. The answer to that would be very clear. She'd gut him for sure, with any sort of utensil she could find, maybe even gore him with one of the burning embers.

At least the horse had stopped nudging him. Duncan slicked his hand over his hair, tightening the queue that kept it from falling into his eyes.

He, too, was exhausted. But he knew if he lay down, sleep was not likely to visit him. When morning broke, he'd have a decision to make. Lady Ross would be meeting him at an inn at noon. That much was set in stone. He would either be there, or he would not. She'd reminded him that with each passing hour, the coins in the purse would deplete, and if he should be an entire day late, lives would be taken.

He and Heather would have to rise at dawn and ride Blade hard to make it in time.

There was no time to engage the Sutherlands in negotiations. How could he possibly save his abbey *and* the lass?

The Sutherlands would protect Heather, of that Duncan had no doubt. But there was no incentive for them to protect the abbey. They had no stake in his church. Even if he sought the help of Brandon Sinclair, the cousin of Laird Sutherland, with whom Duncan had had dealings in the past, there would still not be enough time to save anyone.

Knowing the Rosses, they'd already gathered a group of warriors to surround the abbey, waiting with salivating mouths for the call to attack. They were a vicious clan, more animalistic than human.

Duncan wouldn't have been surprised to learn that they'd formed a pact with the devil himself.

Heather coughed, the sound bouncing off the walls and startling Duncan from his thoughts. He whirled and in four strides was by her side. Bending at the knee, he pressed a hand to her shoulder.

"Are ye all right?"

Heather's eyes fluttered open, and she stared up at him. "I'm fine."

"Do ye need a drink?"

She shook her head and closed her reddened, swollen eyes.

He should have left her side, gone back to the front of the cave where he belonged, but Duncan couldn't bring himself to do it, couldn't make his legs lift him. Instead, they seemed to have lost all power. He sat down beside her.

"Go away," she murmured. "I'm stuck with ye in this godforsaken cave, at least allow me the privilege of not breathing the same air as ye."

"I know ye hate me, lass," he started, but she cut him off.

"Aye. Now go away."

"But I dinna want ye to hate me. I've not put ye in a spot ye want to be in, I know it."

"That makes two of us, now will ye please allow me to sleep?" The anguish in her voice choked off the rest of Duncan's words.

Heather was still too raw to hear his ideas, to help him figure out how they could get her out of this alive. He nodded, though she didn't look at him. He swallowed past the lump in his throat and had started to stand when a tiny white hand reached out and grabbed onto the bare skin of his forearm.

A tingle shot from the spot, rushing through him. Surprisingly, though he felt his cock stir, the biggest place her touch seemed to influence was his chest. It grew tight, making breathing harder. He stilled in mid-crouch and slid his opposite hand over hers, feeling how very tiny hers was in his palm.

"I know your people mean a lot to ye," she said. Her eyes remained closed, as though by not seeing him, perhaps he might disappear. "And I must be the most selfish woman on the planet to be upset that ye would beg for their lives over mine. I'm sorry for it."

"Och, lass, to ask anyone for their life is selfish. Dinna blame yourself for the reaction ye had, nor the feelings that have risen from it. I've asked too much, and truth be told, I'd have ye live."

She opened her eyes, eyes that showed him the depths of her despair and filled Duncan's soul with repentance. "Dinna say things that will never come to pass."

Could he risk telling her his thoughts?

Nay, not yet. Duncan shook his head. "I never say things I dinna mean."

"Well-meaning has no place when your actions contradict it."

Despite her innocence, her verve for life, Heather was wiser than Duncan had originally given her credit for.

"Ye're a very intelligent woman," he mused.

She rolled over to her other side, breaking contact with him. "Apparently not intelligent enough."

"Despite what ye think," Duncan stood and scooped up the discarded whiskey jug, "I've a great respect for ye, lass. And while I think ye're a pain in the arse, I've quite enjoyed your company."

She grunted halfheartedly. "Words of a man filled with guilt for his actions."

Heather was right, but just because she'd pinned the precise reason for his saying so, did not mean she'd had to voice it.

She was the type of woman who always had to have the last, stinging word. Probably the result of having three older brothers who tormented her and indulged her. They'd molded and shaped her into a harridan, and he was about to lay down his life to spend the rest of it with her.

"Ye're a stubborn little wench," he stated, but lightened his tone. Duncan was well aware that he should stop right there. That he should lie down and try to get some rest. To keep speaking when they were both so exhausted would never result in anything productive. Rest was best, for tomorrow would be one of the hardest days of his life. But he couldn't seem to make himself shut up. Something about Heather made him want to fight with her. "I ought to drag ye through the rain and straight to Ross lands now."

"What's stopping ye?" She rolled over, jumped to her feet, the blanket tangling in her legs, exposing her creamy shoulders. "Let's go!"

"Marry me."

Heather's mouth fell open in a perfect, plush-rimmed O. She stood motionless, silent, as if she'd been stilled by time.

"Marry me, and together we can save them all." Lord, he sounded desperate, and maybe he was, but he'd never wanted to put so many lives in danger — only a few, the Sutherlands — and now he couldn't even do that.

Finally, she seemed to come to from the shock he'd given her. "What?" She sounded exasperated, astonished, offended.

"If ye marry me, we can keep everyone safe."

"Everyone?" She raised a brow.

"Aye." He paused, breathing in a calming breath. "Ye, those at the abbey, your family."

"Because by marrying me ye'll simply forget a lifetime of planning revenge?" She shook her head. "Nay. I won't do it. An hour ago ye were telling me to take my death sentence with a smile. Now ye offer me life?"

"Heather." Duncan took a step forward. "I'm not proud of myself. I hated every cruel word I uttered. I didna mean them. I was at a loss. I dinna want to turn ye over to Lady Ross. Trust me in that. If it weren't for the lives of the monks at Pluscarden, I'd have let ye run away before the storm hit. But I am only one man. I canna fight against a hundred. And this way I see ye, them, all of us being saved."

Her eyes widened. "So, ye would marry me to have my family fight for ye."

Duncan shook his head. "Not for me. With me. For us."

"For us," she said very slowly, as if trying to figure out the meaning of the words. Her gaze fell to the ground where she curled her toes, then stretched them back out again. "I've no wish to marry." Her voice was small, quiet. "I want to find William Wallace. Now ye ask me to marry ye to save my life, to save the lives of hundreds. 'Tis terribly unfair."

"I will help ye relay a message to Wallace."

"I dinna want to relay a message," she shouted. "I want to fight!"

Chapter Sixteen

*D*uncan had ruined everything. And now he sought to take away her future.

He stood silently, not a few feet away from Heather. His lips were pressed in a firm line, hands placed on his narrow hips, and the muscles of his upper body were fully on display, mocking her, showing her exactly what would be hers if she'd only say aye.

Well, a body wasn't what it was all about, no matter how perfect it was, or how it made her heartbeat race.

"My brothers would never allow it," she said, jutting her chin and trying to be as confident as one could be while naked beneath a blanket. "Besides, ye're a priest."

"I will renounce my place in the church, as well as my anger at your family." His tone was even, and there was no display of emotion on his face. Nothing to tell her whether or not he meant what he said. "I was never meant for that life anyway."

"Ye said ye never lie."

"I dinna."

"Ye're lying now. One night at dinner, ye'll thrust your eating knife into my brother's throat, and it will be all my fault."

Duncan narrowed his eyes, boring their darkness right into her soul. "Never."

"Ye're going to hell for that untruth." How could she believe him? He'd lived his life, waiting for the moment he could avenge his family—by killing her family. What cause did she have to trust him at his word?

"Nay, lass, I'm headed there for many other reasons, but that is not one of them. If ye marry me, I vow never to stab your brother with my eating knife."

Heather cocked her head. "Or any other sharp object," she said dryly. "Ye'd have to vow not to kill any of my brothers or cousins, or anyone I love, for that matter."

"Done."

"And ye'd have to vow to take me to see William Wallace."

"I will arrange it."

"Why are ye being so accommodating?" Suspicion rose inside her.

"I want ye to marry me."

No one had ever said that to her and meant it. Wanted her. For life. "If the monks' lives were not at stake, would ye still wish to marry me?" She hated to think what his answer would be, knew it would be negative. Heather started to glance away, embarrassed to have asked the question, but when he spoke he lulled her back into his gaze.

"Aye." A simple, strong declaration in one word.

Disbelief crowded out the part of her that wanted so desperately for him to mean the word. "Aye?"

"I would." His gaze was intense, serious.

"Why?"

"As I said earlier, I've enjoyed your company."

Heather frowned. "Surely, that canna be the only reason. Have ye not enjoyed the company of any other women? Or have ye wished to marry all of them as well?"

Duncan cracked a smile. "Ye see? That is what it is. Your wit, your charm. Ye've enchanted me, lass."

Why wasn't she convinced?

Heather chewed her lip. "I will marry ye to save your men. To save myself. But I canna promise to be a good wife."

He barely seemed surprised to hear it. "What do ye promise?"

She furrowed her brow and racked her brain for something feasible. "I promise to be faithful and honest."

"But…?"

How did he know there was going to be a *but*? "But I will probably never obey ye."

He laughed softly. "I hadn't expected that ye would."

"Truly?" Why was she shocked by his statement?

Duncan winked. "Ye're not the obeying type."

Her belly did a little flop, and every nerve seemed heightened. "What will ye do when ye need me to do something? I'll most likely fight ye on everything."

"I'll have to convince ye to see the merit of my desire."

"How will ye do that?" Her curiosity was piqued.

"In whatever manner is necessary."

Heather frowned. "Ye'd blackmail me."

"I would never." Though he tried for serious, there was a twinkle in his eye.

"Isn't that what ye're doing now?"

"Blackmailing ye? Nay."

"But ye have said I must marry ye to be free and to save your monks."

Duncan nodded. "Aye, but 'tis not blackmail. Ye have other choices."

"Such as?"

"I told ye before, ye're an intelligent woman. I'll not give ye the answers."

"What would ye do if ye're not a priest? How would we live?"

"I suppose we'll have to rebuild what I lost."

"What did ye lose?"

He shrugged, not very forthcoming with information. Heather waited for him to answer, but he only stared at her as though he'd dismissed the subject. "Ye will not tell me?"

Duncan shook his head. "Needs not concern ye."

"It does when my livelihood depends on it."

"Ye will not have need to worry over your livelihood, that I promise."

"I won't marry a stranger."

"Good thing we've been introduced."

He toyed with her, knowing she'd marry him anyway. Heather could threaten until she was blue in the face, but Duncan knew exactly which buttons to press to get his way.

"When will we do it?"

"Tomorrow."

"In the morning?"

"Aye. We'll ride to Pluscarden, and I'll have a message sent straightaway to your brother Magnus. He'll come to protect the abbey, for the following day, we will most assuredly have a visit from Lady Ross and her sop of a husband."

"What if my brother does not come?"

"He will come."

"What if he does not arrive in time?"

"I am a trained warrior. I will help the abbey until reinforcements arrive."

"One man against hundreds. Unlikely odds that ye'll win."

"Then ye might be a young widow, but at least ye'll have saved the abbey and its inhabitants."

An unsettling sense of hopeless started to ebb around her. "It's taken us two days to get this far. My brother will never arrive in time."

"Have faith, lass. Besides we passed the abbey yesterday while ye slept in my arms. If your brother rides hard, all will be safe."

She glanced down at the tattered dress drying on the cave floor, not one of her favorite gowns to begin with, but how she wished it was at least clean and not torn. "I suppose I'll be wearing that gown on my wedding day."

If they'd been at home, she would have been absolutely appalled at having to wear that gown anywhere, let alone at her own wedding.

"Better than the blanket."

Heather laughed then, looking back toward Duncan. "True."

Duncan stepped forward and held out his arm to her. She stared down at it, not sure what to do.

"Let us shake."

She gripped his forearm, her hands curling into crisp hair and hard muscle. Duncan wrapped his fingers solidly around her arm and squeezed.

"To us," he said.

"To saving lives," Heather responded.

"Specifically yours."

"Got any more of that whisky? I could use a few sips."

Duncan chuckled. "Likewise." He found the bottle where it sat beside the opening to the door and uncorked it, but before he took a sip, he handed it to her. "Ladies first."

"Thank ye." Heather grasped the jug, their fingers brushing, sending a ripple of unwanted pleasure to radiate through her limbs. How did he have the ability to do that to her?

She put the rim to her lips and tipped the jug. Duncan watched her intently, making her feel both uneasy and excited at the same time.

Finding William Wallace had been about both a need for adventure and a chance to serve her country. Marrying Duncan would be an adventure all right, but how could she persuade him to help serve their country instead of being a mercenary? She'd be stupid not to admit she was a little worried about how they would live.

"Do ye have a home besides the abbey?" They wouldn't very well be shacking up with the monks.

"Aye."

"Where?"

He shrugged and took the jug from her. "Not sure 'tis habitable."

"Why?" Lord she felt like she was playing a game of questions.

"I told ye, my family was massacred."

"And their bodies are still about?" Heather could have bitten off her own tongue.

But Duncan grinned, though there was a sadness in the curve of his lips. "Nay. It burned, or so I'm told."

"Do ye own a farm? Was it a croft?"

He chuckled. "Might as well be."

The way he spoke was confusing. "It either is or it isn't."

"The place is most likely a pile of ash and rubble, so the answer does nay truly matter, princess." He raised a brow at her. "Does the size of your home matter so much to ye?"

She shook her head without thinking. "Nay, of course not. I just want to know whether I'll have a life of cave living, or if I'll be raising our bairns beneath a roof."

"Bairns." The frightened look that crossed over Duncan's face was about as terrified as she'd felt at the mention of it. "I'm not ready for bairns," she admitted softly.

"Neither am I."

"Then we'll make a truce not to have any bairns for a while?"

"Aye."

A rush of relief filled her. She liked his kisses, was tempted beyond measure by the way he made her feel, but the actual physical act frightened her. She'd spied on a few of the warriors and housemaids as they'd joined together in darkened corners and once saw her older brother and his wife making a big ruckus in the cellar. None of them had seemed to be hurting each other, but… All the same, the thought of a man's pike piercing her insides didn't seem too appealing. "I'm pleased ye agree." She tapped her chin. "We could always prick my finger and smear it on the sheets to prove we consummated the marriage. No one would question us."

Duncan's eyes darkened, and he scowled. "Nay."

"Would ye rather we pricked your finger, then?"

"Nay," he growled.

"Well, ye really aren't being very realistic about this. A finger is likely to heal quickly."

"Nay, woman." With each passing minute, he seemed to grow more agitated.

"What then?"

Duncan closed the distance between them. He pressed his fingers to her chin and lifted her face toward his, their lips only an inch apart. "Ye'll be my wife in truth."

Heather gasped. "But—"

He cut her off with a kiss. A searing, stomach-tightening, heart-skipping-a-beat kiss.

Heather found herself sinking against him, the softness of her curves molding to the hardness of his body. Without realizing it, she'd touched her fingers to his chest—thick muscle and crisp hair teased her senses. She dug in, massaging the muscles, feeling the pound of his heart beneath the sinew.

If consummating a union was half as good as his kiss, maybe it wouldn't be so bad…

Duncan ended the kiss abruptly. "Do ye agree?"

"Agree with what?"

"To be my wife in truth? I'll not rape ye on your wedding night."

He was giving her a choice? "What about our agreement not to have a bairn right off?"

"There are…ways to avoid it."

"How?"

Was it her imagination or had Duncan's cheeks just reddened a little?

"I'll explain later."

"Why not now?"

"How many men have ye been…intimate with?" he asked.

Heather gasped and took an appalled step backward. "That is insulting!"

"Tell me."

She held her head high. "None of your business."

Duncan bared his teeth. "Ye're not a virgin?"

Now it was her turn for reddened cheeks. Heat suffused her face, making her cheeks feel like they'd burst into flames at the snap of a finger. "That is—"

"Dinna say none of my business, because it damn well is."

Heather didn't want to admit she was a virgin. Not to Duncan. Shameful as it was, she wanted him to think she was experienced. He was a man who had obviously charmed many females, and though she had no clue how in all the world she was going to pleasure him, she didn't want *him* to know that.

"I—"

"Damn it, Heather, ye either are or ye're not."

She chewed her lip. This dilemma could easily have been solved with her telling him the truth. Humiliation would have been nothing compared to dealing with his wrath over a fake lover.

"Tell me the bastard's name, and I'll cut him down."

Exactly as she'd feared. With a deep sigh, she let her shoulders sink a little. "I am still…intact."

Duncan breathed a sigh of relief. "Has any man touched ye?"

"I just told ye—"

He shook his head. "In any other way."

"Of course, lots of men have touched me." She rolled her eyes. "What a ridiculous question."

Duncan pressed his hands to his hips, drawing her attention to the area. Slim hips and a line of dark hair on his abdomen that led straight beneath his plaid. She found her mouth watering at the sight of his muscled belly, and couldn't help but wonder what the muscles hidden by fabric looked like.

"Ye mean to tell me ye've pleasured many men?"

Heather jerked her gaze back to his. "More insults. Do ye take me for a whore? Would ye marry a woman like that?"

"I'd marry ye no matter what."

"Well, then, nay, I haven't pleasured any man."

"Lads?"

"Oh, for God's sake, why are ye being such a brute?"

"Who touched ye then?"

"Duncan, really… I kissed a few boys at a feast or two. Otherwise, I am completely innocent and know nothing of the act, save for what I've seen."

"Seen?" He sounded exasperated again. "What kind of house did ye live in?"

"Trust me, they were all trying to be discreet."

"And yet, ye found them. Ye little hoyden."

Her face was fully on fire now. She felt like throwing up her hands, but that would have only made her blanket fly off her shoulders. "Ye got me. I'm a little sneak."

"And a curious one." He took a step closer. "Did ye like what ye saw?"

"What kind of a question is that?"

He gently stroked his hands over her hips, gripping them and tugging her closer. Heather stumbled, unable to find her feet, her mind solely on the touch of his hands.

"Well, did ye?"

She swallowed hard, unable to answer. Of course she had. But he didn't need to know that.

"How many times did ye watch?"

"Ye, Priest, are getting entirely too personal."

His voiced lowered as did his eyelids. Eyes darkened, he was giving her that look again. The one that made her knees knock. "Think of this as confession time."

Heather searched for a way out of this conversation. "But ye're throwing your robes aside."

"I haven't as yet."

He had a point. "I dinna know."

"That many?"

"I never counted. Maybe seven."

His brows shot up. "Seven?"

Heather laughed softly, her embarrassment getting the best of her. "I think so. Could be more."

"Tell me what they were doing."

She gasped. "Nay!"

"Come now," he bent toward her, stroking her hair aside so he could nuzzle her neck, "tell me. Were they doing this?"

Heather sighed, tilting her head further, liking the feel of his soft, heated lips on her skin. She nodded.

"This?" He flicked his tongue out, swirling it in a circle at the nape of her neck.

Again, she nodded. There was no way she'd make him stop, not yet anyway. She liked it entirely too much.

Duncan caressed her hips, moving his hands around and down over her buttocks. "Did they touch their women like this?"

"Aye," she sighed.

"Touch me like the women touched their men." His whispered demand caused her stomach to flip up into her throat.

Tentatively, she stroked her hands over his corded arms, tightening around his upper arms, feeling the bulge of strength, and then moving to his shoulders and around to his back. Every inch of flesh she touched made her curious to keep moving. Duncan's breath quickened, and he skimmed his lips up the column of her neck to her chin, nibbled gently on her jaw.

"Do ye like this?" he asked.

Heather nodded.

"Then ye have nothing to be afraid of."

"I'm not afraid." She whispered the bold-faced lie.

Duncan chuckled, brushing his lips over hers. "I could see the fear on your face when ye talked of being with others. Ye didna want to admit your innocence. But truth be told, love, I want to be the only man to ever touch ye like this. I want to teach ye everything there is about making love."

Love. Making *love.*

Was it possible?

She swallowed, cleared her throat. "Aye. Ye will be the only one."

Duncan groaned and caught her lips in a deep kiss full of possessive desire. He slicked his tongue over the crease of her lips, and when she parted them, he dove inside to taste her. Whisky, heady and intoxicating.

"Say ye'll marry me again."

"I'll marry ye."

"Call me husband."

"Husband," she sighed against his lips.

"And I call ye my wife."

The word, so foreign to her, sent chills of excitement racing along her spine—or was that his fingers dancing over her rib cage?

Heather leaned closer to him, feeling the ridges of his body mold to her own through the blanket. And then he was running his fingers along the two edges where the blanket met, scraping every few inches over the bare skin of her belly. Passion ignited within her. She *wanted* him to touch her bare skin, to feel what it was like to have a man pant for her, to whisper things in her ear and to cry out in pleasure.

Curiosity and desire overcame her fear of the unknown. The way he responded to her kiss, the way he groaned when she massaged the muscles of his back, she must have some bit of talent, else such a response wouldn't have been elicited. At least she hoped that was the case. Duncan had said it best. He was going to teach her. He was going to be the one and only.

Her husband.

She tucked her belly closer to him, letting more of his fingers edge around the shield of the woolen blanket. Duncan took her cue and slid his warm hand flat against her belly and around to the side of her waist. Having his hand on her bare skin was exquisite. She gasped against his lips. He fluttered his fingers, making her delirious with such a simple touch.

He caressed over her ribs until he stopped at the side of her breast. Would he? Oh, God…she wanted him to. Her nipples were taut, tingling. She arched up into him, wanting more, trying to ease the ache in the hardened buds.

"Touch me," she whispered.

Niggling in the corner of her mind was the warning that this was wrong. To let a man who was not yet her husband touch her bare skin in such an intimate manner was a sin. But that caution was brushed aside by the impish element in her that wanted to feel this, to experience the touch of a man. *That* side reminded her that this time tomorrow he'd be her husband, so he would have every right to touch her, and she every right to enjoy it. The little angel inside her head, the one reared by Aunt Fiona, leaped to her feet and shouted of him being a charlatan, only wanting what most men wanted, the prize that only her husband should have.

"I want to," he whispered back.

What was a few hours when he'd be doing this to her for the rest of their lives?

Caution lost.

Heather let go of the blanket, not hearing it fall to the floor around her feet, hearing only the dull roar of blood rushing through her ears and the storm pounding outside.

Duncan groaned. "Och, lass. Why did ye do that?" But he didn't seem to mind, truly. He skimmed his lips over her chin down to her neck and collarbone, then moved away, keeping hold of her hips with his thick fingers as his eyes roved over what she showed him.

Heat curled its way over her chest and neck to her face. In the dimmed light of the cave, she could see desire flicker in his eyes, along with the flames.

"We'll be married. Is this not your right?" Her voice sounded tiny, echoing in her ears.

"Aye, love. A husband's right and privilege."

There he went calling her love again… Oh, if only. A surge of emotion wrapped warmly around her heart.

He took a deep, staggering breath and blew it out slowly as his eyes fell to her breasts and then the dash of curls between her thighs.

"But 'tis also about a woman's pleasure. I'd not make love to ye unless ye wanted me to." His eyes returned to hers, pupils dilated, and a grim expression flattened his lips. "Do ye want me to?"

Heather couldn't tell if his serious expression meant he dreaded her approval or her denial.

She nodded slowly. "Aye. I want ye to." There was no immediate sense of regret like she'd expected. Only a heightened excitement.

"I would say it was necessary to keep us both warm." He gave a slow grin and a wink. "But I doubt ye'd believe me."

Heather smiled. "I might. I've heard of men piling themselves naked on one another when caught in a snowstorm and the threat of frozen limbs hung heavy."

"But I dinna want to make love to ye for the sake of warmth, Heather."

"Nor do I want that to be the only reason."

Nay, she desperately wanted it to be about love, but knew that was an impossibility. For now, she'd take the fact that he cared enough about her pleasure to ask her permission, and the honor and loyalty of his personality. The fact that he'd saved her life. She wasn't being forced. She had a choice.

And she chose him. This. Them.

Duncan slid his hands over her shoulders, down her arms, her skin pebbling in their wakes. He entwined their fingers and pulled them up to his lips, pressing tiny kisses to each of hers.

"I've only ever seen love once, when I was a young boy, before…" His voice trailed off, and for a moment he looked as though he'd traveled to another place. "My parents loved one another. Their marriage was arranged, but my father always told me how lucky he was to have fallen in love with my mother. He told me if I was lucky, if I met a woman who matched me in most ways, I might, too, find love."

Heather's throat tightened, and her mind reeled. Could this be true? Was it possible that one day he might feel even partially what she felt? Was that tight clenching in her chest…love? They'd only just met. Couldn't be. And yet, already they'd shared so much, learned so much about each other.

"Ye're my match in most every way."

A near confession of love and a promise of good things to come.

He pressed her hands to his heart. "I will take care of ye. I swear it. I will not let them have ye."

"Ye're an honorable man." She leaned up to press her lips to his knuckles.

"Ye make me honorable."

She shook her head. "Nay. 'Twas in ye all along. Ye just needed a reason to let it out."

He grinned. "And ye're that reason."

"Ye said so yourself." All of it seemed almost too good to be true.

"There could not have been a better enticement." Duncan pulled her arms up, placing them around his neck.

She curled her fingers into the length of hair tied back in a queue, caressed the pads over the parts on the sides that were shaved, feeling the tickle of soft bristles. Her body sank against his, the wool of his plaid tickling her thighs and his belt buckle pressing into her belly. Their gazes remained locked as they studied one another, perhaps letting them each wrap their heads around the promises they'd made. But within a minute or two, Heather didn't want to wait anymore. She wanted to feel his lips on hers, molding to her, feel that strong press of his rigid length against her.

"I may be a virgin," just saying the word caused her face to heat, "but I believe there is more to making love than pressing my naked body to yours."

"Aye, and I'm going to show ye."

Chapter Seventeen

*S*weet heavens!

Duncan pressed his lips to hers, and somehow, this kiss seemed different than all the rest. Tender, passionate, intense. And this time she knew it wouldn't end with one of them pushing the other away.

He toyed with her mouth while he stroked his hands up and down her ribs, teasing her skin with each passing inch. Shivers raced over her limbs. Places on her body she'd not been aware of before flickered to life. Every inch of her tingled and a deep yearning for more centered in her chest. Between her thighs, twinges sparked, spiraling outward and then cascading back again. She clutched at Duncan's bare shoulders, stroking her hands over the glorious ripples of strength, finding happiness even in the bend of his elbow and the soft skin of its crook.

When he softly stroked the undersides of her breasts, Heather gasped, arching into him. His palm flattened over a breast, warm and tender as he kneaded her, then swiped his thumb over her nipple. She moaned, running her hands over his chest, curious to see if he'd feel the same way when she touched him. Duncan's nipples, too, were hard. Smaller than hers. They tickled her palms.

To think this man would be her husband, and they could do this… every day. Maybe more than once a day. Heat rushed through her. Excitement, anticipation.

Duncan slid his lips away from hers, down her neck and to the top of one breast. She watched him do it, finding a certain allure in seeing his mouth on her skin. He glanced up at her, catching her eyes just as he moved to the center of her breast and licked her nipple.

She choked on a gasp, her body jerking.

Confidence oozed from him. He knew she liked what he was doing, knew that he was giving her pleasure.

He drew her nipple into his mouth and sucked gently. But no matter how gentle it was, her reaction was tenfold. She gasped, dug her fingers into his skin. When she'd thought about him doing this before, she'd never expected it to feel this good. Duncan paid equal homage to her other breast. All feeling of cold left her, and only warm heat rushed through her blood.

While he teased her breasts, Duncan massaged a path from her hip to her thigh. Then her inner thigh. A finger drew an enticing line from her mid-inner thigh to just below her center. He stilled there, waiting. Was he waiting for her to say aye? Heather shifted forward, wanting desperately for him to continue his climb, but he retreated, traced that same line back down her thigh, and then up again. Never touching the apex of her thighs, only hovering on the brink. 'Twas torture. Delicious, wanton agony.

"Touch me," she said, suddenly unafraid to ask for what she wanted.

Duncan groaned, straightening away from her breasts and pressing his lips to her ear.

"Lass, ye'll have me undone." But he did what she asked, caressing against her folds and sliding over some part that made her jump and cry out with intense pleasure at the same time. "God, lass." Every word sent her to trembling as his breath tickled her skin. "Slick and ready."

Aye, she could feel the slickness as he stroked over her, feel her body heated to a thousand degrees and begging for something. Begging for this feeling to never end, and yet she wanted to go beyond this.

"I feel..." She didn't know, couldn't answer.

"Tell me."

Her breath hitched when he slid a finger inside her. She couldn't tell him, could barely think beyond that sensation. He dipped in again, pulling slowly out, then in again. At the same time, he rubbed the pad of his thumb over that sparking part, the part that made her—

"Oh," she moaned. Heather pitched her hips forward, rocking against his hand even more when she realized it heightened the sensations.

Her muscles clenched, and she held onto him, certain he was taking her somewhere, but then he abruptly left her, stepping back a couple of feet. She opened hazy eyes, concentrated on keeping her balance, though her legs shook.

"I'm going to lay out the blanket, lass," he said. "Then I'm going to lay ye down on top of it. I'm going to remove my plaid."

Every sentence generated a vision in her mind, making her tremble with the anticipation of it.

"When I lie down beside ye, climb on top of ye... There's no going back from that."

Heather chewed her lower lip. "I know."

"I need to be certain that ye want this. That ye want me. That ye would call yourself my wife."

"I do. I will."

His eyes were heavily lidded, and the expression on his face made her want to rush forward and lay the blanket out herself. He desired her, wanted her, was willing to give up so much for her. Just as she was willing to give up things for him.

"I want ye," she said again.

Duncan gave a short nod, then laid down the blanket, spreading it flat. He stepped forward, took her hand in his and led her over to it. Just as he said he would do, he laid her down on the blanket, giving her a soft kiss on the lips before he stood.

He gripped his belt and pulled it off, letting his plaid unravel around his hips and fall to the floor. The cave was dim, but even in that dimness she could see his arousal jutting forward. Her eyes widened, and she sucked in a staggering breath.

Standing before her like the statue of a god, he said, "There is still time to turn back."

Heather shook her head, certain now of one thing. She wanted Duncan to be her husband, no matter the cost. An honorable, fiercely loyal warrior, he was her destiny.

"I dinna want to turn back. I want to go forward."

In a matter of a breath he was lying beside her, pulling her into his arms as he kissed her. The clash of his nude body against hers sent fresh tingles of awareness skating over her limbs. She moaned against his lips, slid her tongue over his.

Duncan rolled her onto her back and moved to hover above her, his thighs pushing hers apart as he settled between them.

"I've never taken a virgin," he admitted. "I fear I'll hurt ye, but I promise to go slow."

Pain… She'd heard of the pain. Knew there would be blood. Suddenly, fear filled her, and she wanted to change her mind, wanted to push him away and tell him that this was a mistake, maybe they should try another time.

But then he was kissing her again, sliding his body against hers, his arousal pressing against that triggering bit of flesh between her thighs, and she answered with her pelvis rocking up and down. Fear of the pain was overshadowed by the pleasure he gave her like this.

Duncan slid his hands between their bodies, stroking over her folds and entering her again, this time with more than one finger. He stretched her, a delicious pang that was instantly replaced by a throbbing need.

When he withdrew his fingers, she felt the void keenly. She canted her hips upward, begging for him to come back. And he did, but this time he returned with his shaft, guiding it against her folds. He pressed it gently against her opening, pushing against her. Heather clamped down, stiffening every muscle.

"Shh, lass, 'twill be all right. I've heard the pain is brief. I promise to go slow." He kissed her nose, her cheeks, her lips. "I will stop if ye ask me, even though I said there was no going back."

She shook her head. Even if he stopped, she'd agreed to marry him. This moment would come again and again. How many times would she be able to deny him? He slid his shaft upward over her sensitive folds, and she moaned, liking that sensation so much.

This time when he slid back down, he pushed into her opening a fraction of an inch, hitting the barrier of her maidenhead.

"Say ye want me, lass."

"Aye, Duncan, aye," she whispered.

He surged forward, past the barrier, and she cried out from the pinch of pain. An aching throb pounded in her nether region. He filled her to the brim. Too big. She wanted him to get off of her, out of her. Duncan remained still, unmoving.

"I'm so sorry," he whispered against her lips, kissing her tenderly and then wiping at the tears she hadn't realized had spilled. "Does it hurt overmuch?"

She shook her head, afraid to move and feel that sharp pinch again.

Duncan made her forget the discomfort, though, as soon as he pressed his lips to hers and kissed her deeply. The touch and swirl of his tongue, the slide of his lips, and the press of his weight on her chest sent her back to the moments before the pain, when pleasure had radiated through her limbs.

Then he moved, withdrawing slowly before gently sliding back inside. Heather gasped, the thrilling sensations tenfold. The pain was gone, replaced by a subtle ache that was quickly overpowered by pleasure.

Duncan guided her legs up around his hips, which only brought him closer to her, deeper. He kept his pace steady. Slow and deep. Above her, his breathing was much the same. He pressed his forehead to hers, locking eyes. He groaned when she gasped, grit his teeth when she moaned. 'Twas obvious he was working hard to keep himself in control. Heather had no such power. It felt too good to hold back. Clutching his back, she moved with him. Her body coiled tight, muscles clenching, and she could barely find her breath.

When Duncan slowed to a torturous pace, she arched her back against him and begged. "Please, please."

"Och, I canna," he answered.

"Ye must," she said.

"Nay, I dinna want to get ye with child."

How could he remember a thing like that at a time like this? She was on the precipice, the edge of a cliff, ready to fly off and fall deeper into the ecstasy he brought her. Instead of quickening his pace, he drove in slowly, but deeper, arching up into her, his pelvis grinding against hers.

"Oh!" she cried out, as ripples of decadent, foreign sensation resulted. "Dinna stop," she demanded.

"I won't. I canna."

He continued to rock into her, until Heather could barely breathe, and her mind centered squarely on the pressure building deliciously between her thighs. Suddenly, it hit her. A tidal wave of pleasure, like the storm outside, it pounded against her, soaking her. A feral cry ripped from her throat. She rode out the waves, unable to catch her breath. And then Duncan was pounding into her with earnest strokes, faster, harder. She thought she'd die from the impact. Another storm of ecstasy was upon her, ricocheting relentlessly around her insides.

Above her, Duncan groaned. Shouting out, he withdrew from her suddenly, pressing his thick shaft against her belly. Warmth spread over her flesh as he collapsed on top of her, his forehead pressed to the crook of her shoulder.

They panted in unison, unmoving other than the rise and fall of their chests.

"Lass…that was…" He cleared his throat and pulled away from her shoulder to look her in the eyes. "That was amazing."

"Beautiful," she whispered.

"And I made sure not to…put my seed inside ye."

Heather nodded. "Thank ye."

"Dinna thank me, lass. This was…God, I can barely think."

She laughed. "Nor can I."

"Let me clean ye." He pulled away from her, climbing to his feet. He picked up one of her chemises. "Can I sacrifice one of these?"

"Aye." She'd already decided that when they left here, only one of her chemises was coming with them.

Duncan tore off a few strips and held them both out in the rain. Returning to her with the wet cloths, he wiped one between her thighs. She turned away when she saw the blood.

"Dinna be embarrassed." She looked back at him, seeing a satisfied grin on his face. "Ye were perfect, Heather."

"I have the best teacher."

Duncan cleaned off her belly and himself, then tossed the rags into the fire. He stretched out beside her, tossing his unraveled plaid over top of them both, and pulled her into his embrace. Warmth spread through her. Happiness.

His flesh against hers stirred up more of the yearning, hungry sensations she felt when he kissed her. Lord, she was a wanton to already want more of him. But…"When will ye be ready…to do that again?" she asked.

A deep rumble of a laugh sounded in his chest. "Och, lass, dinna tease me. I'm ready now."

"Me too."

Duncan sat upright, jolted awake by something. A cursory glance around the cave showed Blade sleeping by the door, his head hanging low, and Heather curled up beneath the blanket beside him.

What had woken him?

He stood up, stretching his tight muscles. Grabbing hold of his sword, which had lain beside him, he crept toward the entrance to the cave.

The tempest had subsided, and a gentle, warm breeze blew in, almost like there had been no storm at all. There did not appear to be anything out of place in the woods—no flashes of metal—but from a distance he could hear the sounds of horses, dogs and whistles.

A hunting party?

Ballocks! Could it be the Sutherlands had followed them here?

"Get up, my lady," he called. He hated to wake her like that. After their night of lovemaking, she'd needed her rest.

Heather sat up straight, her golden hair a riotous mess around her head. He held his laughter in check.

"Time to go. Now. We've been followed."

She opened her mouth to say something, but he cut her off. "Could be your family, aye, but could also be the Ross clan, or worse, hungry outlaws."

Heather scrambled to her feet, gathering her chemise. "Turn around."

He raised a brow, about to remind her of all they'd done the night before, but the way her face colored, he chose to oblige her.

Duncan turned on his heel to find his own shirt, tugging it over his head, and then wrapping himself in his black robes. The wool of his priest's robes was warm, but the weave was loose enough that a breeze flowed through. He felt like a fraud wearing it now. "Are ye ready, lass? We've not time to waste."

"Dinna look."

"We're to be married."

"Dinna look!"

Duncan groaned, and with his back to her, went about packing what he could.

"Are ye done? We need to be on our way."

"I'm done," she grumbled.

A plaid hit him in the head, and again Duncan had to keep from laughing. The lass was not a morning person in the least. He was going to have a right good time teasing her about it over the years, but right now they had to get the hell out of here.

There had never been a hunting party this close to his cave before. Gut instinct told him they weren't looking for a stag.

He saddled Blade in record time, and just as they were ready to depart the cave, the voices sounded closer.

"Damn," he muttered. They might have to wait out the group. And he prayed they didn't see his cave. The brambles and tree hid the opening from most. Unless one knew where it was, it could be overlooked.

But the Sutherlands were known for their thoroughness, and Duncan didn't have hope the cave would be missed.

"Who is it?" Heather whispered from behind him. Her small hand pressed to his back as she tried to peer around him.

Duncan shifted his feet, moving himself further into her line of vision so he could be sure she didn't see outside the cave. "I'm not sure."

A sudden panic seized him. If they were discovered by her family, Duncan would be completely at her mercy. He'd never been at the mercy of a woman. God and church had ruled him. Murderous men had sought to overpower him. Coin had governed him, to some extent. But a woman? Nay. And he couldn't be sure which way she'd lean.

Would she go willingly back to her family while they cut him down? Even after what they'd shared? He'd fight like the devil, taking as many as he could with him. Or would she claim him as her husband, use the fiery spirit he knew she possessed to convince her brothers she wanted him?

'Twas more the not knowing than anything else that was slowly driving him mad.

"Stay back," he whispered. "Your golden hair is sure to alert any of them, whoever they may be."

Heather retreated a distance, her hand no longer warm on his back. The void felt empty, and he almost wished he could tell her it was all right to touch him.

Two Highlanders stopped their horses in front of the cave's opening, neither having yet noticed that it was there. Duncan waved Heather further back into the cave, but he crouched low, trying to listen to what they said.

"We need to find her. Tonight," one growled to the other.

They were after a woman. They wore neutral-colored hunting plaids, nothing to distinguish them from one clan to another.

"How the hell did she make it this far on her own?" the other answered.

"She's not alone." The deadly serious tone reminded him of someone he'd met before, and Duncan had a pretty good idea that it was Magnus Sutherland not a few feet away from him.

He glanced behind himself at Heather. She didn't appear to have heard and instead looked at him anxiously. He shook his head and crept to the back of the cave.

"Hunters, I think. I'm going to distract them away from here. Ye stay put."

Heather nodded.

Duncan slipped from the cave. He rounded the gorse bushes and pretended surprise at seeing two heavily armed Highlanders in front of him.

"My laird," he said. "What a surprise."

Magnus narrowed his brows. "Likewise."

Duncan recognized the man beside Magnus as his younger brother Blane. "What brings the both of ye to these parts?"

"I'd ask ye the same."

Duncan stretched. "On my way to the abbey. Been riding all night. I heard the Ross clan has issued a warning to the prior that he must pay a certain amount of tax or they'll attack on the morrow at noon."

"Ross clan?"

"Aye. The lady is planning on wedding a cousin of hers to a young lass, and they need the money for a dowry, I'm guessing." Lying came easy to Duncan. Another of his many sins.

"Young lass?" Magnus's eyes widened a fraction of an inch.

Duncan nodded. The Sutherland laird was taking the bait. "Aye. At Pluscarden Abbey. Noon on the morrow. Good day to ye."

He turned, prepared to go back to the cave.

"Wait, Priest." Magnus' voice was commanding, sending the thrill of a challenge rippling over Duncan's spine.

"Aye, my laird?" he asked.

"We'll accompany ye."

Duncan shook his head. "I'm afraid I canna allow that. I must journey on my own."

"How can we trust ye?" Blane asked.

Duncan shrugged, fingered the thick cross hanging from his neck. "I have served your family before and will in the future. I'll not bring fear to my brothers by arriving with an army on my heels. If ye must attend the abbey, then do so on the morrow just before noon."

Magnus grunted. "If ye come across the lass…"

"The Ross bride?"

Magnus nodded, looking as though he wanted to say more.

"My laird?" Duncan pressed.

Magnus pressed his lips in a firm line. "Nothing. A blessing?"

The two Highlanders dismounted and knelt on the ground before Duncan. How easy it would have been for him to end their lives at that moment. To take from them what their family had taken from him. To punish them the way he'd dreamed of doing for years.

Thoughts of Heather stalled him. She was not ten feet away, safely tucked into the cave. He could not raise a sword to her brothers. He'd given her his word that they would be safe from his vengeance, and he meant to keep it.

Duncan pressed a hand to both of the warriors' heads and said a prayer for safe passage. On the inside he said a prayer to keep him at his word.

The Highlander's Sin

The men thanked him, mounted their warhorses and took off through the forest, issuing whistles as they went.

When Duncan turned, a crown of golden hair greeted him. Heather stood right behind him, hands on her hips and murder in her eyes.

"Princess..." he drawled.

"Dinna call me that. Those were my brothers," she accused. Heather opened her mouth to scream, but Duncan rushed to press his hand over her mouth.

"Aye. They were your brothers. But I did what I did for many reasons."

"Ye sent them away," she garbled through his hand. Anger made her eyes bright and skin flushed.

Duncan nodded. "If I let ye go, will ye scream?"

She shook her head and he trusted from the look in her eye that she meant it. Duncan slowly released his hand from her lips, surprised she didn't try to bite him in retaliation.

"Why the hell did ye do that?"

"Language, my lady, ye're in the presence of a man of the cloth."

"Man of the cloth, my arse."

Duncan swallowed a laugh and reached out for her, but she took a leap back.

"I thought ye were going to do the honorable thing," she said through bared teeth.

"And what is that, my lady? Give ye up to your brothers?" He shook his head. "If I had done that, they'd not help the abbey defend against the Ross clan."

"They might have. Ye kept me safe."

Duncan grew serious. "And I intend to keep ye safe for the whole of our lives."

He watched her throat bob as she swallowed. "As my husband." It was more a statement than a fact, a reminder to herself of what they'd promised. Her face colored, and he could guess at what she was thinking—about how they'd made love. He'd not been able to get the remembrance of it out of his mind for more than a few seconds at a time.

"Aye. Is the thought so abhorrent to ye?" A man's ego could only take so much bruising.

"Nay. Not abhorrent."

"What then?"

She shrugged, chewed at her lips. "'Twill just take some getting used to. I…" She ran a hand through her hair, which seemed to have settled somewhat since she'd woken. "I want to marry ye."

Shock ricocheted through Duncan. For some reason, he'd fully expected her denial. "Good," was all he could manage to say. He should have come up with something romantic, endearing, but he wasn't that type of man, and he was afraid whatever he tried to say would only come off sounding confused and odd.

"Good?"

Damn. He should have at least tried for romantic.

"Aye, love. I want ye to want me."

"And what about ye? Am I only a convenience to ye? An answer to your prayers?" She was mocking him. He hated to be mocked.

A sizzle of anger raced from temple to temple. "What shall I say? That it was love at first fight?"

She crossed her arms over her chest. "That would have been better than *good*."

Duncan took a step toward her and steered her behind the bushes before the Sutherlands decided to come back to see what he was all about. He locked his gaze on hers. "I'll tell ye this much—I'd not marry another. Seeing ye upon your knees in the chapel, ye admitting that ye were a naughty lass… I couldna have found a woman more to my liking. 'Tis not just about the abbey." He took a breath, swiped his hand over his face, trying to find the right words. "Everything feels right with ye. Even when we fight."

Heather pressed her lips together, trying to hold back a smile, but she was slowly losing the battle as her lips curled. "That was *a lot* better."

Duncan tweaked her nose. "Good. Now let's get to the abbey afore your brothers do. Else, I might have to go back on my promise to do no harm, for I'll not let them take ye away from me."

They mounted Blade outside the cave and took off in the opposite direction of her brothers. Duncan knew a shortcut to the abbey that would get them there before the evening meal, and if all went well, they'd be married before they supped.

Holding Heather felt right, as much as it disturbed him. Marrying her was the right decision to make. But now he had to figure out how he would take care of her. He couldn't ask her to partner with him in mercenary duties, couldn't risk her being harmed.

'Haps now was the time he took his place as the head of the MacKay clan. Would they welcome him back from the dead? Guilt soured his gut. There was every possibility that they wouldn't. Hell, he'd turned his back on them. He could have gone back at any time over the last twenty years, and yet he'd hidden away.

But he belonged there, owed that much to his father. If he was not going to be able to avenge their lives, at the very least he could rule his clan.

Their acceptance was a risk he'd have to take. And together he and Heather could rebuild his castle, rebuild his clan. She'd make a good mistress. The lass was certainly bossy enough.

"Why do ye want to marry me?" He'd not asked before and wasn't sure he wanted to know her answer. Women were supposed to do what they were told, and he'd told her to marry him. She should comply as the fairer sex, but knowing Heather, she'd comply only to poison his soup later. There had to be an ulterior motive for her.

"To save myself. To save your people." Her voice was bland, banal.

"For a normal woman, I'd take your answer at face value, but ye're a lot more complicated than that." He leaned forward, catching the scent of her hair as it blew about in the wind. "Tell me, princess, is there another reason?"

She huffed. If she'd not been holding on to the saddle for balance, he guessed she might have crossed her arms over her chest.

"Well, is there?" he prodded.

"My life before ye lacked adventure." She shrugged. "I want more from life than chasing my brothers' bairns. I dinna want to be told who to marry. I wanted the choice to be my own."

Duncan frowned, staring down at her crown of golden hair. "I fear I've failed ye on the last account."

Heather shook her head. "Nay. Remember, I told ye I wanted to marry ye."

"For the adventure of it? Or to be released from your brothers' hands? Is that why ye didna sneak from the cave until after they'd gone?"

When she spoke, he could practically hear the smile in her voice. "Aye."

"Ye trust me." The fact resonated deep within him. No one had ever trusted him. The monks didn't count. Her trust was a gift he'd cherish and strive never to destroy.

"Aye, warrior priest. I trust ye."

Duncan swallowed hard. He'd just been given a gift and a curse. The lass expected much of him, and he feared he'd only disappoint her.

"Do ye trust me?" she asked.

The Highlander's Sin

"Aye." There was no pause in his answer. She'd proved herself today when she could have set herself free. His mind still reeled with that understanding.

Heather was proving to be a lot more complicated than he'd originally thought. Not simply a spoiled hellion, but a strong, intelligent, considerate temptress. Her kiss was enough to make a man toss his clerical robes and fall to his knees before her. And her lovemaking was enough to make him beg entrance to her heaven every second of every day.

Now he understood why so many men did abominable things just to be with a woman. But such a notion made him realize he had to be more careful. Falling for Heather was dangerous in so many ways, and just because they'd exchanged trust didn't mean he or his abbey were out of danger yet.

"Duncan," she started, a nervous edge to her tone. "Will they let ye renounce your position in the church?"

He cleared his throat. "I believe so."

"Why?"

"Because I've not yet taken my final vows."

"Then are ye truly a priest?"

"Aye, I just had not pledged my life to the church as yet. They knew who I was when I arrived. Prior Samuel didna want me to give up everything until I was truly ready. But now I think it best to claim back my identity."

"Your identity? Who are ye really?"

Chapter Eighteen

Duncan had not answered her question, and it'd been nearly four hours since they'd ridden away from the cave. He veered off the road, pulling his horse to a stop in a copse of trees. Blade was covered in a lather of sweat, and Heather thought she just might not make it to the nearest bush. Besides her urgent need to seek privacy, her stomach grumbled loudly.

"We'll take a short break here. Then we'll ride another hour to an inn where we can grab a decent meal."

Judging by the sun, it was just before noon. She'd be lucky not to lose consciousness by the time they got to the inn. Heather nodded and waited for Duncan to dismount. He reached up, wrapped his hands firmly around her waist, bringing her instantly alert. Her body awakened, recalling every touch from the night before. Chewing the inside of her cheek, she shoved away the sensations churning in her center. Duncan set her on her feet, and she pretended to barely notice his hands around her waist before she leapt behind a thick, lichen-covered tree.

"Dinna look at me!" she called.

Was he laughing?

She went about her business and then rejoined him and his horse, who was being fed a nice apple treat.

"Are ye familiar with the inn?" she asked.

"Somewhat. They've a nice rabbit stew." His voice had grown distant, as though he mulled some deeper thoughts.

Heather's stomach grumbled in answer. Duncan raised a brow.

"I didna realize ye were so famished." He reached inside the bottomless satchel of his, pulled out a shiny green apple and tossed it her way.

Heather caught it with one hand and took a huge bite. "Mmm."

Duncan grinned. "Have never seen a woman enjoy an apple so much."

"And I never have." Truly. She was famished, thirsty, and the apple helped to alleviate both.

They remounted Blade and continued on their way. The hour didn't drag on as the previous ones had, partially because she'd had a snack, though her belly still grumbled. Having had a taste of food, she was ready for more. They'd worked up quite an appetite with their...nightly activities. She imagined every way in which the rabbit stew could be cooked. With carrots and potatoes or without. With a touch of sage and thyme, or more of a bland, peppery flavoring. Heather couldn't give a fig what blend, as long as it was warm and accompanied by bread. That made her frown. There was every possibility that it would be cold and not a crumb in sight.

Before she had a chance to really work herself up over how the stew would be produced, they arrived at a large croft with a small wooden barn. A wooden sign staked into the ground outside the inn read: *Crofter's Inn.*

As they rode up to the door, a young boy of about fourteen summers rushed from the barn toward them.

"G'day, Father MacKay." He bowed his head in Duncan's direction.

"Blessings to ye, my lad." Duncan pressed his hand to the boy's head and then dismounted. He winked up at Heather as he reached for her. "We were hoping ye're mother has made some of her rabbit stew."

"As always, keeps a pot boiling for ye. Let me take your mount to our stables." The boy trudged with Blade toward the barn—also, apparently, the stables.

Duncan held Heather's elbow, heat suffusing the spot, and led her toward the front door. Would there ever come a time when he touched her that she didn't think about the both of them naked and his mouth upon her flesh?

An older gentleman and his wife spilled out followed by a brood of at least a dozen girls and boys. A ton of bairns in this household—Dunrobin did not seem half as bad as this.

Heather plastered on her best smile, fully aware she looked like a beggar beside Duncan in his magnificent robes.

"Father MacKay," the woman exclaimed. "We are so blessed to have ye with us." Her eyes roved over toward Heather.

"Many thanks. Ye've always been very hospitable." Duncan did not make mention of Heather.

She felt her face coloring, wondering what these people must think of her. Glancing down toward the ground, she examined the hem of her gown. Dirt-smudged, torn. She most definitely looked like a beggar. All the better, should her brothers come looking for her here. The innkeepers would make mention only of a poor, sad lass with the priest.

"Come inside. Ye must be famished." The woman spoke while glancing at Heather, but on the last word, she turned her gaze to Duncan.

"Aye, madam, we have ridden hard."

She smiled cordially and waved them inside. They walked past a long line of children whose cheeks were reddened, as though they'd just scrubbed the grime off their faces at seeing riders approaching.

Inside, the inn smelled musty, like spilled beer and unwashed bodies, but above all that was the succulent scent of stew. Heather detected an essence of sage, rosemary and pepper. It would appear the innkeeper's wife was a fan of spices, all the better.

"The regulars will be in soon. Ye might wish to avoid their rowdy behavior."

"Aye. My thanks," Duncan said.

She led them through a wooden door to a diminutive room past what looked to be a common dining hall. The room was cozy, private and dimly lit by a small window with homespun curtains pulled back. Duncan drew the windows and lit two candles on the table instead.

He took a seat at a small table with three chairs and pointed to the chair opposite him. "Sit, lass."

Heather nodded and pulled out the chair, arranging her skirts as best she could beneath her. Even arranged, they looked haggard, only fit for burning.

"I'll be back with the stew." The woman left them alone, closing the door quietly.

Duncan gazed over at her like she wore the finest of gowns and smiled. "We'll eat and then be on our way."

Heather returned his smile and then shifted her gaze warily toward the door. "Do ye know the regulars?"

Duncan steepled his fingers in front of his face. "Not beyond a skirmish or two."

"Ye fought with them?" She gave a little laugh. "Do ye fight with everyone?"

"Och, nay. I have to keep up appearances. I took their confessions after."

That made her laugh all the more. "What people must think of ye. A right, honorable man of the cloth and all the while, ye've a sword as long as your leg and sharp as death."

"No one asks about that. Oddly enough." He stared at her lips, pupils dilating.

It would appear she was not the only one who couldn't get thoughts of last night from her mind. "'Haps they think it a family heirloom."

That made Duncan chuckle. "Entirely possible."

A moment later the woman returned with two bowls of steaming stew. She set them down on the table.

"Care for some ale?"

"Aye, please," Duncan replied.

Heather stared down with disbelief into her bowl. Barely two bites filled hers, while Duncan's was near to overflowing. Why had the woman snubbed her?

Duncan glanced over at her. Seeing what must have been a stricken look he turned his eyes to her bowl.

"Well, that won't do," he mumbled. He yanked her bowl toward his and upended his into it, until they both had equal portions. "Better."

When the innkeeper returned, she frowned at seeing what he'd done. Heat filled Heather's face—anger, embarrassment.

"'Tis a sin to judge others and withhold from them what is rightfully theirs." He said the words with his eyes locked on Heather then, at the last syllable, he glanced up at the woman with a reproachful gaze.

The woman straightened her back and folded her hands in front of her. She was stern when she spoke. "Apologies, Father, but I—"

Duncan held up his hand. "This lass is deserving of more than your scorn."

The woman bit her tongue. They engaged in a silent battle, his eyes boring into hers, and the woman seemed set on not backing down, until finally, she relented. "Aye, Father." She shifted her gaze to Heather. "Apologies."

Heather smiled weakly, unable to find her voice. She nodded, wishing she could sink into the floor.

The woman turned without setting down the mugs. A moment later, she returned with the mugs full and frothy. A boy followed with a plate full of freshly sliced, still-steaming bread.

"On the house," she said softly.

"Blessings to ye," Duncan said with a genuine smile.

The woman backed out of the room, her gaze on the ground, fully regretting her previous actions.

"Why did she do that?" Heather asked, genuinely confused as to why she had been disparaged. Certainly a dirty gown did not mean she should starve.

"Sometimes people judge others by their appearance and not by their hearts."

"And what would she have seen with my appearance?"

Duncan took a slow sip of his ale. "Not what ye would have hoped."

Heather's eyes widened, and her stomach plummeted. "They think I'm...a..."

"Aye. A harlot."

"Because I have a dirty gown? A few tears?"

"Because of that, and because ye're beautiful, because ye travel alone with a priest. I must be escorting ye to a convent or returning ye to your family."

Her stomach soured, losing some of the hunger she'd felt keenly. "That's mad."

"Nay, princess, I assure ye, 'tis not."

Heather was suddenly sad for every woman who may have looked a little down on her luck and could have been turned away by someone like the innkeeper's wife. She hoped she hadn't ever looked at someone and judged them by their appearance. Hoping wasn't settling, for she was certain that at some point in her life she'd judged someone by their outward presence. She gazed down at her bowl of stew, now filled near to the top. Duncan had shared with her. How many small things such as this had he done for her to show the kindness of his heart?

Mercenary by trade, sinner, as he professed, Duncan MacKay was a good man.

Heather flicked her gaze up to him, seeing how he observed her intently. Her stomach fluttered. "What?" she asked softly.

"Will ye take the first bite?"

"Oh. Aye." She lifted the spoon to her mouth and was met with a surprisingly delicious taste. 'Haps the innkeeper's wife had left a sour taste in her mouth, but no matter. The rich, decadent flavor of the stew flowed welcomingly over her tongue. "Delicious."

"I am glad ye think so. When I've been on the road for a long time, I often find my way here, simply so I can have something hearty and good before I take another bite of an oatcake."

Heather smiled and tore off a piece of steamy, buttery-smelling bread. "How can ye be sure 'tis truly tasty and not the works of your imagination after days of bland sustenance and hunger?"

Duncan chuckled, taking the piece of bread she offered. "Right ye are. This may be the worst stew in all the Highlands."

They shared a laugh over that. Heather watched Duncan eat, loving the enjoyment he took in each bite, and struck by the thought that he'd brought her to a place that was special to him. With that thought, the idea that he would be her husband startled her once more. She'd known it. Agreed to it. But the notion had yet to sink in.

Her. Married.

She shook her head and shoveled another bite of stew into her mouth, chewing without tasting.

Married.

The word repeated in her mind again and again. She was bound to make a terrible wife.

And she was determined to find out more about this man she was supposed to marry — before they said *I do*. There was an air of mystery around Duncan. He was hiding from his past. Hiding from his demons.

Could they be so hellish that even he refused to face them? Besides her brothers, and maybe even a smidge more so, Duncan was the most fearsome man she'd ever come to know. Imagining him afraid of anything was enough to make her scoff, but it was clear that whatever skeletons were buried beneath his bed, kept him awake at night.

Heather took a hearty swig of her ale, but before she could swallow it, a banging sounded at the door. She glanced from the wooden barrier back to Duncan, whose lips had gone firm, his eyes narrowed. He leapt from his chair and pulled his sword from its sheath on his back, and he moved to stand in front of her. Protecting her.

And he waited.

Heather scooted her chair back in order to reach the knife in her boot. She was prepared to fight. 'Haps the innkeeper's wife had told the locals there was a whore among them, and they now clamored at the door for her attention. Were men such wolves? The thought seemed too ludicrous to give it merit.

"Stay behind me," Duncan demanded.

Heather nodded, then realized he couldn't see her. "All right," she managed, though her voice was hoarse with fear. She gathered her skirts in one hand, prepared to lift the hem and grab the knife if the need arose.

But there was no other sound. Not even a scrape of boots outside the door. Fear built inside her, making the stew curdle in her belly and her lips tingle.

"What is happening?" she whispered.

Duncan did not answer, but he did walk with quiet steps toward the small window with its drawn curtains. Setting the tip of his sword on the ground, he steadied the claymore with one hand and slowly pulled aside the curtain until a tiny shaft of light stabbed across the floor.

The frown on his face deepened, creases burrowing in his brow, and his jaw clenched so tight she could see the ridges of the muscle there.

She feared speaking, feared what he would say waited outside for them.

"I'm afraid we'll likely not finish our stew, lass. Grab the bread. We're leaving."

Heather sucked in a breath. "What did ye see?"

"Trouble."

Visions of warriors descending upon them, Lady Ross at their head, terrorized her mind.

"How shall we leave?" she asked.

Duncan turned in a circle, then faced the small window. "This is the only way out. I'll not chance walking through the inn." He glanced back at her, his eyes hard. "Sometimes coin is more precious than honor."

Heather was haunted by his words. Who was outside? What was happening? She felt blind in a room filled with fire. Anywhere she turned she might get burned.

"Come here." His voice was strained, gravelly.

Heather approached on unsteady feet. His nostrils flared as he dragged in a heavy breath. She breathed out, not realizing she'd been holding hers.

"Ye'll climb through first. Get to the stables and find Blade."

"What about ye?" Fear made her knees knock.

"I'll follow."

She shook her head. "Nay, ye need to come with me."

Duncan smiled, stroked the backs of his fingers over her cheek. He leaned down and pressed a tender kiss to her lips. "Whatever happens here, know that though my intentions at first were ignoble, they are nothing now but honorable."

Heather nodded. His talk was ominous and sent fear to shake her where she stood.

"Ye're talking nonsense." Fear took control of her teeth, making them clatter.

That noise, that clicking, seemed to bring her full force around. She had more backbone than this. A Sutherland born and raised, Heather had to cease acting weak and bring out the strength she knew she had.

"I speak the truth." He pulled her into his arms, pressed his lips to her head and took a deep pull of air. "I'm going to lift ye as soon as the courtyard clears. Run toward the stables. Dinna stop. Find Blade. Mount him."

"But—"

"No buts." He pushed her away from him, his eyes stern and locked on hers. "I need to know I can trust ye in this."

Heather nodded. She wanted to squeeze him close but refrained, afraid if she held onto him, she'd never let go.

Duncan swiped back the curtain and looked outside again. "I dinna know how much time ye have left." He knelt in front of her. "Put your foot on my knee."

As he knelt, his robes parted in the middle, falling to the side and between his legs. A sprinkle of hair graced the exposed knee he bent for her. Heather swallowed, remembering she'd promised herself that she'd be brave from now on. Brave for him. For his people. For them.

She lifted a boot and pressed it to his knee, feeling the solidity of him beneath the ball of her foot.

"Put your hands on my shoulders."

Heather did as he instructed, curling her fingers into the wool of his robes, the sinew of his shoulder muscles.

"Lift up."

She hoisted herself up until she stood on his knee. The window was small but big enough she was certain she could wriggle through it. A cold knot tied around her spine. Duncan would never be able to fit through its center. She pushed the realization aside. He'd go out the front. His robes were a shield. They protected him.

The window sill was jagged with splinters in need of sanding, and they stung her fingers as shards buried in her flesh. Wincing, she held back her cry of pain, trying as hard as she could to be tough.

Voices and the scuffling of boots sounded outside the door.

"Ye have to go now, lass." Duncan stood, lifting her halfway through the window. "If I dinna follow within ten minutes, go to Pluscarden. Keep heading north on the path we were taking, and ye'll find it."

Heather didn't say anything, her sole concentration on getting out the window. With Duncan's help, she wriggled through, and then fell the four feet to the ground, catching herself on her hands and knees in a pile of muck—obviously they discarded rubbish outside the window.

Sucking in a breath, she pushed to her feet, wiping her hands on her soiled gown. Only a few children stood in the open courtyard, curious gazes on their ruddy faces. Heather waved and gave them a tentative smile as she ran toward the stables. While she ran, she kept a keen ear for sounds of fighting in the inn behind her. Was that Duncan's booming voice?

She reached the stables and rushed through the doors, momentarily blind in the dim light, a stark contrast to the sun shining outside.

At first it appeared empty, but from within a stall she spied the eyes of the lad who'd come to greet them earlier, his eyes filled with fear.

"Lad, the horse. I need the priest's horse."

He stepped out from the stall. His voice shook. "They're looking for ye."

"Me?" She whirled back toward the door. Her brothers. That's who had come. And Duncan would have her run rather than face them.

Irritation bristled.

"Are ye Lady Heather?" the boy asked.

Relief flooded her. "Aye. My God. They've found us." She needed to get back to the inn, explain to her brothers that Duncan was not the enemy, that he was to be her husband.

"Tsk, tsk. Didna your brothers tell ye not to talk to strangers?"

Heather turned back around slowly, the raspy female voice familiar. She dreaded who it belonged to—and wasn't surprised to see Ina Ross standing there before her. She had dark hair pulled severely back at her nape, sharp-edged cheekbones and brown almond-shaped eyes. If not for the bitterness etched on to her face, she might have been beautiful.

Ina walked out of the stable the boy had been hiding in—or, rather, had been held hostage in. Her gown was made of the softest wool, a dark blue with silver embroidery trimmed at its hem and collar.

"Never leave a man to do a woman's job," she sneered. "Leave us." Her hardened, malevolent gaze fell on the stable hand, who took off running outside.

Behind her, Blade lifted his head over the gate of his stable, his black eyes glowing like coals. If Heather could just get past Ina, she could mount the warhorse and ride out of here. Duncan had told her where the abbey was. He'd told her to meet him there, and, by God, she would. If she was followed by Ross warriors, the Sutherlands would hopefully be there in time to save them all.

Oh, Duncan!

How would he make it past the Ross guards? Her own safety was not a question in her mind. They wanted something from her and would at least keep her alive for as long as it took for her to figure out a plan of escape. That was, if they even caught her. But Duncan… How many warriors had he seen crowding the courtyard? Enough for him to make the decision she was to flee. He'd put himself in the line of danger.

The knife in her boot seared her skin, begging to be let out.

Ina licked her lips, ending with a tight suck to her teeth. "I had a feeling things would go badly with the priest." She shook her head as if really disappointed. "I know how ye Sutherland harlots behave." The bitch had the nerve to wink.

"Ye know nothing of my family."

Ina waved the words away with her hand. "I knew enough to guide that hulking waste of breath into your castle, enough to have him steal ye and bring ye here to me."

Heather's ears buzzed. Here? He was supposed to bring her *here*?

"Och, honey, did ye think he was going to set ye free? He was meant to meet with me here, at noon."

Heather refused to answer, though her mind reeled, and the already curdled stew made a slow rise up her throat.

"Never trust a man when coin is involved. They turn faster than a rat toward a hunk of cheese."

The blood drained from Heather's face. Ina Ross had just uttered nearly the same words Duncan had before he'd sent her through the window.

His proposal of marriage… Their lovemaking. Oh, she felt sick to her stomach. It had all been a ruse to get her here. To bring her to those who wanted her, those who'd paid him. He'd manipulated her. Tricked her. Stolen her innocence as a ploy to

The Highlander's Sin

gain her trust. Magnus—Blane—they'd been *right* there. Close enough she could have called out their names, and they would have turned, cut Duncan down and taken her home to safety.

A painful fist squeezed her heart tight enough she thought it would burst. Her throat swelled painfully as she tried to hold back tears.

It mattered not. Not now, anyway. Duncan's betrayal could be dwelled upon later. The evil witch in front of her was another story. Heather had to get away from her.

"Now, where were we... 'Twas before your soul was crushed by the broken promises of one sinful Highlander." Ina tapped her chin as if deep in thought.

Heather hated her then, more than anyone else. The woman had caused her brother Magnus mountains of misery when she'd refused to let him break their betrothal contract and now she was here to heap on another load. This time, she wouldn't get away with it.

"Take me to your lair then, witch," Heather said with mock meekness. "Oh," she pressed a hand to her heart, "I am ever so fearful of ye, and my heart has turned to dust at the mention of love's broken promises."

Heather was proud of how strong her voice sounded. She was certain it would crack at any moment, as her heart truly was shattered behind her ribs. Little fortification those bones provided. Duncan had buried himself deep inside her, and for her to learn he'd led her here only to give her up to her enemies was the worst of fates.

Holding out her hands, she wiggled them toward Ina. "I'm unarmed. Easy for ye to subdue. Shall we go?"

Ina eyed her with speculation. "Ye can try for bravado if it makes ye feel better, but I know ye for what ye are."

Heather cocked her head to the side. "And what is that?"

"A spoiled brat."

Heather smiled. "'Haps I am. But what does that matter to ye? Will ye not take me based on my attitude? I should think as an evildoer, ye'd have more practicality than that."

Ina gnashed her teeth and took a threatening step forward. "Shut up."

With much exaggeration, Heather closed her lips. Keeping them pressed tightly together, her arms still outstretched in front of her, she glanced around the stables.

"We're all alone," she mused. "Did ye hide in the stables in hopes I would come? Was it all a show? Or did ye hope to garner all the credit for my capture?"

Ina swallowed, showing a moment of vulnerability.

"I guess it does not matter. Can we get this over with?" Heather tinged her words with boredom.

Ina took large strides toward her, baring her teeth, her cheeks reddened with anger. "I told ye to shut your mouth."

When Ina reached for her, nails long as daggers scraped painfully over Heather's forearms, but she didn't let Ina get hold of her. Instead, she twisted her arms and stepped sideways.

"Going to have to try harder than that," Heather taunted. Why not have a bit of fun with Ina before she used a defensive maneuver Arbella had taught her one winter evening when they'd been snowed in for days and both had been tired of sewing and playing the lute.

"Ye'll pay for this," Ina said, rushing toward her again. This time she'd tugged a sgian dubh from within her sleeve, the thin blade aimed straight for Heather's heart.

Patience was apparently not a virtue Ina Ross possessed. Heather let her think she'd gained the upper hand but leapt out of the way at the last minute, raising her arm and slamming the side of her hand down as hard as she could onto the spot where Ina's neck met her shoulder.

Ina gave a squeak of a shout, and then collapsed in a heap of woolen skirts. Unconscious.

Heather wasted no time in locating Blade's saddle and harness. Surprisingly, he allowed her to ready him, mount him and direct him out of the stables.

She gave a long, last, painful look at the inn, where angry shouts and cries of pain sounded from within. If only Duncan hadn't betrayed her.

She glanced down at Duncan MacKay's prized warhorse, the one who let no one ride him other than his master.

"Ye've a new master now, Blade. Call it the price of betrayal."

Chapter Nineteen

*H*ow in bloody hell had they found him?

Duncan had instructed Lady Ross to meet him at Fir Tree Inn, a good several hours' ride from Crofter's Inn. And yet, when they were supposed to be separated by miles, Marmaduke Stewart stood not two feet from him, sword drawn and spittle droplets on his lips.

They were surrounded by at least half a dozen groaning warriors that Duncan had already cut down. The small dining room was overcrowded by far at the moment. As soon as they'd rushed the room, he'd been prepared and had issued them all the same verses he now repeated to the bastard standing before him.

"*Son of man, speak to the children of thy people, and say unto them, When I bring the sword upon a land, if the people of the land take a man of their coasts, and set him for their watchman: If when he seeth the sword come upon the land, he blow the trumpet, and warn the people...*"

"Dare you recite such verse to me?" Marmaduke said, anger making his lips form a sour shape.

"Then whosoever heareth the sound of the trumpet, and taketh not warning; if the sword come, and take him away, his blood shall be upon his own head. He heard the sound of the trumpet, and took not warning; his blood shall be upon him. But he that taketh warning shall deliver his soul."

"Stop it!" the Sassenach screeched. His sword shook as his hands started to tremble.

Duncan grinned. *"But if the watchman see the sword come, and blow not the trumpet, and the people be not warned; if the sword come, and take any person from among them, he is taken away in his iniquity; but his blood will I require at the watchman's hand. So thou, O son of man, I have set thee a watchman unto the house of Israel; therefore thou shalt hear the word at my mouth, and warn them from me."*

"Kill him!" Marmaduke shouted.

Duncan was prepared. He swung his sword in a wide arc, slicing through another man's shield and shoulder, all the while continuing with his litany. *"When I say unto the wicked, O wicked man, thou shalt surely die; if thou dost not speak to warn the wicked from his way, that wicked man shall die in his iniquity."*

Marmaduke stood, quivering in his boots. He was a thin man, not built for fighting, and his hair had thinned much, creating a crown of fringe around his head.

"Where is your wife?" Duncan demanded.

The man was suddenly filled with confidence, a vile grin curling his lips. "In the barn."

And Duncan now knew exactly why the bastard should be confident... Heather.

Her safety was first and foremost in his mind, a dangerous circumstance given he was being attacked by twos as men ran at him from either side of Marmaduke. After a brief pause, Duncan swung into action. The men did not cease to come, either, as Marmaduke bellowed orders. When two came, behind them two more waited, and others were yanking those who'd fallen out of the room by their ankles.

As he cut through one and parried another, all he could think about was Heather, alone in the stables with that madwoman. Ina was not right in the head. Demented, vengeful and mean. If she got her alone, surprised her, Heather would be caught. Defenseless.

He pushed forward, having fought over a dozen men now. His muscles balked at the exertion, but anger and panic fueled him on.

"Wonder how we knew where you were? Ina had a feeling ye'd betray her. Thought it best to come here instead, knowing if we were wrong you would wait at the Fir Tree a day or two. Choosing this inn was simple, really. We had scouts visit every inn within range of your abbey to find out if ye were a regular. You really should choose to dine where they don't cave so easily. Well, no use in keeping fighting," Marmaduke taunted. "We've got her now." The man flicked his gaze toward the window. "Bet you want to see her tied up on the courtyard to the hitching post." The man licked his thin lips. "I bet your bag of silver that you'll want to watch my wife cut that bitch's throat."

Anguish formed a dangerous storm inside Duncan, and he bellowed his rage to the rafters of Crofter's Inn. Marmaduke had the temerity to jump a little at Duncan's battle cry.

"My lord! 'Tis the lady!"

Marmaduke's face looked stricken as he heard the call of one of his soldiers outside the doors.

"My lord!"

Duncan head-butted the last man who'd entered the room, leaving him face to face with Marmaduke.

"Are ye going to see what's happened to your lady?" Duncan said through gritted teeth, pushing his face within inches of Marmaduke's. "'Haps ye spoke too soon."

The man growled under his breath and backed out of the room, his gaze never leaving Duncan's. The man was too cowardly to walk out with his back to him, afraid Duncan would slice him down as he retreated. Bastard. Duncan wouldn't cut down a man who had his back turned. He faced his enemies every time, wanted them to see his face as they took their last breath and know it was him who'd put them there.

But that didn't mean he wasn't going to advance on the bastard to see what the noise was about. Had Heather managed to escape? Was it possible? Lord, he hoped so.

He wiped his bloody hands on his robes, ignoring how they shook, wiped the hilt of his sword but didn't sheath it. The Ross warriors were always itching to start a fight. He edged out of the small private dining room to see that the innkeeper and his family had all but disappeared. In their place stood at least another dozen Ross warriors eyeing him like starving wolves. A few of them reached for their swords, but stilled their movements when Duncan bared his teeth and made a move like he would retaliate. Keeping his eyes trained on not just the jumpy warriors but the ones who looked too calm, he followed Marmaduke out the front door of the tiny inn.

The courtyard to the left of the door had a growing line of men laid out on their backs, bleeding from Duncan's sword. Duncan made a sign of the cross to see so many who'd fallen by his own hand. A warrior's duty came with a price, one that weighed heavily on his soul.

"Ina!" Marmaduke's distraught call pulled Duncan's gaze toward the center of the courtyard, where Ina rested upon the arm of a larger warrior.

"Found her staggering out of the stables."

Duncan couldn't help the sense of triumph that pumped with a vengeance through his blood. Heather had gotten away. She'd beaten Ina and escaped.

"What happened, my darling?" The English sop's voice was whiny and repelling. How had Ina managed to enjoy it over the few years they'd been married?

"She…she hit me." Ina pressed the back of her hand to her forehead. "I'm so dizzy."

"Where did she hit you?" Marmaduke asked, then turned to the warrior holding her up. "Is she bleeding? I don't see any blood."

The warrior looked just as perplexed. Ina did not appear to have any outward signs of injury.

"Ye fool," Ina managed to screech, and then wailed at the pounding it must have caused in her head. "She did not cut me. She *hit* me."

As the two idiots argued over the merit of her injury and their warriors looked on with avid fascination, Duncan managed to slip inch by inch toward the edge of the croft. If he had to run all the way to Pluscarden he would, for that was where Heather would be.

When he rounded the corner, not a single one of the stupid Ross clan seemed to notice. Their mistress and her husband were now in a full-blown screaming match, replete with wails from them both. Dear God, their household had to have been a nightmare to live in.

He hurried to the back of the croft, prepared to duck into the woods, but the innkeeper stepped in front of him.

"Dinna make me hurt ye," Duncan said. "Step aside."

The man looked contrite. "My wife and family…"

Duncan waved the man away. "Ye're forgiven."

The innkeeper shook his head. "Nay, Father, we wish to offer ye the use of our horse in exchange for full forgiveness for having given ye up. The lady took your horse."

The Highlander's Sin

Thank God for that. Blade would get an extra barrel of apples as his thanks. Duncan nodded.

"I'm sure ye did only what ye saw fit as best for your family. But I'll take the horse all the same. Ye are forgiven, the lot of ye, and blessings be upon your household for a long and prosperous life."

Duncan grabbed hold of the older saddle and hoisted himself up onto the horse's back. He inclined his head to the family who'd betrayed him, letting bygones be bygones and vowing never to return to this particular inn, and also deciding on a personal quest to find better stew.

He set off at a gallop through the trees toward the path he hoped Heather had taken toward the abbey. With her on Blade, she was likely to beat him there by a good solid hour. Not once did he hear the sounds of warriors following him. Their idiocy would have been comical if it hadn't been so damn pathetic.

The horse trudged through the green forest as though Duncan had asked him to climb a mountain in an ice storm. No amount of clucking, thigh-squeezing or heel-nudging seemed to quicken the nag.

With luck, the damned horse would make it in time — before the Sutherlands arrived and took Heather away from him forever.

Blade seemed to sense their destination, or at least he acted as though he did. Heather was completely turned around, certain she'd passed the same lichen-covered boulder four times now.

"Do ye play games with me?" she asked the horse, pulling him to a stop.

Alone in the woods with only a small knife and a horse for protection, Heather tried not to let panic take hold of her. When she'd had a direction to go in, she'd felt better. Now she was simply lost.

At first she'd stuck to the trees, but a road had been made through the forest and seemed likely to take her the direction she needed to go. That had been an hour ago.

How did one get lost on a road? Heather had always been directionally challenged. She had been lucky when she'd gone out exploring that one of her brother's guards had always trailed behind and brought her back after she'd gone in circles. But there was no one here today to help her.

There were lots of scary things in the woods. Wildcats, boars, bears, outlaws, Englishmen, poisonous spiders…

Blade stomped his feet, scraping them in the dirt of the road, showing the darkened dirt beneath.

"Dinna be irritated with me," she said. "I've never been in these woods before." That she knew of. "Ye're more likely to have been here than me. Take me to the abbey."

But the horse simply stood there, still as a statue, his ears perked back.

"Oh, nay…" Heather held her breath and tried to listen.

What did the horse hear?

A light breeze rustled the leaves, and birds made calls to each other. Squirrels scurried. Nothing else. Except—*that*. A whistle, a shrill sound in the distance.

Had she been followed?

Heather nudged Blade, shook his reins, but the damned animal wouldn't budge. Did he want her murdered just as his master surely had been?

"Go, ye blasted horse!"

Still he remained.

Heather couldn't risk being found by the Ross clan. With the stubborn warhorse planted in the middle of the road, her best bet would be to run.

She dismounted, much to the chagrin of the horse. "I asked ye to help me, ye wouldn't, and if I climbed back in your saddle, ye'll likely just keep on standing there. Best of luck to ye."

And she was off, lifting her skirts as she ran up the hill to the right leading back into the woods and hiding behind a thick oak as the sound of an approaching rider rounded the bend in the road. The rider slowed, and a horse whinnied. She dared not move in case whoever had come upon them saw her, even just a glimmer of movement.

"Heather!" Duncan's voice boomed through the forest, and her knees buckled, heart leaping to her throat.

She grasped onto the thick trunk for support and peered around the tree. He was looking right at her. She jerked her head back into hiding and cursed under her breath, praying he'd not actually seen her, as futile as it was.

"Come down from there. 'Tis not safe."

"Ye're the most dangerous thing around," she called back.

"Likely not," he said.

She'd take her chances. Heather turned and ran deeper into the forest, her feet crunching loudly over fallen branches and sliding on slick moss. Stealth was not one of her virtues. She stopped for a second, hopping on one foot to pull the blade from her boot. Lucky for her, she'd not had to use it as yet, saved it all this time for the man who'd stolen her virtue, her heart and then spat on them.

Behind her, Duncan called to her as he came crashing through the forest like a bear. A quick glance back, and she saw he was indeed crashing through the trees—on Blade. *Zounds!* The animal was likely to crush her, especially since she was going against his master. Well, she wasn't going to let that happen.

Heather tried to pick up her pace, but she was no match for a warhorse bent on mowing her down. Seconds later, she was lifted into the air and slammed down onto hardened thighs.

"Nay!" she cried, kicking and swatting, but Duncan was immune to her abuse.

He quickly gained the upper hand, his thick grip holding both of her wrists in one of his hands. He pinned her legs beneath one of his. Stuck, immobile, helpless. Her throat burned with the need to scream and call him every horrible name she could think of.

"Should have tied and gagged ye when I had the chance."

Chapter Twenty

*H*ow dare he?

"Let go of me, ye slimy whoreson!"

"There's the lass I know and lo…" He trailed off.

And why shouldn't he? She was well aware his love had been false.

"Enough games. I know ye betrayed me. I know ye'll do so again. I should have known from the start that a priest with your wicked tendencies could never actually be good."

Duncan had the nerve to look confused, hurt at her words. He tightened his hold on her. Narrowing his brow, he frowned at her fiercely. "Silence those harsh words, princess."

"I'll not listen to your orders any longer. Ye've no claim on me." Why did her words sound weak? She wriggled against him, though it seemed hopeless. He held her tight, and the warmth of his body, the sturdiness of it, drew her in, made her feel safe, even if he gave her no indication to feel that way.

With his free hand, he curled his fingers around the back of her neck and brought her face close to his. His scent surrounded her, intoxicating her with its heady masculine effect.

"No claim?" he growled. "Ye're to be my *wife*. We made love last night. I've every claim."

A shiver stole up her spine. Wife. His. His admission that he'd stolen her innocence made her lightheaded with internal pain. "I'll never be yours."

Anger darkened his gaze. Beneath her buttocks and on top of her thighs, she felt his muscles twitch. "Not the right answer."

As best she could with arms held high, she straightened her back, attempted to square her shoulders, and set her jaw firmly. "*Not* in all of eternity."

Duncan grinned, but it wasn't a happy expression. Nay, this was intense, angry. "Wrong. I've bedded ye already, voiced my wish to marry ye, and ye did the same. Ye're as good as my wife in the eyes of God."

Her breath caught at the truth he revealed. All the words her brothers would need to hear. They would believe her to be married. But that didn't mean they wouldn't challenge Duncan all the same, make her a widow before nightfall. Despite her anger, her heartache, the thought of him lying dead, her brothers meting out the punishment, made her dread waking in the morning. She hated him, despised every breath he drew, and yet, she'd be torn to pieces if he were killed.

"By the end of this day, ye'll wish ye'd never been born." She glared daggers at him through tears that shimmered. Dear Lord, why did she care so much? Why did she have to love the bastard?

He drew his face another inch closer. "Och, lass, but ye see, I've already wished that for a lifetime," he whispered. Pain laced his words and etched in the corners of his eyes. "Ye'll have to do better than that."

Her heart reached out to him, but her mind screamed for her to run away. She wrenched in his embrace. Why wouldn't he just let her go? Heather wasn't certain she could handle what he was putting on her. To spend her life with him...it was the stuff of dreams. And to set aside everything else that mattered to her...for him. It was a lot to ask. And before he'd fed her to the wolves, she would have willingly given her life for him. Duncan had ruined that. Duncan had changed their future. Duncan was at fault. Not her.

"My brothers will kill for me." Yet she prayed they'd stay their swords if she begged.

"A risk I'm willing to take." He was deadly serious. The man was willing to risk his neck for her, even after she'd told him she wished he were dead? How deep did his feelings for her go? How much was he willing to risk in order to be with her? Why, in all of the world, had he betrayed her? Questions fired with screaming accuracy through her mind, but she was getting no answers within her head.

"Ye would risk your life for me?" Why did he play such games? Confusion warred with anger and forgiveness.

"I proved I would when I jumped into the water to save ye. And again when I fought off Ross warriors. Again when I chased after ye. I'm here. Holding ye to me, making ye see that, aye, I would risk it all."

Heather shook her head. "But ye led them there, to the inn. Ye told them to meet ye at noon." Her voice had grown soft. He was saying all the right words, making her forget the pain and anger she hugged tight to her chest.

"Nay, lass. Ye've got it wrong. I did not lead them there."

"But they *were* there. Ye canna deny it."

"I canna deny they were there." He let go of her hands and stared into his palms. "I canna deny it, nay."

Rather than letting her hands fall to her lap, Heather placed a palm on either side of his face, forcing him to look at her.

Their eyes locked, and she wished that while staring into those dark pools, she didn't see so many monsters waiting to tear their way out.

"Then stop lying to me," she whispered. "Stop this charade ye're playing. Let me go. Ina Ross will certainly give ye no coin now." She hated the pleading in her voice, and with her next words, she sought any strength left inside her to bolster her. "I've already given ye much, Duncan. Dinna ask for my soul."

His eyes darkened, mirroring her own feelings of betrayal. How could he look at her like that? How could he be the one suffering? "I'm not the devil nor a god. Your soul is yours to keep."

A painful wrench squeezed inside her chest. "Then dinna pretend anymore. Let me go." Her hands fell to her lap.

Duncan intently searched her gaze. "Tell me ye dinna love me."

Why did he have to ask that of her? Her lies were easily read upon her face. If she told him she didn't love him, he'd be able to see that. Even if he'd broken her heart, she couldn't shove aside the strong emotions that took over every time she thought of him, much less was held in his arms.

Heather pressed her lips together, formed the words in her mind and then let them spill out, each word a jagged tear in her heart. "I dinna love ye, Priest."

But Duncan smiled, the expression irritating in its cheerfulness. He'd seen through her. "I ought to give ye a penance for lying."

She tossed her head, pretending to flick a strand of hair from her eyes, and looked around the forest, seeing nature in its prime beauty. But her words were ugly, disenchanting and cruel. "I dinna lie. I feel nothing for ye. I agreed to marry ye only to save your stupid monks and to keep myself out of the hands of evil."

Duncan spread his hands wide, shifted his legs off her, causing her to look back at him, see the hope shining in his beautiful eyes. "Well, then, I suppose 'tis your lucky day, since I myself have two hands and an evil disposition."

Heather frowned, biting the tip of her tongue to keep the next few choice words from echoing around them. Duncan had made a mistake — he'd let go of her.

Wrenching her arm back, she prepared to hit him the same way she had Ina Ross and then leap to freedom, but damn the man, he was quicker than that, catching her arm in midair. He squeezed and brought his face close to hers.

"Ye know, princess, at the same time I want to kiss ye, I want to wrap my hands around that pretty little neck and squeeze. No one's ever made me feel the way ye do. Made me angry and filled with an intense need to have ye all at the same time. Made me wish I was anywhere else but with ye, only so I could tear apart the earth looking for ye. Ye know what I think?"

She tentatively shook her head, out of breath, his words having stolen all the air from her lungs and paralyzed her with fear and need.

"I think it must be true love," he drawled.

A gasp escaped her lips. "Ye're mad!"

"Mad for ye, darling." Duncan grinned, his eyes twinkling as though he'd discovered some deep, dark secret. Was it the truth that he'd only now realized how he felt for her? The true meaning of it?

Love soared through her, her heart reaching from inside her chest toward his, but she hunched her shoulders, trying to draw it back in without success.

"Nay." She shook her head, totally denying everything he'd said. He couldn't love her. Couldn't make her tell him that she loved him so very much. "Nay," she said again.

"Oh, aye, love. I didna realize it until that bastard Sassenach told me Ina waited for ye in the barn. Thinking that I'd sent ye to your death made me sick with fear. As mad as it may be, I canna think of living another day without ye. Not another second. Not an hour. To think I might never feel your lips on mine, or hear ye call me a bastard, is the stuff of nightmares. Hell, I'm giving up my entire purpose for living just to be with ye, princess."

"Dinna call me that," she croaked out. Every single word he'd said shattered the hard shell she'd been trying to keep around her heart since the moment Ina had muttered those vile words. "Ye were going to give me up. Ye canna speak of love, of wanting me, needing me, if ye were going to give me away."

Duncan let go of her wrist and wrapped his arms around her. "Dinna ye see, lass? I didna give ye up. I was to meet Lady Ross at an inn miles from here. But the bitch was being cautious. Must have known I would never be able to stay true to our arrangement once I'd laid eyes on ye."

"I dinna believe in coincidence."

"Nor I. The woman is demented. In her mind, she knew I'd fall for ye, and she planned to be here when I did."

"Why?"

Understanding dawned in his eyes. "'Haps seeing your pain, your loss of love was a bit of revenge on her part. The woman thrives on others' misery. One Sutherland's pain was good enough. Just like myself. I was willing to kill any Sutherland to avenge my family. Revenge makes us mad, insane. I canna explain it more than that. It's senseless, illogical. But I dinna care why she did it, only that ye got away." He blinked slowly and swallowed. "I'd never have forgiven myself if ye'd not lived."

Heather flicked her gaze to his lips and then back to his eyes. She wanted to kiss him. To let out all the pent-up frustration and fear that sat cold in her chest.

"I'm glad ye were not killed," she said. "When I heard the shouts and fighting… I was certain they would cut ye down. I was so scared. Devastated."

"It would take a lot more than a dozen lame warriors to take me down."

"And Ina, when she told me ye'd betrayed me, I was heartbroken."

"I'd never break your heart."

She touched his cheek, rubbing her thumb gently back and forth. Escape. She needed to get away from what had just happened. Her pain and fright. "Kiss me."

"Gladly."

He tucked her against him as he lowered his mouth to hers. But the gentle brush of lips was not what Heather wanted. She wanted commanding, powerful. Their encounter with death demanded it. Wrapping her arms around his neck, she curled her fingers around the base of his skull and urged him forward. Duncan groaned, thrusting his tongue deep into her mouth just as she opened hers to meet him. Passion ignited, spurred on by their desperate need to be with one another.

To think if things had gone differently at the inn, or he'd not happened to find her upon the road. That they'd not be here together and she may have gone to her grave thinking he'd betrayed her…it was unthinkable. Heather clung to Duncan, afraid of ever letting him go. She wanted to meld to him, make them one, and never let another soul tear them apart again. They hung on to each other, whispering words of endearment from the heart and need as they kissed and stroked, as if forever burning this moment in each other's minds.

"God, love, I need ye now." Duncan tore his mouth from hers, dragging his lips over the line of her jawbone down to her neck. "Desperately."

"Oh, aye," she said, delirious with passion.

"Right here…"

Her eyes popped open. "On the horse?"

"Aye, he will not mind," Duncan crooned.

Heat filled Heather's face. Riding a horse would never be the same again. Every rock of its gait would bring her back to this moment, a moment she would not mind living repeatedly.

"Aye, now," she answered.

Duncan pushed his robes open and tossed up his plaid, revealing the heavy length of his shaft, already reaching toward her. Heather stared down at it, knowing what pleasure it would bring her. Not having touched it before, she needed to now, needed to feel his solid length in her hands. She stroked over his length, feeling the velvety, hard skin against her palm and fingertips.

"Och, lass…" he ground out. "Ye torment me with your touch."

"I hope in a good way?" She smiled up at him.

His lids were half lowered with pleasure, and a slow, wicked grin curled his lips. "Aye, verra good."

Duncan gripped her skirts at her thigh and tugged until the fabric was hiked up around her hips.

"Shall I torment ye?" he asked, stroking a finger between her thighs, over the dewy folds of her sex.

Sharp, pleasurable sensation riveted her. Heather moaned, canted her hips forward, urging him on. Tugging at her gown, he freed a hardened nipple to the summer air and his waiting, velvet tongue. Duncan swept the tip back and forth before drawing it into his mouth to suckle. Tingles fired throughout her body, centering in all the right places. She arched her back, succumbing to the magic he induced.

"Ye're ready," he said, bringing his mouth to hers. He sucked on her lower lip. "More than ready."

He lifted her enough so she could wrap her legs around him. As she descended onto his lap, he guided his shaft through the slickened folds of her sex and thrust up, entering her roughly, deliciously.

Both of them cried out at his invasion. Duncan stilled them both, letting her adjust as he gazed into her eyes.

"I love ye, lass. I think since the moment I saw ye on your knees begging forgiveness for being who ye are. I'll never ask ye to change, nor make ye plead for mercy. I love ye just the way ye are."

Sweet music to her ears. Heather smiled, shifting her hips forward, both of them lost for a moment in that delicious sensation. "I love ye, too. Probably from the moment ye made me climb onto your back and face my fears. No one has ever understood me the way ye do, nor accepted me."

"Ye're my wife."

"Aye, for the rest of my days." She pressed her lips to his, staring at his dark eyes for moments, before her eyes closed with pleasure.

Uncertain of how to move, Heather let instinct and Duncan's hands on her hips guide her, rocking her back and forth, up and down. Their mouths stayed locked, swallowing each other's cries between tender nips and decadent sucks. His pace was steady at first but grew to quickened thrusts. She could barely breathe. Sensation whipped through her like the storm they'd ridden out in the cave, pounding her with ecstasy, and just when she thought she'd had enough, another gust of pure pleasure would knock her down.

She gripped tight to his shoulders, her head thrown back in a moan of decadence as each thrust brought her closer to the edge of release. Duncan drove in harder, his fingers gripped tighter to her hips. And then she was there, crying out her pleasure for all the forest to hear, and not caring a fig for anything but the pleasure they created together.

"Oh, Duncan!"

He sealed her mouth with a kiss, drinking in her moan. He tasted her, sweeping his tongue inside to meld with hers. Duncan thrust harder, vigorous in his effort, bringing her completion full circle, until her body wound tight again and suddenly sprang free once more. Then he left her suddenly, and with a heavy, masculine groan, he spilled his seed into his hand. Even in such a moment of delirium, he'd recalled her desire to put off conceiving children.

"Thank ye," she murmured.

He touched his forehead to hers, their gazes locking, breath heavy, hearts pounding in unison. "I should be the one to give my gratitude."

Heather smiled, touched her fingers to his lips and shuddered. "We please each other."

"More than ye know."

Chapter Twenty-One

"Shouldn't we hurry?" Heather asked.

Duncan held tight to her hand, feeling immeasurable comfort in her small grip and knowing she walked beside him. He'd led her a short distance farther into the woods away from the road, where a thin, winding creek cut through the trees.

He tugged a piece of cloth from one of his satchels the innkeeper had been kind enough to find and attach to the saddle of the nag. Bending toward the creek, he washed his hands and dipped the cloth in the water, soaking it.

"Aye, we should hurry, but first I want to wash ye." He caressed Heather's ankle with his free hand and glanced up at her, feeling overwhelming emotion tighten his chest. "Lift your gown, my lady."

Her face colored prettily, but she did as he asked, slowly dragging the fabric up over her lithe legs. A vision he could stare at all day.

"Beautiful," he murmured. "I wish we could stay here the rest of the day, and possibly tomorrow."

"That would be the death of us."

He nodded, knowing the seriousness of their peril. "We'll ride hard to Pluscarden. I will not let harm come to ye, Heather." Duncan slid the cloth over her calf, up her inner thigh, and settled on the juncture covered in dewy curls. "But, first, I want to clean ye."

"All right," she sighed.

"If we were safely ensconced in a chamber of our own," — he trailed the wet cloth down her opposite thigh and then dipped it back in the water, — "I would have bathed ye in a tub of scented water."

"That sounds heavenly. Would I have bathed ye, too?"

He grinned up at her, every wicked thought probably showing on his face. "Och, aye, lass. Again and again."

"Then we'd best arrange to have a chamber and a warm bath soon." Eagerness brimmed her words, and a smile tugged at her lips.

"I'll see that we do." And, damn, if he wasn't going to keep her up all night as soon as they closed the door.

"Will we be going to your home? Away from the abbey?"

Duncan stilled. His home. He'd not been there in nearly twenty years. Not since the day his family had packed for their journey to Dingwall. "My home," he said, barely above a whisper.

"Aye, Duncan. Ye've yet to tell me anything about it."

He stared at her feet, dainty things encased in brown leather boots.

"Nay, I haven't." A cold rock settled in his gut.

"If we are to marry, dinna ye think ye might share it with me?"

"A conversation best left for another time." He wrung out the cloth. "For now, we must make haste to the abbey."

Heather frowned and crossed her arms over her chest. Stubborn lass. "I'll not leave where I stand until ye tell me. I've already agreed to marry ye. I love ye, Duncan. Nothing ye can say will make me change my mind, nor will it make me despise ye."

Duncan stayed knelt on the ground, his gaze fixed on hers. "That is not what I fear."

Heather bent down, her knees touching his, and took his hand in her grasp. Duncan fixed his gaze on their enfolded hands.

"What do ye fear?" she asked.

"I fear my clan will not forgive me." The words spilled out without his permission. He swallowed hard, hearing the sounds of his family screaming as they were cut down by Heather's own blood. "I fear they will not accept me. They think me dead these past twenty years."

"What horror have ye done?" She pressed gentle fingers to his chin and forced him to gaze at her.

He was never so immobilized, so weak with fear, than when he thought about that day.

Swallowing hard, he opened his mouth to speak, but no words came out. No matter what she'd said, Heather would look at him differently now. Of that he was certain. That inevitability made it hard for him to form words. He couldn't live with himself, if she were not to love him.

"Their death. 'Tis my greatest sin."

She sucked in a breath. "Ye killed…people from your clan?"

He nodded, shook his head. "Not directly."

"What does that mean?" Her voice was soft, begging for explanation.

"Their deaths are on my hands."

She shook her head. "But ye said my uncle—"

He waved away her words. "Aye, 'twas his sword, but I allowed them to have access to my family. All of them. I left the gate open, and the enemy snuck inside."

The stricken, horror-filled expression on Heather's face was too much for Duncan to bear. He thrust her hands away and jumped to his feet.

"Dinna ye see? I dinna deserve ye or your love. I deserve no more than what I am. A mercenary. A man of death and a man offering redemption for everyone but himself."

Heather, too, leapt to her feet, the look on her face enough to make him take a step back, though he kept his feet firmly rooted to the ground.

"Ye're an idiot!"

"Dear me," he pressed his hand to his chest, "let us cut straight to the bone with insults."

"Nay, ye listen. Ye were but a boy. 'Twas an accident leaving the gate open. Not intentional. The guards should have been on the lookout. Should have warned of men approaching, breaching the walls. Was not my uncle meeting there with your clan willingly? Your laird and he discussing a truce? How could one boy be at fault for the evils of men?"

The words she spoke were true, they made sense, but even still, Duncan could not heed them. He shook his head.

"There was no time. They snuck in through the door."

"Or perhaps your laird's men were not true to him. Could it be that they led the men to that gate? Or maybe another gate? 'Haps the men even climbed over the wall as your laird's guards turned a blind eye?"

"They would not betray my father!"

Heather gaped, taking a step back. "Your...father?"

Duncan glared at her. "Aye." He bowed. "Laird MacKay at your service."

"Laird MacKay," she whispered, eyes wide and mouth slightly open. "Ye...ye're a laird?"

"By birthright only." Damn it. He'd not meant to tell her like this, not with such anger. Surely she would turn tail and run.

"Your people… They think ye're dead?" she whispered.

How long until she upended her belly? "Missing. Presumed dead."

"Who stands in your place?" With each question, her voice grew stronger. What was the lass about?

Duncan shrugged. "An uncle."

"Ye must take your place. 'Tis your right. Your duty." The demanding Heather had returned.

Duncan studied her for a long time. She didn't understand the situation, couldn't, if she thought it so simple. "They will not accept me, knowing I was the true reason behind the death of their beloved laird."

"But they will. Ye must explain it to them."

He crossed his arms over his chest. "I will not."

"Is there no one who can speak for ye?"

"The only man who could have spoken for me saved my life on his last draw of breath. The monks at Pluscarden, they know who I am, what I've become. I could never expect them to vouch for me."

"Ye must try."

He ground his teeth in annoyance. "Why? Why should I take my seat as laird? Because ye want to be a princess and live in a castle?"

Heather took a step away from him, her lips set in a grim, sad line. "Nay, Duncan. Because it is your duty."

"Duty? It was my duty to protect my family then, and I failed. They will not believe I can do it again."

"Ye're a coward. Ye dinna believe ye can do it yourself. Ye're the only one holding ye back."

Her words struck a deep chord. He was scared. He'd admitted that much to her already. Looking his people in the eye and facing his past… He'd never planned to do it. He'd sought only to avenge his family and live out his life alone. But Heather had changed all of that.

"Why do ye have to be such a meddler?" he grumbled. "I will nay do it. End of discussion. We need to leave afore we are found."

She said nothing, only gave a curt nod.

"Ye can ride the nag." He lifted her onto the horse. "Stay close to me."

Again, she gave him the curt nod. Damn, but he wanted to know what she was thinking. Then again, he dreaded knowing her thoughts.

"We'll marry as soon as we reach the abbey. Then we'll face your brothers side by side," he said.

"I dinna need ye to protect me from my brothers," she said.

"Nay," he chuckled. "But I may need ye to hold me back when they try to take ye away."

"They will not take me away." She stared straight ahead as she spoke so matter-of-factly.

"They will try." He gripped the reins tight, the leather biting into his palm.

Heather locked her solemn gaze on his. "I will not let them."

He returned her gaze. "Neither will I."

Duncan mounted Blade and spurred him forward. They followed the creek, crossing over a quarter mile down then riding up a hill through the forest. He had no plans to go back to the main road. Riding through the trees was the best course of action for their safety. They were pursued on all sides, he had to assume, by two very different enemies, one of whom he'd have to embrace.

"How much longer to the abbey?" Heather asked a few hours later.

They rode overtop a ridge and, in the valley some distance away, he spotted the motte and castle ruins where they'd camped together the first night. How he'd admired her then. The way she'd stood up to him, attempted to run, and hopped on the wooden stool as a deadly rat had threatened their lives. He'd loved her even then, listening to her rant at him and call him names. The moment they'd first opened their mouths and exchanged words had been profound. She was someone who kept up with him, understood him. No two minds could have been more alike and yet so different.

"Not much longer. An hour or two." When he and the monks had hiked on foot, their journey had taken nearly an entire day. On horseback, the time it took would be cut severely. "We'll make it safely," he promised.

She nodded, still not making much conversation with him. He'd been cruel to accuse her of wanting him to take his place as laird only because she wanted to live in a castle. How many times had she told him she wished for adventure, to live in a war camp with Wallace and his men? Though he'd accused her of being spoiled, there were so many ways in which she wasn't.

Her family had loved her, indulged her, kept her spirit alive, and aye, while it wasn't the norm, he was glad they'd spoiled her in that way. She wouldn't have been the woman he loved if they'd not.

Who knew that upon following orders, he'd find the woman meant for him? Duncan stilled his horse and gripped on to Heather's reins, slowing her mount to a stop. He tugged her closer until their thighs touched and he could wrap his arm around her waist. He nuzzled against her neck, curled a loose tendril of her hair around his finger.

"I dinna know what I'd do without ye, lass. If ye want me to take my seat, I will."

Heather slid her arms around his waist and squeezed. "I dinna want ye to do anything ye dinna want." She sighed. "If there is anything I've learned from my brothers, 'tis that a man is not whole, not true, until he claims all that is his. I'll never truly have all of ye, and ye'll never truly give all of yourself. There will always be a hole inside ye, a need, a question, a guilt.

Leave your fears to chase behind ye, rather than facing them, fighting them, conquering them, and ye're but a prisoner. Set yourself free." She glanced up, large, heather-colored eyes fixing on his. "I'll be here no matter what. I'll wait for ye to battle it out on your own, or I'll come right along with ye, stand beside ye. But only ye can make that choice. Your clan will forgive ye. Ye just have to forgive yourself."

Her profound words struck a deep chord within him. Duncan leaned down and kissed the corner of her mouth. "For a woman, ye're surprisingly wise."

She laughed and slapped at his arms. "And for a man, ye're fairly predictable in your bigotry."

"Precisely why I need ye by my side always."

"I'll never leave your side." She glanced out over the ridge toward the ruins. "Never. Even if a demon rat chases us."

"Of that, there may be many."

"And already we've fought several."

Emotion tightened his chest, and he pressed his lips to her temple, breathing in her scent, finding comfort in something so small as the tickle of her hair on his nose. "I love ye."

"I love ye, too."

The Highlander's Sin

Chapter Twenty-Two

𝓐 gentle breeze blew across Kail Glen, and as Duncan and Heather approached the abbey doors, grasses and flowers lapped at the stone walls of the abbey's sacred buildings. Stained glass depicting scenes from psalms filled the windows. There was a calming air about the place, as though once a person entered there, all would be well. No portcullis blocked its open doors. No guards stood watch upon tower walls. The abbey was so very different than a castle. It wasn't built to withstand an enemy, probably because no one dared breach its walls for fear of being struck down by God himself. Nay, the abbey was built to welcome strangers.

A few dozen sheep and a couple of goats and cows milled in the fields beside the abbey, and several brown-cloaked figures bent stooped in rows, tending crops.

Sounding on the clouds was the chiming of the chapel bell.

"Vespers," Duncan said. "There will be no one to greet us." As he said the words, the monks in the fields followed each other in a line toward the open gate.

"Maybe ye should just climb over one of the transept walls as ye did at Dunrobin."

Duncan chuckled. "Nay, lass. They will leave the gate open as they always do. Monks are a peaceful people, and the house of God is always open to His shepherds."

Heather shivered. "Then we'd best get inside and close them before our enemies arrive uninvited."

"Aye." Duncan spurred his horse down the hill, catching the attention of a few of the monks.

Several of them glanced up and nodded their heads, while the rest kept their gazes toward the rosary beads they counted with their fingertips.

"We'll be welcomed by some, and others will vent at your presence. Not all people are the children of God in some stoic monks' eyes," Duncan said.

She was taken back to the inn when the woman had made her feel lower than dirt. "Then let us pray that those who are accepting are not cowed by those who lament."

Duncan chuckled. "A feat that is easier said than done." He nodded over at her. "Come on, let's go."

Heather nudged the lazy nag forward after Duncan's horse. The mount gave a slow lurch in Blade's direction, compelled each time she pushed it to catch up, though she tired easily.

They rode up the line of walking monks, dismounting from their horses and waiting patiently outside the doors until the last of them had entered. Duncan nodded his head for her to follow behind him under the main doors. He closed the doors tight behind them, lifting a thick block of wood and settling it in its brackets to bar the door. No one seemed to question his movements, as though he often barred their door and they accepted it.

Duncan led the way through a stoned archway until they entered the cloister.

"Wait here," Duncan said. He took the reins of her nag and led the mare alongside Blade to a small stables, disappearing inside.

Heather bowed her head, looking toward the ground, feeling extremely self-conscious of a sudden. If the innkeepers had taken her as a whore, would not the religious and pious men do the same? Duncan had mentioned that several of them, perhaps even more than that, were not of an accepting nature.

Her gown was even dirtier than it had been when they'd arrived at the inn earlier that day, and she was sure her face was covered in grime from their ride. She studied her hands and nails, wishing for a place to wash them, but the only thing readily available with water was the well, and she'd not tarnish these men of faith's drinking water by washing the filth from her face in it.

Duncan came out of the stables and walked over to the well in the center of the cloister, pulling up the bucket. Water sloshed over the side and with it a tin cup. He filled the cup and offered her a drink.

She took it eagerly, glad it was not the slimy mixture he'd served her before. He then poured water over her hands and his so they could wash away the dirt, letting the remnants drain on to the ground.

"I'm going to go into Vespers. When it concludes, I will speak with the prior about the impending danger and the change in my situation. He'll marry us right away."

"But what if the Ross clan arrives before Vespers ends?"

Duncan pointed above her head. She turned to see what he was showing her.

"See that bell? Ring it loud if they arrive."

Heather swallowed down her fear, recalling how he'd said he'd never leave her side again. "I will."

"I'll be at the rear of the church standing by the north transept. First ding of the bell and I'll be by your side." He removed his claymore and handed it to her.

The metal was heavy, pulling her arms down with its weight.

"Ye once asked for my sword to help protect yourself. I give it to ye now."

"But—"

He cupped her cheek. "Dinna worry. Ye will not need it."

Heather nodded, praying he was right.

"I'll be just inside."

She wanted to kiss him, to grab on to him tightly, to somehow find a way to use magic to keep the Ross clan at bay. They would be here today. Tonight. Her brothers wouldn't arrive until noon the following day. If they arrived at all.

Duncan entered the church through the north transept and stood by the door, hands pressed together in prayer, head bowed.

Prior Samuel began the service by making a sign of the cross. It felt like hours before he ended with the Paternoster, but while he recited the Lord's Prayer, his eyes locked on Duncan's, and he gave a slight nod of his head. The prior had been at Pluscarden since before Duncan had arrived. He'd been one of the only men of the abbey to welcome him, and it remained so to this day.

Duncan was well past the time he should have taken solemn vows, becoming a monk in truth, and many of the men had taken issue with that, lamenting often that Duncan should have just parted ways with the abbey altogether. He had never understood why the prior had seen fit to keep him there, always offering words of advice and a bed—not always warm, but at least he'd had one.

The men filed out, but Duncan remained behind, waiting until they'd all left. Prior Samuel motioned him to the front of the church.

"I'm afraid I would like to speak with ye in the cloister," Duncan said.

The prior frowned, and Duncan hurried to apologize with a bow of his head. "I would not ask it if it were not important."

"Verra well." Prior Samuel walked slowly down the aisle toward Duncan. His gait looked more shaky than before. He was nearly twice Duncan's age, and though his face was not lined with wrinkles, his stiffness showed he was getting up there in years.

"My thanks, Prior."

Prior Samuel nodded and led the way out into the cloister, finding a private spot where they could stand. Heather stood beneath the bell, looking as though she'd been put in a corner like a berated child.

"I've come for two reasons," Duncan started.

"Is she one of them?" The prior nodded toward Heather.

"Aye, Prior. She is."

"Who is she?"

"Lady Heather. Youngest sister to the Earl of Sutherland."

Prior Samuel nodded. "A woman worthy of ye, though she looks a bit worse for wear."

"We've had a bit of trouble on the road."

"The other reason why ye're here?"

"Aye. The Ross clan is headed this way, and I've reason to believe they will attempt to take the abbey."

"We must pray for safety." The prior looked solemn.

Duncan forged on. "The Sutherlands have been summoned to protect ye, but I'm not certain they will arrive in time."

"I remember when ye first arrived here, lad. Tired, dirt streaking your face and an anger so deep I thought ye'd join the Father in heaven afore your twelfth year. Ye grew up just as angry but have somehow managed to control it. All of us here, even those loath to admit it, owe our lives to ye. Without ye, we'd have suffered more at the hands of foul men than with ye."

Duncan bowed his head. "I owe ye my life."

"Ye owe me nothing," Prior Samuel responded.

"I will do whatever it takes to protect ye and the abbey." Duncan knelt before the prior.

"I know ye will." He pressed his hand on top of Duncan's head. "I bless ye my son."

"I wish to marry."

"As a novitiate, ye can renounce your vows, my lad." The prior did not seem at all surprised. In fact, he sounded quite the opposite, as if he'd only just been waiting for this day. "If that is what ye wish, then I shall marry the two of ye now, afore we are interrupted by any guests. We've plenty of witnesses."

"Thank ye." Relief flooded him. He'd not been aware before how much he'd feared the prior's response.

"Rise, Duncan. Dinna thank me. I've waited twenty years to hear ye say it. Ye're not a monk. 'Tis not in your blood. Ye're a laird. I tried hard to get ye to return to your clan. Gave ye extra work, took the wood out of your hearth. Hoped to make ye miserable so ye'd leave this place and return to where ye belonged. To your people, who need ye verra much, but ye just would not go."

Duncan laughed and stood. "Took a woman to tell me."

The prior smiled. "As I said, ye're no monk."

"Nay, canna say I ever was."

Prior Samuel nodded. "Bring the lass inside. Let me bind ye within the eyes of God and bless your union."

Duncan couldn't help the beaming smile that creased his lips. He ran across the cloister toward Heather, gathering the eyes of over a dozen monks.

"He will marry us now," he whispered with excitement.

"Now?" Heather paled, looking down at the sword in her hands.

"Aye, lass. Now." Duncan took his sword back.

"But I've not washed my face. I canna marry ye with a dirty face."

"I dinna care if your face is dirty. I'd marry ye even if ye were submerged in muck."

Heather laughed and ducked her head, but Duncan pressed two fingers beneath her chin, lifting her up to look at him.

"Would ye do me the honor of becoming my wife in truth?"

"Aye. A thousand times, aye." She beamed up at him.

Duncan offered his arm and led her toward Prior Samuel. "Wait," he said, stopping. He undid the pin at his throat, unraveling his robes from his shoulders and revealing his true self beneath—a Highland warrior. A chief.

"Immeasurably improved," Heather said. "I was beginning to feel like quite the sinner when I kept kissing a robed man."

"There can be no sin in kissing each other," Duncan whispered. "Let us say our vows so we can do more than kiss."

Heather blushed and glanced toward the ground, biting her lip. Duncan chuckled and led her toward the man who'd mentored him over the years.

"Prior, this is my betrothed, Heather Sutherland."

"Prior." Heather bowed her head and curtsied, not rising until he'd pressed his hand to her head and whispered a blessing.

"Would either of ye like a confession before we begin?"

Heather glanced up at Duncan. "I believe we'd already confessed just before entering your doors."

Duncan's chest tightened. Damn, he loved her. "Aye, we did."

The prior summoned several monks forward and led them all into the Lady Chapel, where he ascended the altar and gestured for Duncan and Heather to kneel before him.

"My lady, Heather Sutherland, do ye come here willingly and honestly to marry his lairdship, Duncan MacKay?"

"Aye."

"And do ye, Laird Duncan MacKay, come here willingly and honestly to marry her ladyship, Heather Sutherland?"

"Aye."

"Then let us proceed."

A short quarter hour later, they were pronounced man and wife, and Duncan, unable to resist, bent Heather backward over his arm and kissed the sin out of her. She wrapped her arms around his neck and eagerly kissed him back, washing away all doubt. She was his, now and forever.

"How dare ye!" The chapel erupted with the booming roar of Magnus Sutherland. "Scoundrel! Get your maggot-infested hands off my sister!"

Duncan nearly dropped Heather in his shock, but quickly gripped on to her tight and shoved her behind his back.

"No weapons in the church!" Prior Samuel called out, his own voice booming off the rafters.

Magnus muttered something under his breath and left the chapel but poked his head right back inside.

"Outside. Now."

Duncan took orders from no one and was about to shout just that when Heather scurried from around him and headed down the aisle toward the door.

"Wife! Get back here!" But she ignored him.

Prior Samuel stepped beside him, suddenly calm now that the armed men had left his chapel. "I am by no means an expert

The Highlander's Sin

on the subject, but it would seem to me, with that one in any case, demands and orders will rarely get ye what ye want."

Duncan grunted and headed out of the church after his wife and, less eagerly, toward his new brother-by-marriage.

In the cloister, a half-dozen Sutherland warriors stood, fully armed. All the monks had disappeared, most probably expecting blood to be shed.

Magnus stood, glaring down at Heather, who spoke softly and calmly. Duncan could not hear what she said until he was nearly upon them. Even Magnus' glare to stay back did not make him cease his advance.

Magnus pointed at him, threats dripping from his stance. "Ye're dead."

Duncan grinned, though not with humor. "I'm quite alive, in fact."

"Not in a few moments ye won't be." Magnus pulled his sword from its sheath.

"Magnus! Stop. Duncan is my husband, and I love him." Though she pressed the news upon her brother, he did not seem to have any care in it. Pure rage filled the man's eyes, inciting in Duncan an intense desire to fight.

"Come, now, wife, let us men talk it through."

Magnus cringed at his use of the word wife, making Duncan grin all the wider.

"I'll have this sham of a marriage annulled. Ye've only just recited your vows. There's been no consummation." He glanced at Heather. "Ye'll be coming home with me."

"I stole her from ye once. What makes ye think I won't do it again? No locked door or dungeon cell could keep me away from her."

They advanced on each other, stopped only by Heather, who jumped between them. She pressed a hand to each man's chest.

"Magnus, I'll not be going with ye. We have, in fact, consummated this marriage…twice now."

That only seemed to ignite the man's rage all the more. Duncan kept his gaze steady on him.

With deadly intent, Duncan said, "The only way ye're taking her away from me is over my bloodied, dead body."

Magnus snarled. "Then let us begin."

Chapter Twenty-Three

*T*here would be a bloodbath.

Heather's heart plummeted to somewhere around her feet. Her eldest brother facing off with her husband? Bile rose in her throat. Neither would survive. They would fight each other even when both lay bloody and dying upon the cloister ground.

"Stop this!" she shouted, pressing against both chests so hard her arms hurt. "There will be no fighting!"

Prior Samuel tried to intervene, but his voice was drummed out by the insults Duncan and Magnus slung back and forth. Her older brother was particularly sour about men stealing his sisters—especially since Lorna had been seduced by a man only a few years prior. A love match, just as Heather's was.

She stared up into her brother's face, a snarl on his lips and murder in his eyes. "Magnus, ye must stop. I love him. He saved me from Ina Ross."

That got his attention. His snarl slackened, and his eyes widened a fraction as he turned his surprised gaze on her. "Ina? What are ye talking about?"

"She had me abducted. From the chapel at Dunrobin." She failed to mention, on purpose, who had done the abducting.

"And how, exactly,"—he glanced at Duncan,—"did ye end up married to this sot?"

Heather turned to stand in front of Duncan, facing her brother. "He saved me."

"Saved ye?" Magnus stared over her head, skepticism in his voice. "How, exactly, did he save ye?"

"I abducted her." Duncan said the words before she could reply. Damn him!

That only made Magnus angry once more, and he jerked forward, barely stopped by the press of her hands on his chest. "I was right. Ye stole her, ye maggot!"

"She went willingly. The lass was preparing to leave Dunrobin on her own. I merely provided a means to depart."

Dear heavens, would her husband ever stop talking? Did he not realize he was only making things worse?

"Trickery!" Magnus shouted.

Heather whirled around to her husband. "Please, Duncan, let me handle this."

The blasted man barely looked at her.

"Och! A man who canna even be a man," Magnus taunted.

Duncan's eyes darkened, and she saw the same angry rage in his eyes that she'd seen in her brothers. She rolled her eyes and turned back to Magnus.

"Really, brother. Ye must not taunt a bear." Placing her hands on her hips, she went for the same posture she'd seen her sister-by-marriage use with Magnus many a time. "Now, that is enough. I have married the man. I will stay married to the man. How I came to meet him is none of your concern. Only know that he treated me honorably and that he is now *bound* to the Sutherland family, and he shall cause *no harm* to ye." She emphasized the words for her husband's sake, hoping he heard them past the roar of revenge burning through his mind.

"A bear? The man's barely a cub. Is he English?" Magnus's taunts grew worse by the minute.

Heather was fairly certain this was going to come to blows, no matter how much she wished it wouldn't.

"Bastard," Duncan seethed.

"Hand over your weapons. All of them," Heather demanded. She reached for the sword at Magnus's hip, wrapping her fingers around the hilt. "I see that neither of ye will begin to see reason until ye've beaten each other into the dirt. Therefore, ye must relinquish all weapons afore ye do so. I'll not bury my brother and my husband on the same day."

She'd hoped the men would see reason then and just shake hands, but as if they were children and she'd offered them a sweet, each man eagerly discarded every weapon on his person, hidden knives and all. They tossed them at her feet, making quite a clatter with all the metal. As they discarded one weapon after another, they did so without taking their eyes off each other, as if they measured who had a longer sword and who had more knives and other wicked means of defense. Duncan won that battle when he unstrapped the devil ax from its fastening on his chest.

"Has it really come to this?" she asked, exasperated.

"Get out of the way," Magnus ordered her.

"Dinna speak to my wife like that," Duncan snarled. "Wife, step back."

Heather threw her hands up on the air and turned to see her brother Blane with his arms crossed, looking on with eager interest.

"Are ye all mad?" she said to him. "Make them stop. 'Tis ridiculous."

Blane shifted his gaze to her, hands on his hips, lips in a firm line, annoying annoyed her beyond measure. "This must be done."

Were all men daft? For heaven's sake, would they all just let blood be spilled without a care for her thoughts?

"Blane," Magnus called.

That was when Heather made the mistake of turning around to see what her eldest brother was about. With her back to Blane, he was easily able to march up behind her and toss her over his shoulder. She screamed, hammered at his back, kicked, but he didn't relent, only took her where a crowd had gathered in a ring around the men.

"Do ye wish to watch or shall I find a quiet spot to lock ye up?" he asked.

"Ye're a terrible brother!" Fury laced her words and ran rampant through her veins. Now she wanted in on the fight.

"Hush, lass, the men are about to begin."

"Put me down." Closing her eyes tight and taking as deep a breath as she could while stomach-down on his shoulder, she said, "I want to watch."

Her admission was the furthest thing from the truth. She had no interest whatsoever in watching her husband and brother pummel each other.

Blane grunted and set her on her feet, keeping a tight, restraining grip on her elbow.

"Promise me something?" she asked, fear settling in the pit of her belly.

Duncan and Magnus were circling one another.

"What?" Blane's voice was edged with irritation.

"If it looks like they are going to murder each other, please intervene."

He only grunted again.

"Now is not the time for manly responses, Blane. I'm worried."

"It will not come to that." Was he trying for reassuring? For his voice fell flat.

"Promise me," she urged.

"I promise."

Before she could thank Blane, a resounding crack yanked her attention back to the two brawling men. 'Twas the sound of a fist hitting flesh. Magnus had socked her husband.

"That will be the only hit I allow freely," Duncan said, serious and calm. "And only because 'twas your right as the brother and guardian of my wife to have given her away. I deserved that one hit."

"Damn right," Magnus said.

"But ye'll not get past me so easily again."

The men continued to jab their fists, ducking, throwing near-misses, hitting full-on. It was painful to watch. But Duncan remained true to his word. He didn't allow Magnus to hit him without working for it.

She also noted that he'd never told her brother who he was or about his personal vendetta against the Sutherlands. Why?

But she could no more think on it, just as she could not cease their fight. Each bled from a bloodied lip. Each boasted an eye slowly bruising and swelling and two pairs of bloody knuckles.

Heather had to bite her cheek every time she wanted to shout for them to stop. Duncan bounced back, Magnus missing, swinging into the air, and just as his fist finished its descent, Duncan swung upward, cracking Magnus in the jaw. The hit had him stumbling backward. She thought for sure he'd lose his footing, but he didn't. Instead, he lowered himself into a tackling position and ran at Duncan, who braced his feet, waiting for impact.

Magnus barreled into him with a move that should have knocked Duncan from his feet, but her husband seemed prepared for it and grabbed hold of Magnus's back instead. They wrestled on foot until it seemed they both lost their balance at the same time, and they went rolling to the ground.

One on top of the other, they punched, blocked, retaliated. It was a nonstop, brutal attack that seemed never-ending.

Heather's heart had long since ceased beating, and her stomach had taken up permanent residence in her throat.

A sheer whistle took all of their attention, even the two brawling men on the ground. Everyone turned to face Prior Samuel, who stood by the main door.

"Your guests have arrived," he said calmly.

Following his announcement, a loud banging sounded on the doors.

"Dinna open it," Duncan ordered.

Prior Samuel nodded his head. "Keep us safe, my laird."

"I will," Duncan and Magnus said in unison before turning to glare at one another.

"Your husband is a laird?" Blane asked.

"Laird who?" Magnus asked Duncan.

"Laird MacKay."

The courtyard grew silent, save for the banging that resumed on the front doors.

Magnus frowned, swiped at a trickle of blood from his lip. Duncan mirrored him.

"Am I good enough for her now?" Duncan sneered.

"No one will ever be good enough for her. But I think I understand now why she was worried about ye harming us. I know your history."

Duncan grunted. "And?"

"'Twas unfortunate that my uncle disobeyed direct orders. Truly. On behalf of my clan, I do offer ye an apology, and gratitude for not seeking revenge." Magnus glanced at Heather. "Although, I canna say as ye got the better end of the deal." He winked at her.

Duncan chuckled. "She's a hellion. But she's mine."

Magnus stuck out his arm. "Take care of her."

"Until my dying breath." Duncan grabbed hold of Magnus's arm.

Her husband. Her brother. Making amends. 'Haps a good beating had been all they'd needed. She decided then and there that when it came to certain things, men really were daft. Heather ran up to the both of them, lifted up on tiptoe and slung her arms around their shoulders.

"Thank ye," she whispered, holding back tears of joy. "Now don your weapons and dispense of the pests that Ina Ross and her English husband have become."

"Become?" Magnus chuckled. "Nothing's changed."

Duncan smirked. "Right ye are about that."

Magnus sauntered toward the gate, leaving Heather a moment of privacy with Duncan. Well, as private as it could be, surrounded by warriors.

"What will ye do?" she asked, worry creasing her brow.

Duncan pulled her into his embrace. "We'll attempt to settle this peacefully first. No need to shed any more blood on our wedding day."

"And since ye're dealing with the Ross clan, what will truly be your plan?"

"Predictable, are they?" he teased. "We'll dispatch them as soon as we can."

Heather smoothed away blood from his lip, seeing it was bruised beneath. "Kiss me for good luck. Gently."

Duncan pulled her tighter against him and leaned down, brushing his lips on hers. "'Tis hard to kiss ye gently, lass, when all I want to do is delve inside and devour ye whole."

"When ye come back."

"When I come back."

Heather watched him go toward the gate to join her brothers.

But they were back sooner than she'd expected. It had taken Ina and Marmaduke only a quarter hour to decide they'd not enough men to fight the Sutherlands. It also helped that Prior Samuel had told them they both had a straight ticket to purgatory, and he was going to make sure their clan chaplain knew about it.

As assurance, Ina's cousin Padrig, whom she'd originally planned to marry to Heather, was taken into the church as a novice monk. One wrong move from Ina or Marmaduke, and the lad would be turned over to Duncan. Ina cared for her cousin like a sibling—and heir—and had not been accommodating at first, but she'd known she did not have enough manpower to withstand a battle. It was agreed that on the young man's twenty-fifth birthday, he could be returned to her.

The Sutherlands and MacKays had five years of peace, at least, to look forward to. But Heather couldn't help but wonder how long it would take for Ina to break down and forfeit the life of her beloved cousin in the name of revenge.

"Let us sup before Compline," Duncan said. "The monks will not be pleased to see us milling about when they go into their evening prayer."

The Sutherland warriors set up camp outside of the abbey walls, and only Heather's brothers Magnus and Blane remained behind. Prior Samuel led them all into a public dining hall, where they ate a plain meal of cabbage stew and brown bread. The meal was short and quiet, and once completed, the prior met them outside of the hall once more. Bells tolled as the sun bade its farewell to the day. The cloister was lit by a few hanging lanterns, light enough to envision the path to take but dark enough that anything along the path was not visible.

Magnus and Blane wished them a good night and retreated toward their men.

"We have a small guesthouse available to ye both this night," the prior said. "But on the morrow, ye'll leave. While the lot of ye were fighting, I sent word to your clan that we've been keeping ye safe until the time ye were ready to return. They'll be expecting ye, my laird."

"My thanks," Duncan said. "For everything."

Duncan and Heather bowed their heads, kneeling before the prior, who blessed them both before wishing them good night.

Duncan took Heather by the hand and led her to the guesthouse, a small building just past the prior's lodging. 'Twas a small but cozy house with a bed just big enough for two of normal size. A man of Duncan's height would definitely have feet hanging off the end.

Once inside the small house, Heather froze. They'd made love before, even slept beside one another. But tonight they would do both of those things as man and wife.

Man and wife.

Married.

Duncan lit a trio of candles set in a candelabra on a small square table and then poured them each a goblet of dark red wine. He handed her the goblet, their fingers brushing, igniting a new and heightened nervous excitement. She supposed the difference between this time and every other was that those times had been ruled by emotion, not actively sought out.

"To us." Duncan touched his glass to hers.

"To us," Heather repeated, taking a sip. She crinkled her nose at the bitterness of the wine, but took another sip all the same, hoping to calm her nerves.

"We made it through the day with little bloodshed."

"And blessings from my family and the church."

"A successful day."

Heather nodded, taking another bitter sip. Funny thing was, with each subsequent sip, the wine seemed to lose its bitterness. An effect of the wine, or was her tongue simply becoming numb?

Duncan stepped closer to her, wiping a droplet of wine from her lip with the pad of his thumb. "I want ye to know how verra happy ye've made me today. I've searched nearly my whole life for the feeling of completeness, and once I found ye, ye made me a whole man."

Heather smiled as he inched his lips closer to hers.

"Now let me kiss ye until we're both unable to breathe." He rubbed her nose with his, and then kissed her.

The press of his lips was more intoxicating than the wine, filling her with warmth and making her head swim. Wobbling on her feet, she clutched at him with her free hand, her fingers finding purchase in the center line where the leather of his jerkin split.

Duncan took her wine, leaving her lips briefly to set both their goblets aside.

"As laird… I know your duty to your clan is to produce heirs," she said softly, nervously.

"Aye."

"Then…tonight…"

Duncan stroked the sides of her face. "Lass, my clan has gone two decades without a laird. They can wait awhile longer for an heir."

She blew out the breath she'd been holding, relief lightening her chest and shoulders. "Thank goodness."

"Dinna be so thankful. Ye'll give me a complex. Now, enough talk of making bairns. Let us simply enjoy each other tonight." He spread his fingers around her waist. "And get ye out of this gown."

Heather tugged at the leather lacing on his jerkin. "We could do without this, too."

Duncan grinned. "A woman after my own heart. Ye first, though."

He walked to a waiting basin and poured water into it, then took a folded linen, dipping it into the water.

"We'll wash each other as we disrobe."

Heather was relieved to hear it. She felt as though a layer of dust covered her.

Duncan undressed her slowly, his lips following the path of the clean cloth over her neck and collarbone. He peeled her gown down over her arm, kissing her bare shoulder beside the thin strap of her chemise.

"Your skin is so soft," he murmured.

His fingers glided over her skin as he removed the sleeves from her arms and once her hands had been freed, he tugged the gown over her hips and let it drop. Normally, she would have felt a cool rush of air, but not this time. The way he touched her, savored her, kissed her, made her burn with a passionate fever.

He went about the same process with her chemise, washing, kissing down the length of her arm until he reached her hand, where he pressed his lips to each of her knuckles, giving her index finger a tiny nibble. Heather gasped and jerked her hand away.

But that subtle movement let the slip of fabric that served as her chemise fall to the ground. Naked as the day she was born, she gulped, her gaze fixed on the center of Duncan's chest.

He drew in a deep breath and then let it out slowly. "Good God, lass… I'd no idea."

"What?" She flicked her gaze up to his, afraid there was something wrong. He'd seen her naked before. What had changed? She didn't see concern in his eyes—only awe, and raw desire.

"Ye're perfect." As he said the words, he reached for her. One hand pressed to her hip and the other trailed over her ribs with the wet cloth.

Gooseflesh prickled where he touched. Lightly, he caressed the sides of her breast, then beneath it, chilling her and exciting her.

Perfect. He thought her flawless, and yet he talked much of how he loved her fiery nature. For him, her flaws made her perfect. She smiled to herself, sinking further into him. He cupped her breast, brushing a thumb softly over her puckered nipple. Heather sucked in a breath, trying hard not to pant. But it was hard to control her breathing with him staring at her, touching her. He took a step closer, dipped his head and captured her lips in a tender kiss. Their lips slanted over one another, tongues lightly stroking, and all the while, he caressed her breasts, rubbed the cloth over her back.

"So eager," he murmured against her lips.

Duncan trailed his fingers lower, in time with his lips, which traveled over her chin and neck down to her collarbone. He tickled her belly, circled her navel. By the time the cloth reached the apex of her thighs, his lips wrapped around her nipple, tongue swirling over the taut bud and he gently swept the cloth over her sex, replacing its chill with the press of his fingers. He stroked through wet folds and pushed up inside her. Wicked, delicious sensation from so many places. Heather could not hold in her cry of pleasure.

It was simply too much and yet not enough. She wriggled, shifted. Demanded more with her hands gripped tight to his shoulders.

And Duncan didn't disappoint. In fact, he shocked her.

Cold air hit her breasts as he left her nipples behind and trailed kisses down to her navel. His swirled his tongue around the indent, and then he dragged his velvet heat lower.

He knelt before her, hands splayed on her hips and lips poised over her woman's center. Dark, hungry eyes gazed up at her.

"I want to taste ye," he said.

Heather licked her lips. Dare she hope he meant what she thought he did? She'd never guessed that a man could…kiss a woman there, but just seeing him poised over top of her mons made her knees quake, and somewhere deep in her core clenched tight with need. Her breath hitched. "All right."

Duncan smiled up at her, wicked intent etched in the curve of his lips.

The heat of his mouth centered on her, and then his tongue flicked out over that part of her that fired white-hot sensation, sending jolts of pleasure coursing through her.

This was so much more than a simple kiss. Fingers massaged at her hips while his tongue massaged at the very heat of her. Tasting, licking, nuzzling. He swirled that velvet length over her again and again. With each stroke, she moaned. With each stroke, she felt her legs give way a little, until Duncan all but held her up. And still he tormented her, lapping at that little bud.

Heather gasped, trying desperately to pull in a decent breath, but she couldn't. Every draw of breath was a gasp, a moan, and he never relented, only increased her pleasure. Just when she thought she'd lose consciousness, so intense was the sensation whipping through her, an overpowering climax took root, shaking her where she stood. Her nails dug into his shoulders, hips canted forward, knees buckled, and she cried out, riding the potent waves of pleasure his tongue provided.

"Beautiful, lass." Duncan dragged his mouth across her inner thigh, nibbling at her sensitive skin. "Exquisite."

Heather bent forward, her forehead dropping on to his. "Amazing," she said, still panting.

Duncan stood up, rinsed out the cloth and handed it to her.

"Will ye wash me, wife?"

Heather nodded, speechless. She curled her fingers into the wet cloth and watched as Duncan shed his jerkin and shirt. Before she'd caught her breath, he took her hand and pressed the cloth to his chest. She did as he'd done, cleaning him gently, but didn't have the courage quite yet to kiss his nude flesh. When she had at last found a normal breathing pattern, he removed his belt and his plaid fell to the floor. Again, her breath hitched. Her eyes widened as she studied him, taking in the wide expanse of his shoulders and chest, the chiseled muscles of his abdomen. Where before she'd not been able to look him over too closely, this time she did, her gaze roving over the jutting length of flesh that gave her so much pleasure.

"I want to…" She trailed off, didn't bother to finish. Instead, she closed the distance between them and knelt in front of him. If he could taste her, she was going to taste him.

"*Mo chreach*," Duncan groaned.

She stared up at him, suddenly wondering if it was all right. His gaze had darkened all the more, and the look he gave her said it was more than all right. He was eager for it.

Heather took him in her grip, marveling at the combination of solid velvet. She washed him from root to tip, going slow so she could feel every inch of his length. Then she tossed the cloth. Doing exactly as he'd done, she breathed hotly on his skin, touching her tongue to the tip and swirling around it. She teased and tormented him, kissed his hard length, running her tongue from root to stem. Duncan groaned, pumped his hips forward so his erection slid back and forth in her hand as she kissed him.

"Och, lass…" He wanted more, she could tell.

Just like she'd wanted more, wanted to reach that pinnacle moment of release. And she wanted desperately to take him all the way into her mouth. To suck on that rigid length. Was it proper? Would he resist?

Only one way to find out. Heather centered her lips on the tip and then opened her mouth to him. Duncan jerked his hips, groaned loud, but pushed his way inside.

"Heather," he groaned. "Ye have to stop."

She pulled back and stared up at him. "Why?"

"Because I want to make love to ye slowly."

"Isn't that what we're doing?"

"Aye. But..."

"Let me finish."

"Nay. Not this time."

He grabbed her hand where it wrapped around him, then slid his palm up her arm, coaxing her to stand but not let go of him.

"I want to make love to my wife, in a bed, for the first time. And if ye keep kissing me like that, I'll not make it to the bed."

Heather grinned, feeling proud of herself for having made him feel just as undone as she'd felt.

He lifted her into his arms and carried her to the bed, where he laid her down. The wood creaked, and a cloud of dust plumed with their weight.

"My guess is, it has been awhile since any other guests have visited." Duncan chuckled.

"If ever," Heather laughed.

But they didn't let a little dust or a little creaking delay them. Duncan kissed her madly, making her feel as though he needed her desperately, a feeling she experienced every moment. Hands stroking everywhere, Duncan settled between her thighs, gently guiding her to hug them around his hips. She stroked the backs of his calves with her toes, tilting her hips upward, needing to feel him inside her. But Duncan had told her he wanted to make love to her slowly, and he didn't back down, no matter how much she coaxed him.

When they were both shaking with need, he finally did drive deep inside her. As their bodies molded into one, the bed shook and creaked, wood scraped across the floor, but neither of them cared. Once inside her, he did relent on one promise— he didn't go slow. He drove inside her, relentless in his pursuit of their pleasure.

Heather felt that familiar sensation again, the one that told her she was about to fall off a cliff and into a cloud of pure ecstasy. She cried out, arching her back, matching his thrusts with the rocking of her hips.

"Are ye close?" he asked.

Without having to ask, she knew what he was asking and where he wanted to take her. "Aye," she answered, feeling the first tremors of her peak. "I'm there."

Chapter Twenty-Four

One week later...

"Kyle of Tongue," Duncan said, pointing to the loch. "Look there, at the top of the ridge."

Stone walls jutted toward the sky, a thick stone wall surrounding a castle upon the highest point. "Your home?" Heather asked.

"Aye, lass. Castle Varrich." Duncan felt both relief and fear approaching the place that would only remind him of such pain and suffering. At least here, the memories of being in this castle were all good. Not like if he were ever to visit Dingwall. There, he'd likely have nightmares.

Heather rode in front of him and slid a comforting hand over his thigh. They'd decided to leave the nag at the abbey. The journey had been longer than it should have been, as they took it slow. A honeymoon, of sorts. They'd spent hours bathing and swimming in lochs, making love in glens. The Sutherland clan had promised to meet them at Castle Varrich, following at a respectable distance to give the new couple privacy.

At first Heather had been embarrassed by their insatiable need for one another, wondering what her brothers must think. Duncan didn't give a fig for anything other than his beautiful wife. Neither of her brothers had rushed their camp to find out what was taking so long, and within the first two days, she told him that she'd realized that when her brothers had both married, they'd spent just as many hours enjoying their newfound wedded bliss, so she didn't need to worry about them anymore.

"Are ye ready?" she asked softly.

"Aye. Too long a time has passed." He was as ready as he'd ever be.

"They will love ye, just as I do." Heather leaned her head back against his chest and gazed up at him.

Her eyes shone with merriment and peace.

"Thank ye, love." Duncan kissed her forehead. He felt like the luckiest man alive.

The Sutherland warriors melted from the trees, not surprising either Duncan or Heather. Magnus and Blane nodded to Duncan giving conspiratorial nudges, which, thank goodness, Heather didn't notice.

They rode in two lines up the winding road to Castle Varrich. Just as Prior Samuel had said, the clan was awaiting them. Guards called out orders, and the portcullis was raised, and the gate doors opened. The place looked just as it had when he'd left it. Busy, bustling and fully fortified. His uncle had done well by the clan in keeping them safe. Lord, he prayed the man wasn't upset with Duncan's return.

Inside, clansmen, women and children cheered. Duncan couldn't shake his shock at their pleasure in seeing him. He dismounted swiftly, turning to face his bride.

"I have to tell them," he said to Heather as he helped her dismount.

She shook her head. "They accept ye as their laird, their chief. They know what happened to your family, to your people. They know ye feared returning, that ye sought sanctuary with the church." She pressed reassuring hands to his forearms. "Ye must first forgive yourself and then accept their acceptance."

What would he have done without her? He never would have returned here, that was a certainty. "Have I told ye today how much I love ye?"

Heather giggled, tried to duck her head, but Duncan wasn't going to let her get off that easy. He tipped her chin and planted his lips on hers in a demanding, possessive, very thorough kiss. The crowd erupted in cheers. Even the Sutherlands shouted out bawdy barbs and hoots of appreciation.

"Welcome home, Laird and Lady MacKay!"

Duncan turned Heather to face the crowd, lifted her hand with his in victory. "MacKays!" he shouted.

"MacKay!" they returned.

An elder gentleman stepped forward, the lines of his face familiar to Duncan. "My boy," he said, "we've long awaited your return. When we didna find ye amongst the...well, we had hope."

"Uncle Andrew!" Duncan hurried forward and enfolded the older man in a back slapping hug.

"When so many years passed, our hope faded. We'd feared ye were dead."

Duncan pressed his lips together, not allowing that day to rush forward in his mind. "Part of me was."

"Your people love ye, lad. Always have, always will." The way his uncle spoke the words, so matter-of-fact, without question, struck a chord in Duncan's chest.

"Thank ye."

Uncle Andrew nodded. "None required." He turned his gaze toward Heather. "And who is this beautiful lass?"

"Lady Heather, my wife. Youngest sister to the Earl of Sutherland." Duncan introduced Magnus and Blane to his uncle, who couldn't take his eyes, nor his hand, away from Heather.

"'Tis a pleasure to meet ye," she said, a charming smile on her face.

Duncan grinned with secret wonder. This woman amazed him. Charming, shrewish, seductive, all of it in one inspiring package.

"Now we feast!" Uncle Andrew shouted, followed by a deafening roar of agreement from the crowd.

Surprisingly, another man stepped into line with the MacKay clan, his hands folded behind his back—William Wallace.

Duncan immediately turned to see his wife's reaction. Heather's eyes widened. He nodded to the Sutherland men and then introduced himself to Duncan. "William Wallace, my laird. I've heard much about ye."

Duncan grunted. "Not sure I want to know what."

Wallace grinned. "A story for another time. Let us simply say ye've helped me and hindered me on many an occasion."

Duncan laughed and took Wallace's arm. "I'm pleased ye came. My wife has been wanting to speak with ye." Duncan had sent a note to Wallace when they'd first gotten to the abbey. Prior Samuel had mentioned that the man had been visiting with allies in the north near Varrich.

Wallace turned his attention to Heather. "I've heard ye wanted to help with the rebellion."

Heather was speechless. She glanced up at Duncan, her eyes saying she'd guessed that he'd made good on his promise to tell Wallace of her desire. Duncan winked at her.

"Aye, Sir William, I do."

Wallace stepped forward. "Then I believe I have a task for ye."

Heather's fingers trembled as she sought Duncan's hand. "All right."

"Can I make ye in charge of our supplies?" Wallace asked.

"In what way?" She never agreed to anything without knowing all the details. Even when her dream was presented as a reality she questioned it.

It only made Duncan admire her more.

"We'll send ye a list of all the things we need. Ye gather them, or have others gather them, and ensure their delivery. We canna survive without our supplies. 'Tis a duty that will keep ye here as well, tending to your new home and husband."

"Aye! A task I will enjoy and give my all to." She glanced over at Duncan with a blush, making his chest puff out with pride.

Damn, but he loved her more than life itself.

"The men of the resistance will be verra pleased to know their livelihood is in such capable hands," Wallace said.

"'Tis a great honor, sir, truly." Heather beamed.

Duncan was more than pleased that Wallace had come through. He'd not been sure if the man would get his message, let alone indulge a woman's desires. Seeing Heather's dream come true made his heart clench. She'd done so much for him, more than she'd ever realize. It was the least he could do for her.

Wallace grinned, took her hand in his and brought it up to his lips, kissing her gently on the knuckles. "The honor is ours."

Duncan growled, trying to temper the jealous beast inside him. "Och, get your scoundrel lips off my wife."

Everybody with a set of lungs burst into laughter at Duncan's outrage, even Wallace, who made a pretense of pulling Heather into his arms, before quickly thrusting her back at Duncan.

"The lass is yours, my laird, though I canna say that would have been the case if she'd allowed me to court her afore laying eyes on ye."

"I've spent too much time with ye, Wallace, to ever have let that happen!" Heather's brother Blane called out.

"Aye, ye scoundrel," Magnus taunted the highest-acclaimed warrior of their time. "Not on your life." He tilted his head toward Duncan. "And nearly not on his, either."

"Och, the lot of ye are a bunch of braying ninnies," Heather lamented. "Are we going to feast or shall we all perish while ye figure out who's the best among ye?"

"There's my wife," Duncan called out, pulling her into his arms. He lowered his voice so only she could hear. "I've a mind to feast on only ye."

Too late, he realized that she was *not* the only one to hear what he'd said.

"Enticing words, my laird! Shall we have a bedding afore a meal?" Uncle Andrew called out.

Duncan shook his head, while Heather's face colored a shade darker than a beet. He pulled her up into his arms, cradling her against his chest. "A meal," he replied. Pressing his lips to her ear, this time he made *sure* no one else could hear, "and then a bedding."

Heather giggled and wrapped her arms around his neck. "Maybe this time ye'll let me—"

Duncan cut her off before she'd said what he thought was on her mind. Already, his cock was hard as stone. "Hush or I'll change my mind about the order."

"There's one thing I'll never change my mind about," she said softly.

"What's that?"

"How much I love ye."

Duncan couldn't help the smile that curled his lips. "'Tis a fact, I love ye more and more each day, princess."

"Hmm." She tapped her chin. "I just thought of another thing I'll never change my mind about."

"Do tell." Duncan nuzzled her ear.

"That I hate when ye call me princess."

Duncan's head fell back on a roar of laughter. "How about I call ye tart instead?"

Heather shook her head in pretend disgust. "Only if ye want me to call ye a bastard whoreson heathen."

Love poured from every inch of him. She was such a delight, a breath of fresh air. "I think I have changed my mind. We'll feast after I take ye upstairs and whip up your skirts—"

"Shh… They'll hear."

"Too late!" someone called out.

"I'm going to enjoy sparring with ye for the rest of my days," Duncan said with a laugh. "I just never know what ye'll say next."

"Aye, so ye best be on your toes."

"With pleasure."

Duncan led her to the chair where his mother used to sit, and he took his place in his father's. Facing the clan with grim eyes, he lifted his glass of ale and stood.

"The last time I saw most of ye was the morning we trekked to Dingwall. I return here to ye a changed man. No longer a lad, but your laird. We've risen from the ashes of our past to start a new life. God bless my mother and sire. God bless my lost sisters and brothers. God bless our lost men and women. God bless, Clan MacKay!"

The roar of approval echoed through the rafters of the great hall. Mugs clinked and sloshed. Boot heels stomped. And a great weight lifted from Duncan's chest. Everything he'd feared was no longer. He could move forward, live his life the way he was meant to.

"Thank ye, Heather," he said, though his words were dulled by the crowd.

She glanced up at him, a contented smile curling her lips. "Ye dinna have to thank me, Duncan."

"But I do have to kiss ye." And with that said, he claimed his wife's lips in a fiery kiss, knowing from that moment on that he would get to spend the rest of his days in perfect moments, just like this one.

"The End"

If you enjoyed **THE HIGHLANDER'S SIN**, *please spread the word by leaving a review on the site where you purchased your copy, or a reader site such as Goodreads or Shelfari! I love to hear from readers too, so drop me a line at* authorelizaknight@gmail.com *OR visit me on Facebook:* https://www.facebook.com/elizaknightauthor. *I'm also on Twitter: @ElizaKnight Many thanks!*

AUTHOR'S NOTE

A note on the murder of the MacKay chief. According to history, two MacKay cheiftans—father and son—were murdered by a laird of a junior branch of the Sutherland clan at Dingwall Castle. However, this happened around 1371. For the purposes of my story, I used creative license to move the date by nearly 100 years.

A note on Pluscarden Abbey: This abbey is real, and was built in the early 1200's. It is known to have been attacked around the time of my novel by the English, but for the sake of fiction, I made it the Ross clan.

Eliza Knight

The Highlander's Sin

The saga continues! Look for more books in The Stolen Bride Series coming soon! There *were* six planned books in The Stolen Bride Series! BUT due to reader demand, I've decided to keep the series going! Following Book Six: *The Highlander's Sin*, will be *The Highlander's Temptation* – a prequel to the series. That's right! Lorna and Jamie's story.

The Highlander's Temptation – The Prequel, releasing February, 2014

Desire tempted them, but love conquered all…

Laird Jamie Montgomery is a warrior with a mission. When he travels to the northern Highlands on the orders of William Wallace, temptation in the form of an alluring lass, could be his undoing.

Lady Lorna Sutherland can't resist the charms of one irresistible Highlander. Though she's been forbidden, she breaks every rule for the pleasure of his intoxicating embrace.

When their love is discovered, Jamie is tossed from Sutherland lands under threat of death. But danger can't keep the two of them apart. No matter what perils may try to separate them — Lorna and Jamie swear they'll find a way to be together.

If you haven't read the other books, they are available at most e-tailers. Check out my website, for information on future releases www.elizaknight.com.

Eliza Knight

ABOUT THE AUTHOR

Eliza Knight is the multi-published, award-winning, Amazon best-selling author of sizzling historical romance and erotic romance. While not reading, writing or researching for her latest book, she chases after her three children. In her spare time (if there is such a thing…) she likes daydreaming, wine-tasting, traveling, hiking, staring at the stars, watching movies, shopping and visiting with family and friends. She lives atop a small mountain, and enjoys cold winter nights when she can curl up in front of a roaring fire with her own knight in shining armor. Visit Eliza at www.elizaknight.com or her historical blog History Undressed: www.historyundressed.com

Made in the USA
San Bernardino, CA
06 November 2013